**Praise for the l**

"The authentically Southern
deep understanding of humar
— Hank Phillippi Ryan,
Agatha Award-Winning Author of *What You See*

"Boyer delivers a beach read filled with quirky, endearing characters and a masterfully layered mystery, all set in the lush lowcountry. Don't miss this one!"
— Mary Alice Monroe,
*New York Times* Bestselling Author of *A Lowcountry Wedding*

"A complicated story that's rich and juicy with plenty of twists and turns. It has lots of peril and romance—something for every cozy mystery fan."
— *New York Journal of Books*

"Has everything you could want in a traditional mystery...I enjoyed every minute of it."
— Charlaine Harris,
*New York Times* Bestselling Author of *Day Shift*

"Like the other Lowcountry mysteries, there's tons of humor here, but in *Lowcountry Boneyard* there's a dash of darkness, too. A fun and surprisingly thought-provoking read."
— *Mystery Scene Magazine*

"The local foods sound scrumptious and the locale descriptions entice us to be tourists...the PI detail is as convincing as Grafton."
— *Fresh Fiction*

"Boyer delivers big time with a witty mystery that is fun, radiant, and impossible to put down. I love this book!"
— Darynda Jones,
*New York Times* Bestselling Author

"Southern family eccentricities and manners, a very strongly plotted mystery, and a heroine who must balance her nuptials with a murder investigation ensure that readers will be vastly entertained by this funny and compelling mystery."

— *Kings River Life Magazine*

"*Lowcountry Bombshell* is that rare combination of suspense, humor, seduction, and mayhem, an absolute must-read not only for mystery enthusiasts but for anyone who loves a fast-paced, well-written story."

— Cassandra King,
Author of *The Same Sweet Girls* and *Moonrise*

"Imaginative, empathetic, genuine, and fun, *Lowcountry Boil* is a lowcountry delight."

— Carolyn Hart,
Author of *What the Cat Saw*

"*Lowcountry Boil* pulls the reader in like the draw of a riptide with a keeps-you-guessing mystery full of romance, family intrigue, and the smell of salt marsh on the Charleston coast."

— Cathy Pickens,
Author of the Southern Fried Mystery Series

"Plenty of secrets, long-simmering feuds, and greedy ventures make for a captivating read...Boyer's chick lit PI debut charmingly showcases South Carolina island culture."

— *Library Journal*

"This brilliantly executed and well-defined mystery left me mesmerized by all things Southern in one fell swoop... this is the best book yet in this wonderfully charming series."

— *Dru's Book Musings*

# Lowcountry
# BOOKSHOP

**The Liz Talbot Mystery Series
by Susan M. Boyer**

# Lowcountry
# BOOKSHOP

## A Liz Talbot Mystery

## Susan M. Boyer

HENERY PRESS

Copyright

LOWCOUNTRY BOOKSHOP
A Liz Talbot Mystery
Part of the Henery Press Mystery Collection

First Edition | May 2018

Henery Press
www.henerypress.com

Trade Paperback ISBN-13: 978-1-63511-376-1
Digital epub ISBN-13: 978-1-63511-377-8
Kindle ISBN-13: 978-1-63511-378-5
Hardcover ISBN-13: 978-1-63511-379-2

Printed in the United States of America

*For my son,*
*James Gregory Boyer, Jr.,*
*with much love*

# ACKNOWLEDGMENTS

Heartfelt thanks to...

...each and every reader. Because of you, I can live my dream.

...Jim Boyer, my wonderful husband, best friend, and fiercest advocate. Thank you could never cover it, nevertheless, thank you for everything you do to help me live my dream.

...every member of my fabulous sprawling family for your enthusiastic support.

...Gretchen Smith, my dear friend and partner in a great many shenanigans, for things too numerous to list.

...Polly Buxton, for lending me your fabulous bookshop for this novel.

...Julian Buxton, for lending me your equally fabulous tour company and "The Ghosts of Charleston" for this novel.

...Jenna Craig, an early reader, for being a sounding board when I needed one.

...my dear friends Marcia Migacz and Pat Werths, who can see my mistakes when I no longer can.

...my dear friend Martha Rudisill, eleventh generation Charlestonian, for your continued enthusiastic assistance.
...Kathie Bennett and Susan Zurenda at Magic Time Literary.

...Rowe Carenen, The Book Concierge.

...Jill Hendrix, owner of Fiction Addiction bookstore, for your ongoing support. I can't imagine being on this journey without you.

...Kendel Lynn and Art Molinares at Henery Press.

As always, I'm terrified I've forgotten someone. If I have, please know it was unintentional and in part due to sleep deprivation. I am truly grateful to everyone who has helped me along this journey.

# ONE

The dead are prone to secrecy. Eighteen years ago, my best friend Colleen took the outbound train to the next world. She's seen behind the curtain, knows the answers to a great many questions. But since she's been back in her role as guardian spirit, she can't share this information with me. It's against the rules, that's what she tells me.

And then there are times when she keeps things to herself just for the pure-T fun of it—to toy with me. Colleen will be forever seventeen, the age she was that Friday night she drank tequila and went swimming in Breach Inlet. For all her insights into the universe, she won't be getting more mature.

The morning I first laid eyes on Poppy Oliver, it was Colleen's idea to eat at Toast on Meeting Street. It wasn't unusual for Colleen to make restaurant recommendations. She enjoyed food more than you might imagine given that she's passed on and all. At the time I didn't give it much thought. But had my sister, Merry, and I chosen any other restaurant for brunch that morning, our paths would not have crossed Poppy's, and a great many things might be different.

For weeks, Merry and I had planned on having brunch downtown before heading over to King Street for some shopping. She was in the midst of preparing for what our family had taken to calling Merry and Joe's Excellent Wedding Adventure—a three-week trip to Patagonia from which they would return married. Our parents were still sulking about being excluded. Okay, so was I. She was my only sister and she would only get married once. Well, that's always the plan anyway. I digress.

It was a girls' day in Charleston, but, as usual, Merry had no idea there were three of us. I'll always wonder if Colleen knew then where helping Poppy would lead. Colleen's a stubborn spirit. Her lips are sealed.

We were in a booth up front by a window looking out over Meeting Street, sipping mimosas. The cheery air of the restaurant—soft yellow walls, cream-colored pressed metal ceiling, and terra cotta tiled floors—stoked our festive mood. It was midmorning on a Saturday in August, and despite the sultry weather, both the streets of Charleston and Toast were humming with activity. The clop-clop of horseshoes on asphalt and the raised voice of a tour guide floated through the window pane as a horse drawn carriage filled with tourists rolled by.

The waitress had just set plates in front of us, and Merry and I were busy divvying up our food so we could each have some of our two favorite things on the menu. I served her some of my Classic Breakfast—scrambled eggs with cheese, country ham, Carolina stone ground grits, and a massive buttermilk biscuit—while she sliced off some of her Deluxe French Toast with peaches and peach cider syrup for me. Colleen waited none-too-patiently beside me for her to-go order—ham biscuits.

No one but me—and since the day of our wedding, my husband, Nate—could see or hear Colleen when she was in ghost mode, which was her default setting. Nate and I weren't allowed to tell anyone else that Colleen still inhabited our world. As Colleen's skill set had grown, she'd gained the ability to solidify when she needed to be seen, or when it suited her. The catch to that was she could never appear to anyone else who'd known her before she died. Guardian spirits can't eat in ghost mode either. But when she solidified she had the appetite of a horse and a particular fondness for country ham biscuits.

"I swear," said Merry, "you are always carrying a to-go order for somebody. If it isn't Nate, it's Blake or Sonny or Daddy. You need to start charging for food delivery service. You know that's going to be ruined before you get it home. After we've shopped all day...." She gave me a look that suggested I hadn't thought this through.

What she didn't know was how often I told people the to-go order was for her. I shrugged. "Nate loves the biscuits here. What can I say?"

I raised my mimosa and chose my words carefully.

The food forgotten, sisterly love shone in Merry's eyes. She raised her glass.

I smiled, tried not to think about how I would miss her wedding. "To a once-in-a-lifetime trip and—"

The door blew open and in strode Sonny Ravenel. Sonny has been our brother Blake's best friend since forever. He's also a Charleston police detective. Preoccupied by the mail carrier fast on his heels, he didn't even notice us at first.

"Please. If you'd just listen—" Her voice was earnest.

I lowered my glass. Merry set hers down and turned in her seat to check out what was going on.

Sonny smiled, nodded hello to the hostess, then turned back to the postwoman. Sporting twin brown ponytails and bangs, she looked like she was maybe twelve years old.

"Miss Oliver." Sonny's voice was patient, kind. "I promise you, I heard everything you said. But I'm off duty right now, ma'am. I'm hungry, if you don't mind. And I wouldn't want to keep you from your appointed rounds. You have a nice day now."

"But Detective—"

"I'm sure we'll talk again soon." He turned to the hostess. "One, please."

"Sonny," I called.

He caught my eye, lifted his chin. "I'll join my friends." When he walked towards our table, the mail carrier followed. Sonny stopped a few steps away, held two hands up in a halt gesture. "Enough. Please."

Her large brown eyes flooded with tears, her expression forlorn. She was in trouble. My protective instincts switched on.

"Aww, c'mon now." Sonny's voice took on a plaintive note. "Please don't cry."

"Wouldn't you cry?" she asked. "If the police thought you'd killed someone and you knew you hadn't done such a terrible, horrible, despicable thing? You'd cry too." She nodded, sniffled, and blinked back the tears.

I felt my eyebrows creep up my forehead. She was trim, fresh-faced, and neatly dressed in her blue shorts and light blue collared shirt. A ponytail touched each shoulder.

"Surely to goodness Sonny is smarter than that." Colleen employed the universal teenager-of-superior-intellect tone. She knew it all, just ask her.

*Sonny is plenty smart.* I threw the thought at her. This was how we typically communicated when others were around. She frequently jabbered at me in public and liked nothing better than for me to forget who I was talking to and respond to her out loud. She could read minds, and if I focused my thoughts, we could carry on a conversation.

*If Sonny thought this woman was dangerous, she'd be locked up. Anyway, murderers don't always look the part.* I could recall a few surprises in my career as a private investigator. Still, the mail carrier seemed the poster child for wholesomeness.

"Miss Oliver," said Sonny, "perhaps it would be best if you went ahead and retained that attorney after all."

"I already told you I can't afford one. And I didn't do anything. Why do I need an attorney if I didn't do anything but try to help a man who *someone else* ran over?"

"Because an attorney can answer questions, advise you on the process. And perhaps he can convince you how it's a bad idea to stalk the detective assigned to your case," said Sonny.

"You think I'm stalking you?" She straightened her shoulders, drew back her chin. "I am not stalking you. I'm on my route. I bring the mail here six days a week. Are you stalking me?"

"No ma'am. I'm just trying to have some breakfast."

"Fine." She swiped at her cheeks. Her voice swelled with indignation. "You just enjoy your breakfast. I hope you savor *every* single bite. And while you're chewing your eggs, I hope you think about how you're ruining the life of an innocent person who was trying to help. And you think *really* hard about what I told you. Mr. Drayton...he wasn't a good man. There might've been a reason why someone wanted to run over him, but it wasn't me, okay?"

"So you've told me." Sonny stared at her, his look telegraphing how his patience was all used up. "Several times now."

"Fine." She slapped two envelopes down on the counter and stormed out the door.

Sonny muttered a curse, hovered on my side of the booth waiting for me to slide over. He and I were both partial to the side of any booth that faced the door. Colleen popped out and reappeared beside Merry just as he dropped onto the bench next to me.

Our waitress stared at the retreating mail carrier as she handed Sonny a menu. "Bless her heart. It's no wonder the postal workers are snapping, as hot as it is."

He waved the menu away. "Coffee, please. And I'd like the Eggs Meeting Street. And a Bloody Mary, extra bacon."

"I'm surprised to see you here," I said. "Does Moon know you're having breakfast at other restaurants?" Moon Unit Glendawn owned The Cracked Pot, the diner on Stella Maris, the nearby sea island my family called home. Sonny had been dating her for the past few months.

"It hasn't come up" said Sonny. "But I imagine she knows I eat breakfast on days I don't take the ferry over first thing."

Our waitress set Sonny's coffee in front of him. He downed half a cup. "Y'all go ahead and eat now. Don't let your food get cold."

"What's up with the mail carrier?" I put together a bite of eggs and ham.

Sonny winced. "She was involved in a hit and run Thursday night."

"How awful," said Merry.

"She was just trying to help," said Colleen. "She neither hit nor run."

"She said she only tried to help the victim," I said.

"Yeah, well," said Sonny. "Might be she's just too scared to admit she hit the guy. It was pouring down rain—streets were flooded. Maybe he walked out in front of her, who knows? But he's dead, and she was on the scene."

"You said it was a hit and run," I said. "But clearly she didn't. Run, I mean."

"To be perfectly honest with you, I don't know what happened," said Sonny. "Yet. I'm calling it a hit and run for the time being because I do know the victim was hit by a car. If it wasn't her car, and so far I haven't proven that it was, then it was a hit and run."

"We need to help her," said Colleen.

"Where was the accident?" I asked.

"Near the Lower Battery. Murray Boulevard and Lenwood. Outside the victim's home," said Sonny. "Phillip Drayton is the deceased."

Phillip Drayton. That name rang bells. "Banker of some sort? On the boards of several local charities?"

"You're thinking about his father," said Sonny. "One of the pillars of our community. He passed five years back. Phillip junior was more a professional man about town. Restaurant critic on the side."

"I think I've read his blog," said Merry.

"Since when do you read blogs?" I asked.

"What's a blog?" Colleen looked through the ceiling and into the vast database in the sky where she submits such inquiries. Her resource was far superior to Siri or Alexa.

Merry shrugged. "It was a fluke. One of my kids is working at a restaurant he reviewed." Merry was the executive director of a local non-profit that provided all manner of services to at-risk teenagers.

"What was that the mailwoman was saying about someone having a reason to run over him?" I asked.

"Who knows?" said Sonny. "She's certifiable."

I looked at him for a long moment.

"What?" he asked.

"That's a little harsh, don't you think?" Merry said.

"The woman makes me think of bunnies," I said.

He ran a hand through his hair. "I guess you're right. It's been long couple of days. I haven't slept more than three hours since Thursday night. She's just...she keeps showing up. Everywhere. I'm waiting for the forensic reports to see if we can tie her car to the accident. But she won't leave me be."

"Does she have any connection to Phillip Drayton?" I asked.

"Oh yeah." Sonny raised both eyebrows, nodded. "She was his mail carrier."

"That's it?" I asked.

"Poppy Oliver is not your average mail carrier," said Sonny. "She takes a keen interest in the folks on her route. But I haven't found evidence of any other connection."

"Why does she think someone had a reason to hit him with a car?" I asked.

He closed his eyes. "She imagines he abused his wife."

"She imagines that?" I asked. "That's a pretty serious allegation. What does the wife say?"

"No. No. No." Sonny shook his head, then looked around in desperation. "Where is that waitress? What the hell is wrong with me? I need more coffee. And some breakfast."

"What?" I gave him an innocent look. "I'm just making conversation while we wait. Merry and I are downtown to find her some hiking boots for her wedding trip, not fiddle with your hit and run."

"That's right. It's *my* hit and run. This is not your case." Sonny turned to Merry, studied her like she was a puzzle he was trying to solve. "I never figured you for a woman who would want to rough it on her honeymoon. Or anytime, come to think of it. Isn't that trip a bit...rustic for your tastes?"

"What? You think I can't handle an afternoon hike?" Merry asked.

"Most high maintenance women want five-star hotels and room service on their honeymoons," said Sonny. "Not tent camping and communal showers."

Merry, Colleen, and I burst out laughing. My sister was definitely not the tent type—neither was I, for that matter. Not that there was anything wrong with tents. Colleen's unique bray-snort laugh got me even more tickled.

The harder I laughed, the harder Merry laughed. Soon tears ran down both our faces. I reached for the tissues in my purse, handed one to Merry, and dabbed at my eyes. Finally, we composed ourselves.

"The tour company we're going with has us booked in very nice hotels." Merry managed to get the words out as she caught her breath.

"Huh." Sonny raised his eyebrows. "I thought visiting that part of the world was all about exploring untouched nature."

"Well, it is," said Merry. "We'll get to see plenty of the great outdoors."

"They'll have front row seats to nature," I said. "In the lap of luxury."

"Hey now," said Merry. "It's not a bus tour. We're going kayaking, biking, hiking, horseback riding—all that. We'll see plenty of flora and fauna during the day. Then go back to a hot shower and a nice bed."

"Except on spa days." I grinned at her.

"Exactly," said Merry.

The waitress approached with Sonny's egg platter. He moved his arms off the table and sat back to give her plenty of room.

I eyed his breakfast. "I haven't tried the Eggs Meeting Street. I may order that next time." The fried green tomato, crab cake, and poached egg with remoulade sauce concoction was served with a biscuit and a side of grits. I may have looked at his plate with longing.

He picked up his fork and crowded his food. "Stay back."

"Are you feeling territorial about everything this morning?" I asked.

He ignored me and delivered a bite of breakfast to his mouth.

Colleen said, "That girl's in trouble and we need to help her."

"I guess it's hard to afford an attorney on a mail carrier's salary," I mused.

"They have this new thing called public defenders for folks who can't afford attorneys," said Sonny. "If she's charged, the judge will appoint her one."

"Yeah, I guess a public defender could look into the wife abuse angle," I said. Like that would happen. Public defenders didn't have the resources to run down alternate theories of a crime. That was the province of high-dollar defense attorneys with in-house investigators.

Colleen stared at me, smirked. What was she up to?

"I hope they have better sense," said Sonny.

"The wife say she wasn't abused?" I asked.

"So far she's been too upset to discuss the wild imaginings of her letter carrier. Her relatively young husband just died suddenly. I haven't bothered her with Miss Oliver's theories."

"So, she could be right as far as you know," I said.

"Can't imagine what difference it would make, is my point," Sonny said. "Phillip Drayton is dead. If he ever abused his wife, he won't be doing it anymore. It's not like *she* ran him over."

"You sure about that?" I asked.

He chewed thoughtfully for a minute. "Would you pass the pepper?"

I slid the salt and pepper shakers across the table. "Did the mail carrier see the accident?"

"You see where that new tropical depression became a storm overnight? Idell," said Sonny.

My heart stuttered. I couldn't catch my breath. That made three storms churning in the Atlantic. Most of my life I'd taken tropical storms in stride. They were simply a fact of life on the coast. But recently I'd been having nightmares. And Colleen's cryptic warnings had heightened my awareness.

I took a deep breath, gathered my wits. "Sonny? Did the mail carrier see the accident or not?"

"Could I please just eat my breakfast in peace?" asked Sonny.

I raised an eyebrow at him and forced a bite of the French toast Merry had slid onto my plate. It really was in a class by itself—a hunk of currant bread stuffed with peaches, fried up, dripping with butter and peach cider syrup.

"Save me some of that," said Colleen.

We ate in silence until my natural curiosity got the better of me. "It's a puzzlement."

"What's that?" Sonny smeared butter and strawberry preserves on half his biscuit.

"Why that mail carrier would harass you. Looks like she'd want to stay on your good side, hope you'd take her word for what happened."

"I told you, she's nutty," said Sonny.

"You know her well, do you?" I asked.

"No," he said. "But most people don't hound police detectives when they want to be taken seriously."

"Maybe she's just trying to do the right thing," said Merry.

"How's that?" asked Sonny. "By showing up at the department unannounced, hanging out near the Draytons' house, waiting for me, following me to breakfast? How is any of that the right thing?"

"What is she trying to convince you of?" I asked.

"That Phillip Drayton abused his wife, so someone probably ran into him on purpose. But it wasn't her."

"Why don't you believe her?" I asked.

He was silent for a few minutes. Then he said, "You coming tonight? To The Pirates' Den?"

"Of course we are." Sonny and my brother Blake were in a band, The Back Porch Prophets, that played at The Pirates' Den on Stella Maris once a month. "There must be a reason why you don't believe her."

"There is." He nodded and took another bite of his breakfast.

"You see," said Colleen. "She needs our help."

I pondered that. I couldn't argue with Colleen. And I had strong instincts to do what I could for Poppy. But Sonny was a skilled detective and he was my friend.

It's not that I'd never stuck my nose into his cases before. But I'd only ever done that because someone hired me to do it. Jumping in pro bono felt like me saying I didn't trust him to do his job.

*Sonny's got this.*

Colleen's green eyes flashed. "He's made up his mind already. He's mule-headed. And he's wrong."

*What do you know about this?*

"I know Poppy is telling the truth," said Colleen.

"If you're not going to eat that, can I have it back?" Merry stared at the French toast on my plate.

"I'm eating it." I cut off a bite, swirled it in syrup, and popped it in my mouth with a look that said, *See?*

The blues rift ringtone on my iPhone announced a call from Nate.

"I just got a call from your favorite attorney," he said when I answered. His tone alerted me that he was being facetious.

"Do tell," I said. "And what does Fraser Rutledge, Esquire, want?" I had ambivalent emotions about the Broad Street attorney we'd worked a case for a few months back. His tendency to patronize me worked my nerves.

"To hire us."

"We've already turned him down." Fraser and his partner had offered us a spot as their in-house investigators. Nate and I liked our independence.

"He wants us to look into something for one of his clients—contract work, like before. What do you think?" Nate asked.

I sighed. "I think Rutledge and Ratcliffe pay their bills promptly, we need to set aside money for taxes and insurance on the house, we're going to have to paint soon, and we need a new roof. Why are you hesitating?"

"The man has a habit of antagonizing you, which I don't care for," said Nate.

"I can handle Fraser Alston Rutledge the third."

"He wants to meet with us at one p.m."

"Today?" I asked.

"Yes."

"It has to be today?" My eyes met Merry's. We'd planned this day for weeks.

"If we want the case," said Nate. "That's what he says, anyway. If I tell him we'll be there Monday morning, I'm betting he'll decide that works for him."

"See him today." Colleen went to glowing. That was usually a sign something was important.

I telegraphed regret with my eyes to my sister. "Better tell him we'll see him at one."

# TWO

The law offices of Fraser Alston Rutledge III and his partner, Eli Radcliffe, sat a few doors down from East Bay on Broad Street. The building dated back to 1856—a two-story, rusty-pink stucco affair with large palladium windows. A carved globe, scroll, and book in the parapet testified to its original purpose—a bookstore. I could smell history as we walked through the door.

Mercedes Westbrook, Fraser's assistant, greeted us. Cool, thin, and elegant, Mercedes could've done well for herself as a runway model. She escorted us to Fraser's cypress-paneled office on the second floor. He and Eli stood as we walked in. Fraser wore a pale blue seersucker suit with a navy bow tie. Cut short on the sides, his brown hair stood straight up on end across the top of his head. It wasn't unattractive—it just wasn't a style commonly worn by the gentlemen who ran in his social circle. In a tailored, charcoal grey suit, pale grey shirt, and slate grey tie, Eli Radcliffe might have stepped off the cover of GQ. He was tall and solid, with skin the color of milk chocolate truffles. Both men's families had been in Charleston since long before the building we occupied.

"*Miz* Talbot. Mr. Andrews." Fraser extended a hand. "Thank you for coming on such short notice. You remember my partner, Eli Radcliffe."

We all said hello, shook hands, and settled into the same chairs we'd occupied back in May, the first time we'd done investigative work for the firm. Colleen perched in the same spot on the corner of Fraser's desk. She'd changed into a pink flowered sundress for the occasion. Mischief danced in her eyes.

"What can we help you with?" asked Nate.

"I assume you all have heard the news of Phillip Drayton's untimely death," said Fraser.

I cut my eyes at Colleen. This could not be a coincidence. "Yes," I said.

"No." Nate spoke at the same time, glanced my way.

Colleen smirked. I purely hated it when she smirked.

"Hit and run," said Fraser. "Happened late Thursday night, right at the end of his driveway over on Lenwood."

"Charleston PD is still investigating, I believe," I said.

"That is what I am told, Miz Talbot." Fraser savored every honeyed word that passed his lips so much that he rarely used a contraction. The cadence of his voice brought to mind a tent revival preacher.

We waited for him to continue.

Eli said, "We have a client who would like to offer the authorities assistance by way of additional manpower. This client has authorized us to hire an independent investigative team."

"Naturally, we immediately thought of the two of you." Fraser looked at Nate as he spoke. Then his gold, brown-flecked eyes settled on me.

"We appreciate your confidence," said Nate. "But what makes your client think the police need assistance with this case?"

"I am afraid that information is confidential," said Eli.

Fraser cast Eli a quelling glance. "Why, our law enforcement officers are perennially understaffed and stretched thin, are they not? This is merely a precaution."

"Is there a reason your client didn't come to us himself—or herself?" I asked. "I understand asking for a recommendation, but why not hire us directly?"

"Because this client wishes to remain anonymous," said Eli.

I shook my head.

"I'm sorry," Nate said. "We can't help you."

"What you *mean*," said Fraser, "is that you do not want to help us."

Nate spread his arms, palms up. "I mean that's not the way we do business."

"We don't work for anonymous clients," I said.

"Oh, no, no," said Fraser. "I am afraid you misapprehend the situation. Eli and I would be your clients. Just like on the Gerhardt case."

"Any party who has an interest in this case very likely has information regarding this case," I said. "The first thing we do is talk with everyone involved. Not knowing who wants Phillip Drayton's death investigated—or why—would tie our hands."

"Now, Miz Talbot, I assure you that is not the case," said Fraser. "Our client merely has a soft spot for a young woman who has become entangled in the police department's investigation. A young woman who our client is convinced is innocent of any involvement in Phillip Drayton's death."

"Poppy Oliver. Of course." I raised an eyebrow at Colleen, which naturally, Fraser completely misinterpreted.

"Told you so." Colleen's voice had a sing-song quality.

Nate and Fraser both stared at me, Nate with confusion, Fraser suspicion.

"As a matter of fact, yes," said Eli. "Our client insists that Miss Oliver was merely the unlucky soul who happened upon the scene of a hit and run moments after it happened, in the midst of torrential rain."

"And she tried to help him," said Colleen. "No good deed goes unpunished in this world, that's for sure."

"How could your client know that unless he or she witnessed the incident?" I asked.

"Because our client has known Miss Oliver for a number of years, and can vouch for her moral rectitude," said Fraser.

"Sadly, good character doesn't come with a forcefield against accidents," I said.

"That's true," said Eli, "but honorable people tell the truth about what happened. Our client is certain Miss Oliver is telling the truth."

Nate said, "Just so I understand the facts, Miss Oliver was on the scene when the police arrived? But claims she didn't hit Phillip Drayton?"

"Correct," said Fraser.

"Was her car damaged?" I asked. Sonny had said that he hadn't tied her car to the accident yet.

Eli said, "Miss Oliver drives an older car, which does have a dent on the front end, but that dent has been there since she purchased the car. As I understand it, the unusual amount of rain in combination with a King Tide, which led to street flooding, has complicated the forensic investigation. Miss Oliver maintains that she happened upon Mr. Drayton lying in the street."

"The detective assigned to the case seems disinclined to believe her," said Fraser.

"It's Sonny's case," I said to Nate.

Nate lifted his chin, nodded slightly. "Sonny Ravenel is a solid detective, and a friend. That's one more reason this is a bad idea."

Colleen went to glowing. "Even the best detectives get it wrong sometimes. Poppy needs our help. Sonny too."

Nate closed his eyes, muttered under his breath.

Fraser looked at Nate. "If that is how you feel about it, I suppose I will have to call someone else." He stood.

"That won't be necessary." I kept my voice neutral. "Nate..."

"Fine." Nate shook his head. "Fine."

"We'll look into it," I said.

Fraser looked from me to Nate, then back, unexpressed commentary in his eyes. "Very well then." He raised his voice. "Mercedes."

Mercedes opened the door and glided into the room. She placed some documents in front of Fraser.

"Thank you, darlin'." He nodded, smiled up at her.

Mercedes turned and glided towards the door.

Fraser's smile widened, eyes all aglow. He watched her until the door closed behind her, shaking his head slowly. "Umm, umm, umm. I am telling you."

I heaved a sigh and glanced at the ceiling.

"Not a thing wrong with appreciating the Good Lord's fine craftsmanship, Miz Talbot," said Fraser. "Even my wife tolerates me looking, just as long as I don't touch."

As he flipped through the papers, initialing and signing, he said, "This is a contract for your services, at your standard rate plus twenty percent, plus any expenses. It is an open-ended agreement—not for this case alone."

"Hold on now," said Nate.

"We've already discussed this," I said. "Nate and I—"

"Do not wish to join our staff as in-house investigators. You have made that abundantly clear," said Fraser. "This is not an employment contract. It merely stipulates terms for occasional freelance work, not limited to this case. It allows us to work together on another matter next month, or the month after, without having to execute yet another contract. All of the terms of our initial agreement—terms you set—are incorporated. I trust that is acceptable? There are two originals here." He handed Nate the documents.

Nate passed one copy to me. We both read every word before signing. Nate gave one copy back to Fraser.

"Miss Oliver lives over on Wentworth," said Fraser, "in a studio apartment above Mrs. Aida Butler's garage. Here is the address and Miss Oliver's cell phone number." He handed me an index card. "We do have one further piece of information regarding this case, which you are likely not aware of."

Nate, Colleen, and I all stared at him expectantly.

"Eli?" said Fraser.

Eli said, "There were two calls to 911 regarding the accident resulting in Phillip Drayton's death. One from the victim's phone and one from a burner phone."

I felt my face squinch.

"A burner phone?" said Nate.

Generally speaking, folks who used disposable cell phones had a greater need of privacy than the average citizen. Typically, they were involved in something they needed to hide, sometimes from their spouses, sometimes from law enforcement.

"Poppy Oliver called from the victim's phone?" I asked.

"I am afraid you'll have to ask her that question," said Eli.

"Wait just a minute," I said. "There are only three ways your client could know that two calls were made to 911—about the burner phone. Either your client was a witness to the incident, an accessory after the fact, or he or she is a member of local law enforcement. And I don't think the latter is likely. Gentlemen, if your client is a witness or an accessory, they need to talk to the police. We can't cover up the fact that there *is* a witness."

"Now, *Miz* Talbot, pray do not distress yourself. Eli never said that our client gave us that particular piece of information. Naturally, Eli and I have connections within the Charleston Police Department. We have made preliminary inquiries."

I glanced at Eli, recalled how he and Sonny were good friends. Maybe that's how it happened.

"What are we supposed to tell Poppy Oliver?" asked Nate. "Is she to know why we're investigating this case?"

"She is not," said Fraser. "You are not to tell her that you were hired on her behalf, nor anything about our agreement, nor even that our firm is involved at all. You should tell her only that you have a client who has retained you to look into the matter and, as is your custom, that client is confidential."

"We tell Sonny the whole truth," I said. This was not negotiable.

"I've already told him," said Eli. "We spoke on the phone about an hour ago. I can't say he's enthusiastic about having help on the case. He became less forthcoming after I shared that information. However, he does understand that you don't know who our client is and that we are, obviously, bound by privilege. I don't think he'll expect you to divulge our client's identity."

That would be helpful. Otherwise, it would be like Sonny to clam up until we told him the client's name. He would have the same reaction I'd had—the client knows something. Eli had done us a favor.

"Well, let's get to it then." Colleen disappeared in a multicolored spray of sparks.

# THREE

It was hot as blue blazes on the sidewalk. We crossed the street and headed up Broad towards The Blind Tiger Pub. I wasn't hungry after the brunch I'd eaten, but Nate was starving, and a glass of iced tea sounded really good to me. I called Sonny and he agreed to meet us.

The Blind Tiger Pub has changed owners a few times, but it's been around since 1992. The building itself dates back to 1803. During prohibition, folks would pay an admission fee to see a live tiger—one that didn't exist—and get free drinks at many a Charleston speakeasy. The current pub name is a hat tip to the historic tradition.

Normally in August we'd opt for a table indoors, but it would be easier to hear each other outside. We followed the hostess through the dark-paneled bar into the brick-walled courtyard. It was open to the sky but divided into multiple rooms by still more brick walls with charming arched entrances from one section to another.

Thankfully, the back-corner table under the shade of a lean-to roof was free. Overhead, a ceiling fan stirred the air. As soon as we were seated at the round wooden four-top, I reached into my purse for a hair clip. I couldn't think with all that hair on my neck. We ordered iced tea for ourselves and for Sonny, and a cheeseburger and fries for Nate.

When the waitress was a few steps away, I said, "You realize he's bribing us. Fraser."

"You mean by paying us twenty percent above our standard rate?"

"Exactly. He's hoping that will entice us to take the next case he comes to us with, then the next, and the next one after that, until we're just as good as working for him."

"It's still our choice. Right now, the money comes in handy. As usual, there are several valid reasons to be irritated at him. The extra money...that offsets the irritation somewhat in my book."

"Hmm...an irritation surcharge. That works for me." The waitress set glasses in front of us and I sipped my tea. "Dang that Colleen. You might know she'd cut out without answering questions."

I filled Nate in on the scene with Sonny and Poppy at brunch. "I'm reasonably certain Colleen inspired *someone* to call Rutledge & Radcliffe. Which means she knows who their client is—she's responsible for this entire arrangement."

He rolled his lips in and out, seemed to ponder what I said. "There's a difference between Colleen insisting we work this case and Colleen certifying Poppy's innocence. You're saying she's vouching for her as well?"

"Apparently," I said. "We have so little to go on here. The way I see it, there are only three possibilities: One, Sonny's right and Poppy Oliver hit Phillip Drayton with her car and is scared to tell the truth—"

"It just warms the cockles of my heart to hear that you're willing to consider the possibility that I might be right." Sonny tucked into the empty chair with a tea glass in front of it.

I raised an eyebrow at him and continued. "Two, someone else accidentally ran into him and left the scene. Poppy came upon Phillip lying in the street and stopped to help. Or, three, someone else hit Phillip Drayton on purpose and fled."

"I see a fourth possibility," said Nate. "All this testifying to Poppy's strong moral fiber notwithstanding, we can't rule out that she hit Phillip Drayton intentionally, at least not yet."

"No, we can't," said Sonny. "Especially given that she seems overly involved with the private lives of the people on her route. She insists Phillip Drayton abused his wife. Maybe Miss Oliver thought she was saving the wife somehow, who knows?"

"Seriously?" I said. "Hell's bells, Sonny. You're a better judge of character than that. She strikes me as the sort who carefully scoops up spiders from the kitchen floor and finds them a new home outside."

"You analyzed her character in the, what, three minutes you saw her this morning?" asked Sonny. "I've spent a bit more time with her than you have. And yes, I will grant you, she doesn't seem the homicidal type. But people can fool you. I don't have to tell you that."

The waitress arrived with Nate's cheeseburger. He lifted the top of the bun and generously applied black pepper to the lettuce and tomato. "Eli mentioned there were two calls to 911. Did Poppy make the call from Drayton's cell? Did you find the burner?"

Sonny stared at the condensation on his tea glass. "It's just like I told Eli. I don't understand why, after less than forty-eight hours, somebody feels like we need extra hands on this case. Let me do my job, would you?"

"Sonny Ravenel." I admonished him with a look borrowed from Mamma. "Did you or did you not advise Poppy Oliver to retain legal counsel this very morning?"

"Well, yeah, but that was just to give her someone to talk to so she'd leave me alone and *let me do my job*."

"We'll talk to her," I said. "She has legal counsel now. And they have hired investigators, like any attorney with the means would."

"Nah," said Sonny. "Eli told me they weren't going to have any contact with her. They're not advising her. She needs someone to talk sense to her."

"And we will—I promise." I offered him my sunniest smile.

"Now, how about this? We'll talk to her. Get her to stop following you around and all that. And you tell us what you know so we don't repeat the things you've already done."

Sonny sat back in his chair. "And you'll give me everything you find?"

Nate and I exchanged a glance.

"You know we can't," I said. "Our report will be attorney work-product. It will be privileged."

"I show you mine and you keep all your toys to yourself." Sonny huffed out a breath, shook his head. "You know, I'm not sure that argument would hold up in court in this case. There's been no communication between Poppy Oliver and Rutledge & Radcliffe. Ergo, no privileged communication."

"I tell you what," I said. "If and when this case goes to court, we'll let the solicitor fight that one out with Fraser. Meantime, you know we'll give you anything we can. Good grief. If it exonerates Poppy Oliver, or points to someone else's guilt, of course our client will want us to share it. That's the whole point of hiring us—to make Poppy's problems go away."

Sonny closed his eyes, sighed, then opened them. "The calls came roughly three minutes apart. First one was from the victim's cell, at 9:42. A woman's voice, extremely agitated—hysterical. Could've been Poppy Oliver. The tape is being analyzed. All she said was, 'A man's been hit by a car. Lenwood and Murray. Send an ambulance. Hurry. Oh God. Please hurry.' The words were practically screamed, but muffled. It's possible she was trying to disguise her voice by holding something over the phone."

"And the second call?" asked Nate.

"Came from a burner phone," said Sonny. "Also a woman's voice. She said, 'Send help immediately to the intersection of Murray and Lenwood. A man's been hit by a large white sport utility vehicle.' The accent and diction indicate it was likely someone from around here. Educated. Could've been a neighbor, but why use a burner? It was raining—hard. The streets were flooded. Any other night I'd say it might be a jogger, dog walker, something like that—a tourist out for a stroll even. But not in all that rain."

"The first caller didn't describe the vehicle." Nate looked at Sonny. "That tells me the first caller was likely the person who hit Drayton. The second caller was a witness."

"That's the way I read it," said Sonny.

"You said the first call could've been Poppy. But you didn't say that about the second call," I said. "Why?"

Sonny grimaced, turned his palms up. "It sounded like an older woman. It was...regal. I made it for a local matron."

"With a burner phone," I said.

"Yep," said Sonny.

"You find either phone?" asked Nate.

"Nope," said Sonny. "Uniforms scoured the whole tip of the peninsula."

"What did Poppy say?" I asked. "Did she say she called 911?"

"No," said Sonny. "Her phone battery was dead. We confirmed that. We searched her car and her person. By the time we arrived, she had no other phone in her possession. She stated that she was searching the victim's clothing for a phone when we arrived."

"It seems unlikely to me that she would've hit him on purpose, then stopped for any reason. Her actions aren't consistent with intent. I don't see scenario four as viable," I said.

Nate shrugged. "Maybe she's that smart. What does she drive?"

"Subaru Outback, 2004, white," said Sonny.

"The color may be right, but I would hardly describe that as a large SUV," I said.

"Some folks might," said Sonny. "Plus, did I mention how hard it was raining?"

"Any damage to the Subaru?" Of course, I knew the answer to

this question, but I wanted Sonny's take.

Sonny winced. "Front bumper's all dented up. Nothing that can be conclusively tied to the accident. Forensics still has the car, but, again, the rain. If there was any trace evidence—fibers, anything—it was washed away."

"Or Phillip Drayton was hit by another car altogether," I said.

"It's possible," said Sonny.

"What about the wife?" I asked. "Where was she when her husband was killed?"

"Mrs. Drayton—Anne Frances Drayton—was at home at the time of the incident," said Sonny.

"And how do you know she didn't do this?" I asked. "Seeing as how she was maybe abused and all? This could've been a domestic disturbance that escalated."

"I know Mrs. Drayton did not plow a car into her husband because when I arrived at her front door at 9:50—just five minutes after the second 911 call—she answered the door dressed in dry pajamas and a robe. She seemed groggy, stated that she'd taken migraine medication and gone to bed at 8:00 p.m. Her hair—nothing—was wet. There was no evidence of water tracked into the home and both cars were in the garage, dry. There were no wet tire tracks. Both engines were cool. No one had driven either vehicle in several hours. I suppose it's possible she borrowed or rented a car, lured her husband out into a rainstorm, and ran him down. She could've then ditched the car, sneaked back inside the house through the backdoor so Poppy Oliver didn't see her, and changed into her pajamas. But if she somehow managed all that inside five minutes, she'd have been wide awake and out of breath when she answered the door, and there would've been a pile of wet clothes somewhere in that house. There was not."

"How'd you get there so fast?" Nate asked.

I knew what he was thinking. Typically, detectives weren't dispatched for 911 calls. Only after a patrol unit along with fire and rescue made an assessment would a detective be called in.

"I was on Ladson—few blocks away. Had just finished taking a statement in another case. I had my radio on in the car. Night like that, I figured it could've taken longer for first responders to get there. Minutes matter." He shrugged. "I was the first on the scene, but patrol and EMTs were right behind me."

"She could've hired someone," I said. "The wife."

"Maybe," said Sonny. "But if she paid them, there's zero evidence of it in any bank account attached to her social security number. No unusual withdrawals. No cash transactions more than two hundred dollars in the last six months, and only a few of those. Trust me. We're looking at her hard. She's the spouse. You know the odds on that. Plus, Drayton's brother made it clear he's suspicious of her."

"Let me guess," I said. "She inherits all the money."

"Yep," said Sonny. "Well, the brother, Daniel Drayton, he's by no means a pauper. He got his half of Phillip senior's estate. But he was also his brother's heir until Phillip junior married five years ago. Their mother passed when they were kids. No other siblings. No children."

"Where did Mrs. Drayton think her husband was?" I asked. "When did she last see him?"

"She says he was in the den sipping bourbon and watching *Breaking Bad* when she went to bed," said Sonny.

"I'm guessing you guys talked to the neighbors," said Nate.

"Everyone who was home at the time. No one saw anything. No one heard anything until the lights and sirens," said Sonny.

"The evidence against Poppy seems awfully thin." I gave Sonny a long, hard look. "What aren't you telling us? I asked you this morning why you didn't believe her, and you blew me off."

Sonny took a sip of iced tea. "Phillip Drayton's injuries include multiple broken bones and internal injuries, plus a fractured skull. The head injury killed him. All of these injuries are consistent with being hit by a car. But he suffered other injuries within an hour of his death that aren't explained by a motor vehicle impact."

Nate and I both squinted at him.

"What other injuries?" I asked.

"Skin marks consistent with a Taser," said Sonny. "His lungs, eyes, and mucus membranes showed evidence of pepper spray. He had a puncture wound to the forearm. No evidence of any of those weapons in the family home. The wife consented to a search."

Nate and I processed that for a few moments.

"Did Poppy Oliver have any of those weapons in her possession?" I asked.

"No," said Sonny. "But whatever happened, it happened across the street from the Ashley River, within an hour of high tide. It would've been real convenient if you were trying to get rid of evidence."

"The wife could have easily run across the street and dumped the evidence." I was thinking aloud. "But she would've had to have bundled up really well to keep dry."

"Not a single wet coat, boot, or shoe in the house," said Sonny.

"But why would Poppy hang around if she was responsible, after she tossed the weapons in the river?" I asked.

Sonny shrugged. "Maybe she ditched the evidence, and when she was running back to her car she worried she didn't have enough time to get away before the first emergency vehicles arrived. Decided to stage a good Samaritan scenario."

"But she would've waited until she had dumped everything before calling 911—if she were guilty and getting rid of evidence," I said.

"That's...I'm struggling to imagine a series of events that would lead to those particular injuries and involve a car collision," said Nate.

"You and me both, brother," said Sonny.

"And why on God's green earth was he outside on foot in the

middle of a monsoon to begin with?" I asked.

"That," said Sonny, "is the sixty-four-thousand-dollar question."

I flagged our waitress down. "I'd like an order of the Bleu Chips, please." I needed to ponder things, and the house-made kettle chips with gorgonzola fondue, crumbled blue cheese, bacon, and scallions were excellent pondering food.

"Looks like we can rule out the accident scenario," I said. What I didn't say is that I knew exactly what Sonny was thinking. He was thinking that Poppy and the wife were in it together.

# FOUR

After Sonny left, Nate and I decided to divide and conquer. Because we hadn't spoken directly to any of the people involved, it felt like we knew less about this case at the outset than any we'd ever undertaken, and we needed to catch up fast—before Poppy Oliver ended up in the county detention center. So far, we only knew of three parties connected to Phillip Drayton: his wife, his brother, and Poppy Oliver. Both women had been in the immediate vicinity when Phillip died.

Later, when we were back at our desks, we'd profile the victim, his brother, and both women. No doubt this would provide additional avenues of investigation. But for now, we'd start with Anne Frances Drayton and Poppy Oliver. Because Poppy had seen me with Sonny that very morning, Nate set out to find and surveil her. It was 3:45 and she would likely soon be finished with her route for the day.

I'd parked my Escape in a metered spot on Broad Street near State. I opened the lift gate and pulled out the duffle where I kept wardrobe options. It wasn't uncommon for me to swap out shoes, jackets, hats, shirts—even entire outfits—especially if I was running surveillance. I traded my Kate Spade sandals for cross trainers and no-show socks, tucked my hair under a pink Life is Good cap, and donned my biggest sunglasses.

Thankfully, I'd dressed in lightweight capris and a tank with a blouse over it. I slipped off the blouse and smoothed on a layer of sunscreen. From a file box, I grabbed a colorful tourist map of

Charleston and stuck it in the back pocket of my capris. Then I closed the lift gate, climbed into the driver's seat, and pulled into traffic, heading west on Broad Street.

Downtown Charleston—the part most people think of when they think of the Holy City—occupies a peninsula bordered by the Ashley and Cooper Rivers. White Point Garden sits on the point of the peninsula, where the rivers converge and spill into Charleston Harbor. South of Broad, the residential neighborhood where I was headed, was made up of a mix of modern streets and cobblestone and brick lanes. Pastel, rich-hued, and brick homes, in a variety of architectural styles spanning every period of American history, lined the streets.

I made a left on Meeting and followed it to where it dead-ended at South Battery, across from White Point Garden. The Drayton home sat in the adjacent block, on the corner of Murray and Lenwood, with South Battery and King Street forming the other two sides of the block. I made a right on South Battery and street-parked a few houses past the King Street intersection. Without a residential permit, I was flirting with a parking ticket. It wouldn't be my first.

I climbed out of the car, grabbed a bottle of water from the cooler behind the driver's seat, and walked back to the intersection of South Battery and King. Across the street, a mix of young mothers with small children, folks walking dogs, girls' weekenders, and old men swapping tall tales sheltered from the August sun in the sprawling canopy of White Point Garden's live oaks. A handful of oiled sun worshipers courted melanoma on brightly colored blankets and beach towels.

I turned right on King Street, quickly covered the block to Murray, then crossed over to join the stream of people strolling along the Lower Battery promenade. On my right, a row of parked cars stretched along Murray Boulevard as if to fortify the Battery. A young man waited as a pretty brunette unbuckled a little girl from a car seat in back of a Hyundai. Alone in a grey Honda with windows rolled down, a blonde stared across the water.

To my left, the water sparkled in the afternoon sun. Sailboats glided and powerboats plowed in and out of the mouth of the Ashley River, heading between the City Marina and Charleston Harbor. A happy couple on board a Catalina waved and I waved back.

As I approached the Drayton home, I slowed my pace. It was a two-story red brick house with black shutters. Dual sets of curved steps swept up from the front walk to a semi-circular covered stoop with white columns. While the architecture had Georgian elements, the raised first floor was all Lowcountry. It was a lovely home, large and solid. Situated where it was, no doubt it was worth multiple millions of dollars. But it wasn't a historic property, perhaps mid-twentieth century. I meandered down the walkway, taking in the lovely wrought iron fence and meticulous landscaping just like any tourist might do. This was Charleston, after all. Everyone stared at homes here.

Was Mrs. Drayton home? I wasn't planning to disturb her—I wanted a lot more information before I sat down to chat with her. I just wanted to get a look at where Phillip Drayton had met his untimely end. And I was hoping for inspiration. What on earth had happened here?

I made a right turn, crossing Murray Boulevard and heading up Lenwood. A row of palm trees lined the street on the outer edge of the sidewalk. Cars with residential permits were street parked on the right side of Lenwood. Two car-lengths from the corner, the Drayton's driveway intersected the sidewalk and led to a two-car garage underneath the house. I stood at the end of the driveway and studied the street. This was where it had happened.

Whoever had hit Phillip Drayton, their vision had very likely been impeded by cars parked along the street—and the rain. But why had he been out here at nearly ten at night in a rainstorm? He must've been running, or he would've seen the car in time to stop. Wait. The pepper spray. His vision would've been impaired, but surely he would've still seen headlights. What—or who—was he running from? Was he running away from his home, or seeking refuge there?

I continued down the sidewalk as I mulled. The backyard of the Drayton home was enclosed in an ivy-covered brick courtyard wall. A wrought-iron gate led from the driveway to the backyard. The only access to the house from the driveway was through the garage. A keypad was mounted on the doorframe.

When Sonny rang the doorbell Thursday night, Mrs. Drayton had heard it and answered. There was no way she'd slept through the kind of ruckus that involved Tasers and pepper spray inside her house, then been awakened by a doorbell. Plus, there'd been no evidence of that kind of struggle in the Drayton home. Where did all that go down?

I made my way around the block. None of the neighbors had heard anything, Sonny said. But what if one of them was involved? Phillip had been attacked somewhere. Was it inside one of these homes? He hadn't driven anywhere. But someone could have picked him up and dropped him off. He was unaccounted for between 8:00 and 9:42 p.m. Theoretically, he could've been attacked anywhere in the county. I kept walking, looking, and mulling.

After I'd circumnavigated the block once, instead of crossing Murray to walk along the Battery, I stayed on the sidewalk that ran right in front of the house for a closer look. The third time around, I went down another block to Limehouse, then turned around and approached from the west to get another perspective before heading back down Lenwood.

On my fifth lap around the block, just as I rounded the corner of Murray and Lenwood, I caught the faint sound of a garage door motor. As I passed by the driveway, the left garage door eased up.

Hmm. It was unlikely anyone aside from Mrs. Drayton would be parked inside the garage. I walked ahead a few steps, then stopped under a palm tree and set my water bottle on the hood of a handy Volvo. I pulled the tourist map out of my pocket, flicked it open, and peeked out from behind the corner.

A silver Lexus sedan with South Carolina plates backed out of the driveway and into the street, turning towards Murray. I made a quick note of the tag number, grabbed my water bottle, then jogged in the opposite direction, towards South Battery. As soon as I made the corner, I broke into a sprint.

I hopped into the car, cranked the engine, darted back down South Battery, and made a left on Lenwood. Naturally, the Lexus was no longer at the intersection of Lenwood and Murray, but I had a better-than-even chance of getting this right. King Street was one-way. Anyone turning left on Murray would have to drive around the point of the peninsula, past White Point Garden. If I were Mrs. Drayton, I'd turn away from the tourist traffic, away from the row of iconic antebellum mansions along East Battery. I made a right onto Murray Boulevard.

From here things would be dicier. Where was she was headed? I glanced up Limehouse as I drove by. No sign of the Lexus. None up Council, either. Rutledge was a one-way street, so I zipped by it. If I stayed on Murray past Ashley, I'd make the switchback turn at the Coast Guard Station, and then be backtracking on Tradd. I made a right on Ashley and accelerated.

I crossed South Battery, then came to a full stop at Tradd. Was that her in front of the Malibu? I continued up Ashley, passing Horse Lot Park on my left. At the intersection of Ashley and Broad, the Malibu in front of me pulled into the left turn lane. I came to a stop behind the silver Lexus. When the light changed, I followed it as it continued up Ashley Avenue, past Colonial Lake, and all the way up to Calhoun Street.

The Lexus turned right on Calhoun, took it to the other side of downtown, and made a right on East Bay. Wherever she was headed, we apparently weren't leaving the peninsula. Eight blocks and two turns later I followed her into the garage at Cumberland and Concord. She climbed to the third level before finding a spot. I snagged one two spots away, which was fortunate since I still had no idea what the woman I was following looked like. I could no doubt google her and see what she looked like at a benefit ball or some such thing. But she likely appeared very different on a Saturday afternoon, two days after her husband was killed.

I pulled off my hat and fluffed my hair. She probably hadn't seen me back on Lenwood, but why take the chance? I swapped out my sunglasses for some sporty, reflective wrap-arounds. When I heard her car door close, I got out of the car and eased mine shut. A willowy brunette with her hair in a loose knot at her neck, wearing white linen slacks, a matching blouse, and a sand-colored scarf walked towards the stairs. I waited a five count and followed, thankful that she wasn't of a mind to take the elevator. This early in the case, I didn't want to be in such close proximity to her for the length of an elevator ride with nothing but mirrored sunglasses as a disguise.

At street level, she went right towards the Cooper River, then turned left at the corner and headed up Concord. A few steps later, she walked into Buxton Books. She wanted reading material? People grieved in different ways. Perhaps she needed a distraction. The space also housed Tour Charleston, one of the city's premier tour companies. One of their more popular tours was a ghost tour. She surely hadn't come for that—or maybe she had. Was she into mediums and the like? Looking for someone to help her communicate with her dead husband? Polly and Julian Buxton weren't conducting séances, as far as I knew. Charleston natives, they owned both the bookshop and the tour company.

Colleen was going to love this.

"Are you going inside or what?"

"Ooh!" My heart seized. "Are you trying to scare me to death?"

Colleen had popped in behind me. "Not really. Though it would be fun for us to be on the same side of the veil again." She sighed. "You've got work yet to do. I repeat. Are you going inside?"

"Do not leave until I've had the chance to talk to you." I pulled the red wooden door open and walked inside. Colleen followed.

The space was light and airy with pale hardwood floors, soft grey walls, and white wainscoting. A Pat Conroy quote was painted above a bookcase on the back wall. I'd been here several times, but it had been a while. It was somewhat unusual, as bookstores go. While the walls were lined with assorted furniture—a desk with a hutch, a secretary, and various tables and bookcases—all housing books, instead of aisles of additional bookcases that filled the space, there were a few tables, some with lovely table skirts, scattered about the room. It was an open concept bookshop, the vibe warm and inviting.

"I haven't read a book since I crossed over." Colleen made a beeline for the display of *The Ghosts of Charleston* by Julian Buxton.

Anne Frances Drayton wasn't in the main room. I glanced to the smaller room to my right. There. She browsed a shelf on the far side of the room.

I recognized Polly Buxton, the attractive brunette behind the cash wrap desk. "Hello," she said. "Is there something in particular I can help you find?" The most striking thing about Polly was her smile, warm and open. She was one of those women whose age was hard to pinpoint. "You've been here before, haven't you?"

"Yes, I have. I'm surprised you remember me. You must meet an awfully lot of people," I said.

"I have a good memory for faces," she said.

Ordinarily, I would've introduced myself and chatted a moment. But I didn't want Mrs. Drayton to catch my name. "I'm just going to browse a bit, if that's okay."

"Of course. Let me know if I can help you," said Polly.

I turned around and scanned the shelves across from the cash wrap desk. This allowed me to keep an eye on when Anne Frances left the corner room. She and I were the only two customers at that particular moment, unless...A silver-haired woman had been standing at the corner of the cash wrap desk. Her skirt suit and low heels told me she wasn't a tourist. The hairdo looked like the variety that involved weekly blowouts at a high-end salon. Behind me, she spoke to Polly in hushed tones. Was she a customer or did she work here?

I moved deeper into the store, positioned myself at the end of an oblong table display. From here I could see all of the main room and the door to the smaller room. I let my eyes slide over the titles, then picked up a book and pretended to read the back cover.

Anne Frances stepped into the main room and moved to the desk and hutch just inside the front door. She picked up a book, studied it, flipped through the pages, then replaced it on the shelf. This was similar to how I shopped for books. If the title and cover caught my eye, I read the inside jacket or the back cover. If that seemed interesting, I'd read the first page. Mrs. Drayton seemed to be reading random samples. She moved in Colleen's direction.

"I wonder if he's going to do a volume two?" said Colleen. "I could introduce him to a ton more lingering spirits."

*That sounds like the kind of thing that falls outside your mission. You're not supposed to be in Charleston following me around on surveillance anyway.* I raised an eyebrow at her.

"Spoilsport," she said. "Can we go on the ghost tour? I could have some fun with that. Really get them to show out."

I just shook my head.

After perusing half a dozen or so books, Mrs. Drayton had worked her way to the secretary underneath the sign that read "Come Walk With Us." The books on display included *The Ghosts of Charleston* and books by and about Edgar Allan Poe, who was stationed at Fort Moultrie on Sullivan's Island while in the Army. A lot of people around here believed that Poe's poem, "Annabel Lee," was written about Anna Ravenel, a young woman from a wealthy local family.

The Ravenel family tree has many branches. If I traced one of them far enough back, I might well find that the object of Poe's desire was Sonny's great-great-great aunt or some such thing. But he refuses to discuss any connection whatsoever to our former state treasurer turned reality TV star.

Legend has it that Edgar Allan Poe and Anna Ravenel were desperately in love, but her father deemed him an unsuitable suitor and refused to allow them to see each other. A man of considerable means and influence, he arranged to have Poe transferred to keep them apart. Not long after, she died from either yellow fever or a broken heart, or perhaps some combination of the two. Her spiteful father hid her exact burial place in the Unitarian graveyard by erecting multiple tombstones to prevent the heartbroken Poe from visiting her grave.

*Is it true?* I threw the thought at Colleen.

"I don't know. I haven't run into either of them so far. But the Lady in White isn't Anna Ravenel—that's Mary Whitridge." The Lady in White was one of Charleston's more active spirits.

I meandered over to the corner shelf, to Mrs. Drayton's left. She was oblivious to the fact that she was rubbing shoulders with a guardian spirit.

Colleen held her ground, studied Anne Frances closely. Anne Frances picked up a copy of *The Ghosts of Charleston*. After skimming a few pages, she slipped it back onto the shelf. Abruptly, she turned towards me. Her eyes were a pale grey/blue. They seemed hard and hollow at the same time. She had the high cheekbones and flawless skin of a model. I flashed her a friendly smile. She slid her sunglasses from the top of her head over her eyes without the faintest upturn of her lips. Her husband had just died. She got a pass on the Southern friendly thing.

Anne Frances walked past me and left the store without buying anything. I didn't dare follow her. She'd surely notice me. I didn't have much to show for the afternoon's work, but at least I'd gotten a good look at her.

Colleen stared after her, but didn't say a word, which was very un-Colleen.

*What do you think?* I asked Colleen.

"I can't read her at all. Her head is all murky."

*That usually means someone is dark inside, right? Not a good person.*

"Not necessarily. Not always. I've told you before. Not all minds are open to me," said Colleen.

*If you say so.* But my memory of the folks Colleen couldn't read was that most of them were up to no good. Before I could ask her if she'd prodded someone into hiring Rutledge & Ratcliffe, she disappeared into thin air.

Dammit, Colleen. Typical.

I browsed for a few more minutes, smiled and waved to Polly and her friend, and made my way back to my car. Mrs. Drayton's Lexus was gone. I called Nate.

"Where are you?" I asked when he answered.

"Wentworth Street. Between Rutledge and Ashley."

"Is Poppy home now?" I asked.

"Unless she climbed over the fence. I followed her here from the post office on East Bay after she finished her route. She's been home about thirty minutes."

"What's she driving?" Charleston PD still had her car.

"A yellow beach cruiser with a basket on the front," he said.

"I bet that was a fun tail."

"Piece of cake. Between the carriage tour and the pedicab I got behind, we were moving at about the same pace. Anyway, it was only a mile and a half."

"Does it seem strange to you that she can afford to live in Harleston Village on a postal carrier's salary?" I asked.

"Studio over a garage? Maybe. Could be something that needs too much work to compete in the short-term rental market."

"Eh—or maybe her landlady prefers one long-term tenant to an endless stream of folks coming for a couple nights. Even still...it seems like the rent would be steep."

"Fair point," said Nate.

"We should talk to her as soon as possible, get her unfiltered version of what happened."

"Agreed. But it may be best if you do that by yourself. Your cover is already blown."

"You want to listen in?" I asked.

"Naturally."

# FIVE

Poppy Oliver agreed to meet with me immediately at her apartment. I had the impression she would've told her story to anyone who would listen. Per her instructions, I parked in the street, opened the gate at the end of the brick driveway and walked to the back of the Butler home. The house was a grey, two-story affair with black shutters and white trim. Unless I missed my guess, it had been here close to two hundred years, though both the house and grounds were well-maintained.

A separate garage, likely originally the carriage house, sat at the end of the driveway, sheltered by an enormous live oak. An exterior set of stairs led to the apartment above the garage. Before I started the climb, I dialed Nate.

"Heading up," I said when he answered. I minimized the call window, tapped the Voice Memo app, and started recording. I loved technology. Nate could listen while I recorded with a different app. I slid my iPhone into the exterior pocket of my cross-body bag upside down, so that the microphone faced up and was unobstructed.

As I climbed the stairs, I ran my hand along the railing. It was solid, as were the steps. From the small landing at the top, I scanned the backyard. Was Mrs. Butler watching from inside the house? I'd always thought living in an apartment above someone's garage would be at the expense of one's privacy.

I started to knock, but the door opened with my fist in midair.

"You." Poppy's eyes held surprise and an accusation. She had changed from her uniform into lightweight cotton lounge pants and a cropped t-shirt. Her cheeks were flushed, either from anger or from delivering mail all day in the August heat and humidity. She looked incredibly vulnerable, and once again, I had the urge to protect her.

"Hey, Poppy. I'm Liz Talbot."

"You were with Detective Ravenel this morning at breakfast," she said.

"Sonny and I are old friends. But that has no bearing on why I'm here. May I come in?"

She hesitated, gave me a doubtful look. "You're a private investigator?"

"That's right."

"Who hired you?" She asked.

"I'll explain everything, but I think we'll be more comfortable if we could sit and talk." I smiled warmly.

She drew a long, slow breath, stared at me from under her eyebrows, then huffed out a sigh that fluttered through her bangs. "Fine. Come in. As long as you understand *I* can't pay you." She stepped back and opened the door wider.

"You won't be getting a bill from me, I promise." I stepped inside.

Her apartment was a perfect little jewel box of a home, maybe 400 square feet total. The walls and cathedral ceiling were done in white painted shiplap siding. Two skylights let in light dappled by the leaves and branches of the tree above. Just inside the door was a galley kitchen with open shelves lined with yellow, blue, and green dishes. A bar with a dark wooden top and two stools separated the kitchen from the rest of the apartment.

A queen-size bed was centered on the far wall. It was covered in a down comforter, with a desert star patterned quilt with blues, yellows, greens, and pops of orange folded across the end. The bed was flanked on one side with an armoire, and on the other, an overstuffed bookcase that reached to the top of the wall. Everything from classics to romance novels to thrillers filled the shelves.

At the foot of the bed, a light-washed denim sofa delineated the living area. A pair of leather armchairs sat on either side of the sofa. Along the far wall, a small flat screen TV hung above a wooden dresser.

"Have a seat," Poppy gestured to the general area of the sofa. "But if he sent you thinking we'd get to talking girl-talk and I'd confess to you that I ran over Mr. Drayton, you and him are both gonna be disappointed."

I perched on one of the chairs. "Sonny didn't send me."

She curled onto the end of the sofa nearest me and reached for a glass on the tea table. She jerked her hand back and jumped up. "I'm so sorry. Would you like something to drink? I mean, would you like some water? That's really all I have, but it's filtered and cold."

"Thank you, that sounds lovely." I hated for her to get back up. She must've been exhausted. But if we both had drinks in our hands, the vibe turned more social. She'd be less likely to hustle me out.

Poppy darted into the kitchen.

I kept up the small talk. My first objective was to make her trust me. "It's a wonder you don't get heatstroke walking around all day in this heat."

"I'm used to it," she said. "The people on my route are really nice, too. They bring me lemonade and, on really hot days, cool towels. They look out for me." She set the glass down on a tea stand by my chair. "And I have no trouble getting my steps in."

I thanked her and she returned to the sofa. When she had resettled, a large grey cat appeared and hopped up beside her.

"This is Ruffles," she said. "Hey sweetie." She stroked the cat and it laid down.

"She's beautiful," I said. "I've never seen a cat with crinkly fur like that." The underside of her neck, chin, and a triangular section of her face around her nose were white.

"I think she's a Selkirk Rex, at least partly," said Poppy. "The breed has wavy hair. But I'm not really sure. Ruffles was a stray. Or maybe I was. Anyway, we found each other." Poppy continued to stroke Ruffles, her gaze resting on the cat. "So, if Detective Ravenel didn't send you, who did?"

"I'm afraid I can't tell you that." I winced, gave her a look filled with apology. "As with most of my cases, my client's identity is confidential. But the important thing is that someone hired me to find out exactly what happened to Phillip Drayton."

"So his brother hired you." She continued petting the cat.

"I really can't say. But if you didn't hit Mr. Drayton with your car, me doing my job can only help you, right?"

"Well, I did *not* hit him." She sighed. Her enthusiasm for telling her story seemed to have waned. "But you might find out some things your client would rather no one knew about. I'm not sure where that will leave me. But what the heck? What do you want to know?"

I sipped my water, then started with the least upsetting topic I needed to cover. "Do you know the people on your route well?"

"We don't see each other socially or anything like that. But we look out for each other. It's what people do," she said.

"Like the water, the cold towels." I nodded.

"Exactly. A couple of the ladies bake me cookies sometimes. One of them tried to fix me up with her grandson." She blushed. Her eyes widened and she looked at the floor with a small smile. "And I...well, I let them know if I see anything out of the ordinary."

"Sure. Like...?" I lifted a shoulder in a shrug of agreement, raised a palm.

She nodded. "Like if their neighbor's package has been on the porch for a couple of days, or a repairman left the crawlspace door open, or someone unfamiliar is hanging around. Or if I see their cat a few houses down, I bring it home with the mail."

"Seems like only the considerate thing to do." I tried to keep her nodding.

"Exactly. Thank you. Who wouldn't keep an eye out for their neighbors?"

"How well do you know Mrs. Drayton?" I asked.

"That poor woman." Poppy shook her head. "She's the sweetest thing. I see her nearly every day. She watches for me. Comes to the door for her mail. They have a mail slot, but I hardly ever use it. She nearly always offers me something to drink. Hot days, she has Gatorade in her hand. If it's cold out? Coffee or hot chocolate."

"Why did you call her 'that poor woman?'"

Poppy bit her lip, hesitated. "I think she's lonely, which is strange because she's a really nice lady, and gorgeous—she could have a ton of friends. I usually get to her house between 12:30 and 1:00. She's usually there. Most women in her shoes would be out to fancy lunches, or shopping, or at the spa. But it's more than that."

I waited for her to continue.

"You know how hot it's been the last two weeks? Mid to high nineties. Close to one hundred degrees a couple of days. But Mrs. Drayton always has on long pants with long sleeve blouses and scarves. No matter how hot it gets. Somedays she comes to the door wearing sunglasses. Don't you think that's strange?"

"It does seem a bit unusual." Anne Frances Drayton had been wearing long sleeves and slacks when I saw her too, but the ensemble was white linen—hardly seasonally inappropriate.

"Yeah, well, more than once, her sleeve has slipped up when she handed me a drink, or her scarf gaped, and I could see the bruises."

"What kind of bruises?" I asked.

"All kinds. *Someone* beats the daylights out of her. A couple of times it looked like someone tried to choke her," said Poppy.

I reflected on that for a moment. "Has she ever said anything? Asked for help?"

"No, of course not. If she had asked for help, I could've called social services or the police. Once I asked her what happened to her arm. It was all black and blue. She said she'd fallen. Said she was clumsy—always tripping over something. Laughed this fake little laugh." Poppy shook her head slowly, stared into space.

"Did you ever meet her husband?"

"Not really. I mean, I've seen him coming and going. He's never spoken to me. He always seems busy, distracted."

"Did you ever see them together?"

"No."

"You told Sonny that he abused her," I said.

She gave a huff of disgust. "Well, someone did. Who else would it be? If your wife had bruises like that and you knew *you* didn't put them there, wouldn't you find out what was going on? Put a stop to it?"

"I suppose so," I said. "But no one really knows what goes on behind closed doors, do they?" In my line of work, I'd seen all manner of marital relationships. Domestic abuse was abhorrent— I'd seen it up close and had intervened on more than one occasion— but one of my guiding principles was never to judge consensual behavior between adults. And there's the problem. In the absence of a complaint, you just never knew.

"Well, if you'd seen what I saw, you'd believe me." Her expression had an air of defiance.

I switched gears. "Tell me about the night of the accident."

Poppy's eyes grew and her lip quivered. "It was horrible. Just the most terrifying thing that's ever happened to me. Not that it happened to me. It clearly happened to him. But I was terrified. Terrified."

"Take a deep breath and start with what you did after work that day," I said. "Take your time."

She nodded, inhaled slowly, then exhaled, her eyes fixed on mine as if I were a life preserver. "It rained so hard all day, that really slowed me down. I didn't get home until after six. I came in, showered, put on dry clothes—I hadn't planned on going back out in that mess. I read for a while. Then, a little after nine, I remembered I'd forgotten to pick up my prescription. I have asthma. I was just so wet and uncomfortable—all I could think about was getting home and into dry clothes. Anyway, I had to go back out to get my inhaler."

"Of course," I said.

"I use the CVS over at George Street and St. Philip. It's on the College of Charleston campus—only half a mile from here. But there's no drive-thru. I couldn't find a place to park. I wanted to just pop in and out, but I ended up having to go into the parking garage. There's one right next to the CVS on St. Philip. When I came out, there'd been a fender bender on St. Phillip, before you get to Wentworth. The street was blocked, so I turned left on Liberty and went over to King Street."

"You did tell her to take her time." Colleen perched on the dresser, in front of the TV.

I ignored her. She purely hated that.

"That's when I remembered King Charles," said Poppy.

"King Charles?"

"The Logans' Pekingese. Mr. Logan had a heart incident Thursday morning. They don't think it's terribly serious, at least that's what Mrs. Chapman said. She lives next door. But when the paramedics were wheeling Mr. Logan out, King Charles darted out the front door. He was a nervous wreck, poor thing. Mrs. Logan couldn't find him, and she had to go in the ambulance with Mr. Logan. Mrs. Chapman was there, and she looked and looked for King Charles, but she's had a bad summer cold, and it was raining so hard. She couldn't just stand out in the rain and look all afternoon. I was out anyway, so I decided to go by there and see if I could find him."

"Where do they live, the Logans and Mrs. Chapman?" I asked.

"On Lowndes Street, just off Lenwood. Two blocks from the Draytons," said Poppy. "I should've gone on home. But I couldn't stand to think of poor King Charles out all night in that weather. So I drove all the way down to the end of King. Normally, I would've turned on South Battery, but it just looked like it was under water. I was afraid to drive through there. By then, I was really scared, you know? And I knew Murray would be as bad or worse, but there was nothing else I could do. I turned right on Murrary and drove up to Lenwood."

"When I turned onto Lenwood, in my headlights, there was Mr. Drayton in the street. I mean, I didn't know it was Mr. Drayton then. I grabbed my phone out of my purse to call 911, but the battery was dead. All I could think was someone was hurt and I needed to get help. So I jumped out of the car and ran over to him. He was unconscious—or worse—how would I know? His head was hurt. Bad. Really bad."

Poppy fanned her eyes and blinked back tears. "There were no lights on at the Drayton house. None at the Hill house across Lenwood, either. Those were the two closest. I just wanted to get help, quick. So I checked his pockets for a cell phone. That's what I was doing when Detective Ravenel arrived. All of a sudden, he was shouting at me to freeze and put my hands on my head. I couldn't do both of those things at the same time. I just panicked. Then a police car pulled up and the EMTs arrived and looked after Mr. Drayton. I know I was babbling and didn't make any sense at all. Detective Ravenel must think I'm unstable—that's why he doesn't believe me. But I was shook up. It's not every day I run across dead people in the middle of the road."

"It sounds like a nightmare," I said.

"It felt like a nightmare," said Poppy. "All I was trying to do is help a sick neighbor whose dog was missing. I swear, I didn't hit

Mr. Drayton."

"I'm really sorry you had to go through that, Poppy," I said. "Did you see any other cars in the area? Taillights maybe?"

"Only the ones parked along the street. No, I didn't see a car down Lenwood. No taillights."

"Can you remember what Mr. Drayton was wearing?"

"A blue golf shirt and khaki pants," said Poppy. "Loafers."

"No raincoat?" I asked.

"No."

"Any sign of an umbrella?" I asked.

"No," she shook her head. "I had my suspicions about him, but I would never wish that on anyone. I didn't want to see him hurt. I just wanted him to stop beating up his wife."

I thought about what Sonny had said, then paraphrased it. "Well, if he was doing that, he won't be anymore."

"That's true." Poppy's voice was small.

"Did you see anyone else at all in the area?" I asked.

She shook her head. "No. It seemed like I was the only person in the city. Alone with Mr. Drayton. Well. Until the police arrived."

"What do you think happened to him?" I asked.

"It could've been an accident, I guess. But it also could be that someone knew he abused his wife. Someone besides me. Maybe they were defending Mrs. Drayton. Someone should look into that. But all I know is I didn't hit him with my car."

"So, you never called 911?" I asked.

"No, I told you. My phone battery was dead. That happens every day lately. A charge doesn't last me all day anymore."

I sat quietly for a moment, to see if she had anything else to add. Presently, I said, "You have a lovely apartment. I love the way you've decorated it. A crisp white background with pops of color."

"Aww, thank you. Some folks would think it's pretty small, I guess. But it's plenty of room for Ruffles and me."

"I have a friend who was looking for something similar—a

carriage house apartment—on the peninsula." Of course, this was fiction. "She never did find anything she could afford. You were lucky."

"Yeah, I was. Mrs. Butler's been really good to me. My mom passed away a few years ago. I had to sell her house to pay the medical bills. There wasn't anything left. Mrs. Butler offered this apartment to me. The rent is really reasonable. I know she could get more for it. But she likes having someone here that she trusts."

Was Mrs. Butler Eli and Fraser's client? "So you've known her a long time?"

"Not really," said Poppy. "She goes to church—Grace Church, it's right down the street—with a few of the ladies on my route. They knew she had an apartment available and introduced us." I was familiar with Grace Church—had attended services there a few times. It was the cathedral for the Episcopal Church in South Carolina, the diocese which St. Francis, the church I was raised in, was a part of.

"The folks on your route really do take care of you," I said.

"Yes, they do. Which is why I want to take care of them."

"Have you spoken to Mrs. Drayton since the accident?" I asked.

A crease settled between Poppy's eyes. "No. She didn't come to the door yesterday or today. I'm not surprised, by any means. Bless her heart, she just lost her husband. And she must've loved him, even if he treated her badly, or why would she have stayed married to him?"

"That's an excellent question," I said. The woman whose eyes I'd looked into earlier at the bookshop didn't strike me as the type to suffer abuse or a loveless marriage. I looked at Colleen.

"Hey, don't ask me," she said. "I told you I couldn't read her. Poppy, on the other hand, is an open book. She's telling you the truth, the whole truth, and nothing but the truth."

The question most on my mind was why Anne Frances

Drayton was inscrutable to my paranormal friend. That, and who had ultimately hired Nate and me. Whoever our client was, he or she knew things we didn't. The very idea of having an anonymous client worked my nerves. Colleen. She had to know.

As quickly as that thought formed, Colleen was gone.

# SIX

Sunday morning arrived on air as thick as Mamma's gravy. Nate, Rhett—our golden retriever—and I ran our usual five miles on the beach, but none of us did it with our usual enthusiasm. At five in the morning, it was already eighty-three degrees.

I filled Rhett's bowl with kibble, freshened his water, and hit the shower. I abbreviated my morning routine as much as possible. Grace Church offered services at 8:00, 9:00, and 11:00 a.m., with Sunday school at 10:10. We had no idea what time Mrs. Butler would leave for church. I dried my hair, slid into a blue sheath dress and a pair of sandals, and applied minimal makeup—just a swipe of mascara and some lip gloss.

"Hey pretty lady." Nate stood at the bathroom door, a grin on his face. "That must be your personal best time."

"You're looking particularly fine yourself." In a light grey suit with a starched white shirt, my husband was a temptation.

"I confess I'm having some very un-churchy thoughts just now," he said.

"Hmm...hold those thoughts for later. We need to get moving."

"Spoilsport."

That was the second time in as many days I'd been called that, and it didn't sit well.

We barely made the 7:00 a.m. ferry from Stella Maris to Isle of Palms. Nate parked the Explorer on deck, and we made our way up the steps to the second level lounge, which was air conditioned. It was far too hot to stay in the car or ride up top in the sun. The ferry had a full load that morning, and everyone was riding inside. We knew most of them and they were all feeling social. We smiled and said good morning but extricated ourselves from conversations related to topics ranging from how Mamma and Daddy were holding up since Merry was running off to get married in the jungle, to who was going to fill Michael Devlin's seat on the town council since he'd put the Devlin place up for sale and left town.

I was advancing straight towards an empty corner when Charlie Jacobs put his hand on my arm. "Liz. Where have you been keeping yourself, girl? I haven't seen you in a coon's age."

My family had a soft spot for Charlie. He'd given my brother, Blake, his first job out of college, mentored him. Charlie had been the Stella Maris chief of police for decades before retiring ten years ago. Blake had been promoted and had held the job ever since.

I turned towards Charlie and smiled. "It's been a while." I might have avoided Charlie once or twice in the aftermath of a recent case in which his grandson had become entangled.

"I hated to hear about Kinky." He shook his head.

"Kinky? What happened to Kinky?" My daddy's potbellied pig was the source of so much controversy in my parents' house, my first thought was that Mamma had called Animal Control to come pick him up.

"You haven't heard?" asked Charlie. "Him and Chumley got into a ruckus yesterday and Chumley backed him up into that big hole. Poor little pig fell in and broke his leg. I was in the vet's office when your daddy brought him in. Had to put him in a cast." Chumley was my daddy's high-maintenance basset hound.

"Wait—hole? What big hole are you talking about, Charlie?" I squinted at him.

He squinted back at me, like maybe I had developed a sudden onset intellectual disability. "In the backyard."

"Mamma and Daddy's backyard?"

"Of course. You can't put in a swimming pool without digging a big hole. The backhoe's been in the yard all week. Your daddy had been keeping Chumley and Kinky both in the house but—"

Oh, dear Heaven. "Excuse me, Charlie. I need to make a phone call." I huddled in the corner, my back to the room.

Mamma answered on the second ring.

"Mamma, what in the world is going on over there? I heard from Charlie Jacobs y'all were putting in a swimming pool."

"Why, E-liz-a-beth, you make it sound positively scandalous. I assure you, it's a perfectly respectable pool—" She huffed, muttered something, which was odd. Mamma was not prone to muttering. She typically said what was on her mind quite plainly. "I'm getting ready for church. Are you coming for lunch?"

"Yes, of course," I said.

"Well then, you can see for yourself," she said.

"But you never mentioned putting in a pool..."

"We were unaware that we needed your approval for home improvements."

"Of course you don't need my approval. It's just—"

"*E-liz-a-beth Su-zanne Ta-lbot,* I will not be late to church because my daughter has nothing better to do than interrogate her mother this morning. Unless you have called to tell me that you've decided to adopt one or—and this is unequivocally my personal preference—all five of your father's pets, and are on your way right this very minute to pick them up, I have to go. God has his work cut out for him this morning."

"Wait—five pets?"

"Oh, that's *riiight.*" Mamma's voice sounded chillingly pleasant. "You haven't met the latest addition to your father's menagerie. He brought Larry, Roger, and Moe home on Tuesday."

"Larry—"

"*Pygmy Goats.* He keeps calling them his goat herd. He can't stop saying the words. Goat herd." It came out as a strangled whisper.

She hung up.

That song from *The Sound of Music* commenced playing in my head—the one about the lonely goatherd. I wondered vaguely if Daddy had taken up yodeling.

"Slugger? Everything all right?" Nate rested a hand between my shoulders.

I grabbed his arm. He was solid, stable, and sane. "I think my daddy has finally lost his mind."

"No surprise there. He's been misplacing it for years." He teased me with a grin.

I shot him a serious look.

"Come on now," he said. "Lots of folks have swimming pools put in. I wish we had one. Lot safer than you swimming in the ocean while it's still dark out."

"No—he's brought home pygmy goats. Three of them." I rubbed my temple. What in this world had possessed him?

Nate flashed me a look that said *Give me a break.* "Now you know that's nothing more than his latest stunt to get your mamma all riled up. That is his favorite sport."

"I'm hoping you're right, but they've been there since Tuesday."

"How did we not hear about this sooner?" he asked.

"All I can think of is Mamma's snapped."

"Nah..." Nate shook his head. "She may snap *him* before this is over."

Times like these, I wished I was better at compartmentalizing. I needed to focus on my case. I took a deep breath. "We're going over there for lunch. There's nothing I can do until then."

Nate rubbed my shoulders. "There's my girl. You know, once we finish this case, we could go to Greenville for a few days. Check on the condo. Maybe see what's going on at the Peace Center."

I nodded, took another deep breath. Then I settled into a chair, pulled my laptop out of my tote, activated the hotspot on my phone, and commenced preliminary research on Mrs. Butler. Nate sat across from me with his back to the room and we both hunched over the computer, communicating with our body language that we were working. Everyone who knew us knew exactly what we did for a living. Not only were they undeterred, they were intrigued.

*High on a hill was a lonely goatherd.*

Nate fended them off while I dug and looked up to smile occasionally. When we were back in the car, I shared what I'd found.

"Aida Rose Amory Butler is seventy-eight years old. Widowed since 1998. No record of a remarriage. Her house has been in the Amory family for one hundred years. Built in 1835 by the George family, by the way. There's no mortgage recorded. As far as I can tell, she's in a solid financial position. Two children, neither of them live locally. Four grandchildren."

"You find a picture of her?" Nate asked.

"Yeah—I couldn't find her on Facebook. Sometimes women of her generation like to keep up with the kids and the grandkids that way. I did find a photo on her DAR chapter website."

"Good," said Nate. "Might come in handy. If she's headed to the eight a.m. service, she'll be in the pew by the time we get to her house."

Poppy had said that some of the ladies on her route went to church with Mrs. Butler. These same ladies had arranged for Poppy to rent her unusually affordable apartment. Nate and I wanted to know who our client was, and Mrs. Aida Butler's church friends seemed like maybe they were good candidates. We wanted to find out who they were. This required us to see who Mrs. Butler chatted with before and after services.

"We can't just go straight to the church—what if she attends the eleven o'clock service? Or just goes to Sunday school? Plus, there's no way to know whether she'll walk or drive. If she drives, where she parks will determine what door she goes in." Like most of the downtown churches, Grace didn't have a large dedicated parking lot. They had arrangements with Memminger Elementary School and College of Charleston for adjacent parking, but many parishioners parked in Wentworth Garage. A lucky few street-parked in metered spots in the adjacent blocks. But Mrs. Butler lived a mere four blocks down Wentworth.

"Grandmothers are tricky to tail," said Nate.

*Lay-ee-odl lay-ee-odl lay-hee-hoo.*

"Why don't you drop me off at the church?" I said. "Then you go wait near her house. Text me if you see her, I'll do the same."

"Sounds like a plan."

At ten minutes 'til eight, Nate pulled to a stop at the corner of Glebe and Wentworth and I climbed out of the Explorer. If Mrs. Butler were here, she'd be settling in for the service that was about to start. I turned down the cut slate sidewalk on Wentworth that ran in front of the church.

The sanctuary was Neo-Gothic and was consecrated in 1848. Built from stucco over brick, it looked like sand-colored limestone. It had survived the War Between the States, the great earthquake of 1886, and countless hurricanes. Over the years, a parish house was added and then enlarged.

Today the compound was an imposing, U-shaped structure. The section closest to Glebe Street held Hanahan Hall, a large room for social gatherings, with another large meeting room and a chapel upstairs. This wing was connected to the original church building by another row of classrooms, choir rooms, and meeting rooms, along the back side of the U.

The Garden of Remembrance occupied the center of the complex. It consisted of a courtyard with a fountain and a columbarium, a tower lined by niches for the ashes of church members, with a ring of ten bells in the center behind frosted glass doors. A covered walkway connected the main church building with the parallel section of the parish house and bordered the front side of the courtyard.

*Loud was the voice of the lonely goatherd.*

I squeezed my eyes shut for five seconds.

It was a lovely church. The most striking things about it were the massive, arched, stained glass windows. I paused on the walkway to admire the great entrance window above the door. As I approached the entryway, a greeter smiled warmly, wished me a good morning, and handed me a program. I crossed the marble-floored narthex and proceeded down the center aisle of the nave between twin rows of dark wood pews with red cushions. The crowd was small this morning, perhaps owing to the time of year. I walked slowly, scanning the backs of heads for a gently teased, ash-blonde bob.

A single possible match sat alone on the right, a third of the way back from the front of the church. I genuflected as I entered the pew. The woman looked up and smiled as I took my seat. It wasn't Mrs. Butler. I returned her smile, then discreetly scanned the pews I could without craning my neck. No sign of her.

I studied my program, then took a Book of Common Prayer from the shelf on the back of the pew in front of me and opened it. Without attracting attention, there was nothing to do now but enjoy the service. I tried to clear my mind and glanced down as I went to kneel. Exquisite needlepoint covered individual kneelers—they were like small stools. Mine was an image of a stained glass window on a gold background. Someone, likely a group of church volunteers, had invested untold hours in that project.

*Lay-ee-odl lay-ee-odl ooo.*

I knelt, closed my eyes, and prayed for my sanity and that of my entire family.

As parishioners filed out after the 8:00 a.m. Holy Eucharist, I contemplated my next move. No text so far from Nate. Had Mrs. Butler left before he arrived at her house, perhaps to meet a friend for breakfast before church? I slipped into a spot in the back right corner to get a better view of folks coming in for the nine o'clock service.

At three minutes 'til nine, there'd been no sign of Mrs. Butler. I slipped out the back and made my way across the covered walkway to the classroom wing. Like every other Episcopal Church I'd ever attended, Grace had a coffee hour on Sunday mornings. According to the website, theirs was before Sunday school. I could use a hit of caffeine.

The first floor of the building adjacent to the church consisted of a large social hall where folks were beginning to gather. I waded into the cluster of conversation clutches, making my way to the coffee table sitting cater-cornered on the far side of the room. Resisting the pastries, I poured myself a cup of coffee and stirred in sugar and half-and-half. I sipped and drifted towards a large window overlooking Glebe Street.

An amalgamation of happy chatter, gossip, and good-natured debate filled the room. I scanned each group, looking for Aida Butler.

My watch vibrated with a text from Nate: *She's headed your way on foot.*

No doubt she was coming for coffee and social hour before Sunday school. Perfect. This was what I'd come to see. She was headed up Wentworth. There was an entrance to Hanahan Hall directly off of Wentworth. I moved to a spot closer to the door.

"Good morning, how are you?" The woman who appeared at my side wore wire-framed glasses and a warm smile. It had only been a matter of time before someone made me feel welcome.

"I'm doing well." I returned her smile. "I wonder, could you point me in the direction of the ladies' room?"

"Certainly, it's right over there." She pointed towards the Wentworth Street entrance.

I placed a hand on her arm. "Thank you so much." I stepped towards the ladies' room. I took my time reapplying lipstick, et cetera, giving Aida plenty of time to get to the fellowship hall. When I reemerged, I made a round through the room, scanning faces.

There, by a window on the left, I spotted her with a silver-haired woman of roughly the same age. Their heads were a little closer together, their conversation more subdued than the others in the room. I slowed my pace and walked by, rummaging in my bag for nothing in particular, but watching from the corner of my eye.

"...can't have that kind of thing...trusted you..." Aida's voice had an affronted tone.

"Aida Butler. The very idea is positively absurd." The silver-haired woman's voice projected better than Aida's.

Were they talking about Poppy? So much was absurd anymore, it could've been anything.

I took a position against the wall not too far away, with Aida and her friend on my right. I turned my back to them, but kept my ears tuned in to their conversation. Frantically, I continued to search my purse.

"...my reputation to be considered..." Aida's voice.

"Don't fret another second about it. Keep our Poppy in your prayers. Everything's going to be just fine. Now tell me, dear, do you have enough volunteers for the community supper?"

I rotated slowly in their direction and looked up from my purse. For the first time, I saw the silver-haired woman's face. It was Polly Buxton's friend from the bookshop. She must be one of the women from Poppy's route who'd introduced Poppy to Aida. And she was another candidate for our unidentified client.

They chatted for another few minutes about the community supper, then Aida said, "I'm going upstairs to get a seat for this morning's class."

"I can't stay," said her friend. "I came to the eight o'clock service."

They bussed cheeks and Aida headed towards the doorway at the back of the room. The mystery woman moved in the opposite direction. I followed her out the Wentworth Street exit, giving her plenty of room.

She went left and crossed Glebe, moving at a brisk clip, her low-stacked heels clicking rhythmically on the sidewalk. A block later she crossed Wentworth, then entered Wentworth garage. When she got on the elevator, I walked on past. I didn't need to rush up the stairs to whichever level she'd parked on. She was coming down. There were two exits, one onto Wentworth and one onto St. Philip Street. Either way, she had to come down the ramp in the center of the garage and make a right. I positioned myself on the far side of the ramp and lingered, studied my phone as if it held the answers to deep questions. I unlocked it and tapped the camera icon.

Five minutes later, a gold S-Class Mercedes rolled onto the ground level and swung right. Using my peripheral vision, I verified it was her, then walked in the opposite direction. With a practiced move, I lowered my right arm, held the phone upside down and backwards, and tapped the button with my thumb. Then I checked to be sure I had her license plate number in the photo and called Nate to pick me up.

"Learn anything?" he asked as I climbed into the Explorer on the corner of Wentworth and St. Philip.

"One of Aida Butler's friends from church—one of the ones who knows Poppy, and very likely vouched for her with Aida—was in the bookstore when I followed Mrs. Drayton there yesterday."

"You know how I feel about coincidence."

"Exactly," I said. "She's my first order of business, right after lunch."

*Lay-ee-odl lay-ee-odl lay-hee-hoo.*

# SEVEN

We pulled to a stop behind Blake's Tahoe in Mamma and Daddy's driveway. Merry's fiancé's Subaru Forrester was there too. We were the last to arrive. Acid rose in my throat.

"I'm thinking word has spread," I said. "It's early yet. Mamma and Daddy have just barely had time to get home from church. Merry and Blake are never here this early. Do you have any Tums?"

Nate gave me a worried look, fished a small package out of the console, and handed me two of the chewable antacids. "Maybe, if we're lucky, someone else dealt with the goats."

We steeled ourselves, got out of the car, and proceeded up the steps. Halfway across the front porch we heard the most mournful howl imaginable.

"Chumley," I said.

"That can't bode well," said Nate.

Daddy's Bassett hound was in deep distress.

I opened the door, calling out to my family as we hurried inside. "Where is everybody?"

Naturally, I knew Mamma and Merry would be in the kitchen, and Daddy, Blake, and Joe Eaddy—I really had to stop saying that in my brain like it was a double name like Billy Joe, but my soon-to-be brother-in-law's name was pronounced Joe Eddie—would be in the den, where the howling was coming from.

I poked my head in. Kinky was sprawled on Chumley's bed, spilling off the sides. Chumley objected loudly. Kinky's bed across the room was empty, but Chumley was having none of that. No one else was in the room.

"Does that pig look smug to you?" I asked Nate.

"I cannot adequately express my alarm at this fact, but yes, I can discern an air of self-satisfaction."

"Shhhh, now," I said to the dog. "Mamma?" I ran to the kitchen. A platter full of fried chicken waited on the island, but Mamma and Merry were nowhere to be found.

"Oh, dear Heaven," I said. "What on earth has happened? Where is everybody?"

Nate walked over to the French backdoor, peered into the backyard. "Blake's out back."

I crossed the room to join him.

"Oh, sweet reason." I didn't recognize the backyard I'd played in as a child.

Less than ten yards from the house, a large piece of equipment with a claw-scooper arm on it, which I could only guess was the backhoe Charlie had mentioned, sat by a hole that looked big enough for an Olympic-sized pool. Three massive mounds of dirt sat on the far side of the hole. My brother climbed the one in the middle, atop which sat a brown and white pygmy goat.

I pulled open the door.

"Blake?" Mamma's no-nonsense voice floated down from upstairs.

"Mamma?" I dashed back down the hall towards the bottom of the staircase.

"Liz, where's your brother?" She looked down at me with an expression that strongly discouraged questions.

"He's outside," I said.

"Nate, would you please help me with these suitcases?" she asked.

Nate looked at me wide-eyed for help.

I had nothing.

"Ah...sure. Of course." He started up the stairs.

"Mamma, no," I said. "Please don't do this. We'll get rid of the goats and get the yard put back to rights. This is—you can't just leave."

She drew back her chin, flashed me an incredulous look. "Leave? Why certainly I'm not leaving. Don't be ridiculous. I've packed your father's bags for him. *He* will be leaving."

"Where is Daddy?" I asked. "Where's Merry?"

"I imagine she and Joe are out back helping to round up the herd," said Mamma.

Nate reached the top of the steps, picked up the largest of three suitcases, and looked at me.

"Wait. Wait." I raised my hands in a stop motion. I needed time to think.

"Wait for what?" asked Mamma. "Your father to come to his senses? That's a lost cause if ever there was one. Did you *see* what's become of our backyard? 'The doctor says swimming is good for your joints,' he said. 'It'll be like living on vacation,' he said. Lord knows I can't blast him off this island to take a normal vacation, like our normal friends. Fine, I told him. Get some bids from reputable contractors. Do you know what he did?"

I shook my head, absolutely certain I didn't want her to tell me.

Chumley continued to howl incessantly.

"*Your* father bought a franchise for a pool company. A *pool company*." Her voice rose on each word. "Then...then..." She inhaled long and slow, then exhaled. Her eyes popped open, large and round. "Then, he hired his cousin Ponder and Ray Kennedy to run the damn thing. And he turned them loose in my backyard."

I felt my face squinch up. "Ray Kennedy? What does he know about swimming pools?"

"*Exactly.*" Mamma nodded enthusiastically. "He may be the only person drawing breath who knows less about them than your daddy's cousin Ponder."

Ray Kennedy—no relation to the famous political family—sold things out of his trunk door-to-door. As far as I knew, that was the only career he'd ever had. A European orphan from some country I could neither pronounce nor find on a map, he'd been raised by religious zealots in rural Pennsylvania. Ray Kennedy had not had a happy life, is what I'm saying.

He and Daddy crossed paths when I was a child. He'd been trying to sell Daddy some damn thing. Daddy brought him home and Mamma fed him. He'd been hanging around ever since. He peddled all manner of things that normal people refused to buy in reputable stores but would sometimes break down and purchase from a salesman standing on their front porch. Last I'd heard, Ray was selling solar panels. I'd been happy he was doing so well. Solar panels were a big step up from Japanese weight-loss sunglasses, flour made from bugs, and cave-man style camping vacations he called re-wilding retreats. Ray Kennedy was a whole nother story.

"Does Ponder even know Ray?" Ponder Talbot was Daddy's Uncle Harrison's love child, and the closest thing Stella Maris had to a town drunk. Or, he had been. He'd been doing real good in his twelve-step program for the last few years, but he'd had a sad life, Come to think of it, maybe he and Ray Kennedy had a lot in common.

"Well, he does now," said Mamma. "Nate Andrews, are you going to take those suitcases downstairs or not?" For the first time ever, Mamma turned The Look on Nate.

Lesser men would've melted.

"Absolutely, Carolyn." His voice was calm, soothing. "I was just waiting to ask where you'd like me to put them." Damn, but my husband was a pro.

"As long as they're out of my house and off my porch, I couldn't care less," said Mamma.

"Mamma, come sit with me and let's talk about this," I said.

"Sit and talk to your daddy if you'd like. Or your sister. Every bit of this is her fault. I have more important things to tend to than conversation at the moment."

"Merry? Mamma, wait. What does Merry have to do with any of this?"

"You know very well your sister has a soft spot for anything with fur," said Mamma.

I realized I was clutching my head in both hands so hard that it hurt. "Yes, but—"

"Your father agreed on the way home from church that he would find a new home for the goats and that ridiculous pig," said Mamma. "When your sister heard that, she started carrying on so that your daddy decided maybe that was a bad idea after all."

"But why is everyone outside rounding up the goats if they aren't going anywhere?" I asked.

"Ah," said Mamma. "While your sister was passionately pleading the goats' case, I fielded phone calls from three different sets of neighbors whose flower and/or vegetable gardens have been vandalized by those creatures. Several sections of our fence are down due to the machinery—not that any fence would keep those little bastards inside, but your father claims he thought it would. And one of them—I suspect Larry—was standing on the roof of Arthur Murphy's Cadillac this morning. Arthur was afraid of the goat and missed church. Apparently there are hoof marks on the hood and roof of the car."

"Surely even Merry now agrees now that the goats have to go," I said. "Isn't there a local farm or something that can take them?"

"All I care about is that they are leaving here immediately. As soon as they're apprehended, they're going to your sister's house. She likes farm animals so much, she can have them all. See how she likes cleaning up after them. She can take your daddy along too, though he's far more trouble than all the rest of them put together. Heaven only knows who'll mind them all while she's off on her grand adventure. It will not be me."

"Mamma, I know this is all completely out of hand, but—"

"Can't you see what I'm trying to tell you?" Mamma's voice had risen to near hysteria.

"I'm not sure I understand, Mamma," I said, keeping my voice soft.

"It's this wedding trip of your sister's," said Mamma. "If she would stay here and get married like a normal person, your daddy would have something to keep his mind and his pocketbook occupied besides random farm animals and unwise investments. If *someone* would set to getting us some grandchildren, none of this nonsense would be happening."

And there it was.

Nate and I exchanged a glance.

"Carolyn, could I trouble you for an aspirin?" asked Nate.

The angle of Mamma's head changed as if she'd been in a trance and someone had snapped their fingers in front of her face. "Of course. I have some in the medicine cabinet. What's wrong?"

"Just a touch of a headache, nothing really," said Nate.

Mamma moved towards the master bath, calling over her shoulder, "What have you eaten today?"

"To be honest, I skipped breakfast. We had some early morning casework in Charleston," said Nate.

Brilliant. My husband was freaking brilliant.

Mamma reappeared on the landing and handed him the aspirin. "Liz, get your husband a glass of water. Then set the table and call everyone inside for lunch. It's time to put a stop to every bit of this nonsense."

"Of course, Mamma," I said.

Nate walked right around that pile of luggage and took Mamma's arm, spoke to her slowly. "Be careful on these stairs now," he said. "Did I see fried chicken in the kitchen?" He escorted her down the steps. "I can't believe you stood over the stove to fry all that chicken in this heat. But I sure am looking forward to it, yessiree."

I hadn't moved from my spot at the bottom of the stairs.

"*E-liz-a-beth.*" Mamma inspected me. "You're looking pale. Are you all right? Let's get lunch on the table. I declare, it's a wonder to me that you children survive the way you eat—or rather the way you constantly skip meals."

Mamma was back, at least for the moment. Nate had given her someone to mother, and that had snatched her back from the brink of some sort of breakdown.

I darted into the kitchen and poured a glass of water. Nate and Mamma came into the kitchen behind me. I handed him the glass. "Be right back."

He shot me a look that said *Go with God.* "Carolyn, why don't you sit down and I'll set the table."

"Don't be absurd," said Mamma. "Here, you sit and drink that water." She tsk-tsked him.

I took a deep breath, opened the door, and dashed into the wasteland of our former backyard. One of the goats was on top of the backhoe, another on the mountain of dirt on the right side of the yard, and the third munched nonchalantly on a container garden filled with Gerber daisies.

Daddy was apparently trying to stare the goat off the tractor. "You little bastard, get down from there."

"*Daddy.*" I looked at him sideways. "What in the name of common sense were you thinking?"

"I was thinking I wouldn't have to mow the grass if I had goats," he said. "All that brush beyond the tree line, where I got my truck stuck a while back? Nice herd of goats could keep all that mess chewed down. But so far, they haven't taken to that. Vegetable gardens are easier pickings, I guess."

"You know very well they eat everything in sight. And besides that, you've had all the grass dug up. There's barely any grass left in the yard. Of course they're foraging in neighbors' gardens."

"Huh." He gave a shot at an innocent look.

"Unh-uh. I'm not buying it," I said. "I know exactly what you were thinking. You were thinking this was a good way to irritate Mamma. What was your plan? You had to know the goats wouldn't be staying here long."

He looked disappointed, like he wanted to play a fun game that no one else was interested in. "There's a yoga studio over on Folly Beach that wants them."

"I'm sorry, what?" I felt my left eye twitch.

"I called the petting zoo up to Summerville. They have plenty of goats, but they told me about some woman who has a yoga studio in Folly Beach, and she wants them for her classes. Don't ask me what the hell that's all about. Damned if I know. All's I know is she wants them."

"Will she come get them?" I asked.

"Well, she made arrangements with the petting zoo people to pick them up. All I have to do is call the man."

The goat on top of the dirt mound sailed over Blake's head just as he closed in on him. Blake let out a long string of curse words.

Merry and Joe came around the back of the house with a leash and a collar.

"Where have you been?" I asked.

"Soothing Arthur Murphy," she said. "And looking for collars and leashes. I could only find one of each."

"I think Mamma was on the verge of a breakdown. Nate's with her in the kitchen. I'm worried about her," I said.

"Yeah, me too." Our eyes met, and I knew she knew what weighed heavy on Mamma's mind—grandchildren.

"Let's just alleviate as much of the stress as we can," I said. "We're not goatherds, for Heaven's sake. How would we contain these things if we caught them? *Daddy*."

"What?"

"For the love of Pete, please make the call and let's all go inside," I said.

"Have it your way." He cussed the goat while he pressed the buttons on his cell phone.

"Someone's coming to get them?" Joe looked so disappointed.

"Not nearly soon enough. *Blake.*" I waved him over.

He joined our huddle, a particularly disgusted look on his face. "We could chase those damned hateful sons of bitches from now 'til next June. You can't catch them. I'm exhausted. *Dammit*, Dad. Dammit to hell."

"Quit your bellyaching." Daddy hung up the phone. "Somebody will be here directly."

"But they're so cute." Merry made a pouty face, stared adoringly at the nearest goat, the one eating the daises. "Look at this little fellow. Look at that face. Don't you just want to mash that face and kiss it?"

"No, I do not," I said. "And you have no idea how close you danced to having Daddy for a houseguest with that kind of talk. Mamma has his bags packed."

"She what?" Daddy looked stricken. "Surely not."

"Oh yes. She ordered Nate to carry them downstairs and get them out of her house. So, I'd advise you to be on your very best behavior for the foreseeable future. You won't eat nearly as good at Merry's house as you do here."

"Hey." Merry looked wounded.

I shot her a look that said *oh puh-leeze*. Merry was likely able but completely unwilling to cook anything more difficult than a turkey sandwich.

"Let's get washed up for lunch," I said.

The backdoor opened, and Nate led a sullen Chumley around the obstacle course to the doggie condo—we never called it a pen. At least he'd stopped howling. The six-foot fence wouldn't keep in goats, but Chumley had never dug out of it.

Back in the house, things appeared normal. Nate had opened

two bottles of a red blend and Mamma had put together a buffet on the kitchen island. Owing to the heat, she served cold side dishes with her fried chicken that Sunday—potato salad, pasta salad, cream cheese and olive deviled eggs, marinated tomatoes, cucumbers, and onion, and roasted corn salad.

We all piled our plates high and settled into our usual places at the dining room table. From her chair at one end of the table, Mamma held out her hands to Merry on her left, and me on her right. We all joined hands and bowed our heads.

Mamma returned thanks, asked for a blessing, and prayed extra hard for patience. We all dug into our food and for the next thirty minutes, Sunday dinner was amazingly normal given the drama that had preceded it. We were having dessert—Mamma's homemade banana pudding—when the goat wranglers arrived with cages on a truck.

We watched from inside as what looked like a father and son team lured the goats with baby carrots, slipped on leashes, and led them into the cages.

"It's embarrassing how easy they make that look," said Blake.

"Carrots," Daddy said. "Of all things."

He went outside and spoke to the men. A few minutes later, they came inside and gentled a squealing Kinky onto her own bed, then carried her out to one of the cages.

"Don't worry," said the older of the two men. "She'll be fine. I've got a boar that'll be happy to keep her company."

Poor Kinky. She was injured. What if she didn't want any company. I looked at Nate. "Do we have tequila in the house?"

He gave me a little shrug, raised his eyebrows.

Daddy tipped the men well and thanked them for coming on Sunday. No one mentioned how sad they were to see the goats go, though Merry looked pouty around the edges. I gave her a look that dared her to protest.

Mamma didn't say a word until the truck had backed out the

driveway and rolled down the street. "Now, about the rest of the mess in the backyard—"

"Carolyn, I'll handle it," said Daddy.

"And by that you mean—" Mamma started.

"I will hire experienced tradesmen to finish the pool and the patio and repair the landscaping. I will pay them whatever it takes to get the yard straightened out lickety-split. But I am not going to take that company away from Ponder and Ray Kennedy. They just need a few experienced hands, is all." I recognized the person speaking as Serious Daddy.

So did Mamma. She smiled brightly. "Well, hopefully those boys will make a go of it."

Those boys were both older than Daddy—somewhere north of sixty.

"I should've gotten them started years ago, doing something," said Daddy.

"You've helped them both over the years," said Mamma. "Many times."

"You know, Mamma," I said, "you should really consider spending tomorrow in Charleston, over at the spa at the Belmond. Relax. Destress."

"Hmmm," she said. "Maybe I'll do that very thing."

Just then I was thinking how I'd give Daddy the name of a good cleaning service so that she came home to a spotless house. It wasn't grandchildren, but it was a start.

"By the way...." Mamma raised an eyebrow at Daddy. "I've cleaned out your drawers and closet. You have things in there you haven't worn in years. I've got some things set aside for you to drop off tomorrow at Goodwill."

"Is that's what's in the suitcases at the top of the steps?" asked Daddy.

"No," said Mamma. "Those are your good things. I just set them aside so I could get to everything. I'll help you put them away after lunch."

"That's awfully nice of you." Daddy's voice carried just a trace of sarcasm.

Merry and I helped Mamma straighten up. Normally, the guys would settle in the den, or maybe the screened porch after Sunday dinner. But today, Daddy hovered, tried to stay out of the way. He didn't attempt to help, just stood there beside the refrigerator with his hands in his pockets. Because he was in the kitchen, so were Joe, Nate, and Blake. Mamma ignored the men, so Merry and I did too.

We chatted about safe topics—the fall festival at the church, the vacant town council seat, and how it was a good step for Tammy Sue Lyerly across the street, who'd recently lost her husband, to take up Jazzercise instruction.

Mamma piled Chinet platters high with food for Blake, Nate, me, Merry, and Joe. None of us argued with her. She wrapped the last of them in foil and looked up, scanned our faces.

"I'm going to read the paper," she announced. "If you children are staying a while, you'd best put this food in the refrigerator in the garage. There's no room in here."

This was our cue to get out of her hair. I was reluctant to leave, but maybe it was best to give her some space. Besides, Nate and I had work to do. Nate raised his eyebrows at me and I nodded. He picked up our plates. Joe and Blake followed suit, and we all hugged our way out of there. But I knew the trouble with Mamma was far from over.

# EIGHT

Back at home, I changed into shorts, poured us each a glass of Cheerwine, and met Nate in my office—that's what we called the large room off the foyer on the right front side of the house. Once the venue for my Gram's themed cocktail parties, the oversized living room now served multiple purposes. The left front side of the room held my desk and a set of client chairs. Two club chairs with ottomans on the far wall by the fireplace, along with the bookcases that lined two walls, served as our library. The white board we used to lay out our cases stood in the corner between my desk and the fireplace.

By the triple windows that looked out onto the front porch, a sofa, two wingbacks, and a large ottoman formed a sitting area. More than anything else, this room was where we talked through our theories, bounced things off one another, and pieced together the fragments of information that held the solution to each case. It was the hub of our business.

Nate settled into the sofa with his laptop while I turned on the computer on my desk. This was the first opportunity I'd had to open a case file. I typed up interview notes from our meeting with Fraser and Eli on our standard form—a clone of the FBI's FD-302. Then I repeated the process from our conversation with Sonny. This was the foundation of our case. I printed the forms, dated and signed each document, and put them in a fresh case folder. Then I turned to profiles.

Normally, the first person I'd create a profile for would be the victim, Phillip Drayton, followed by the client, or, in this case, Poppy Oliver, the beneficiary of our client's generosity. But I had a strong suspicion that the woman who'd reassured Aida Butler that morning was key to our case. I logged on to one of several subscription databases Nate and I used for research and looked up the license plate I'd snapped in the parking garage.

The Mercedes was registered to Tess Camille Calhoun Rivers Hathaway. I typed her name into my primary background database. Rivers. "Oh, sweet reason. No."

"Slugger?"

"That woman. Tess Hathaway. She's Abigail Bounetheau's younger sister." Abigail Bounetheau was the closest thing to pure evil I'd encountered so far in this world.

"That can't be good news," said Nate. "What else do you have on her?"

I scanned the screen. "She's widowed. Husband was into real estate among other things. He died in 2005—heart attack. Tess lives alone, as far as I can tell, in a house on South Battery—across from White Point Garden. One daughter. She lives in Montana."

"I don't recall a sister of Abigail's turning up when we were working the Kent Heyward case," said Nate.

I shook my head. "I dug into Abigail. There was so much there. I must have seen that she had a sister. She just wasn't relevant to our investigation."

"Siblings are often very different." Nate gave me a long look.

Nate was my second husband. A finer man did not walk this earth. My first husband, Scott the Scoundrel, was Nate's older brother. That's a whole nother story.

I took a deep cleansing breath. "You're right, absolutely."

I created a profile document for Tess Hathaway. For the next hour, I researched her background, filling in the puzzle pieces from public records and various subscription databases. When I had a sketch, I shared it with Nate.

"I'm hoping hard not to find anything that changes my mind about this, but Tess may be the anti-Abigail. After her husband's death, she created a non-profit foundation to help victims of domestic violence. Zelda's Safe House. Tess owns a resale shop on King Street. The proceeds go to the foundation. Apparently there's a shelter for women, but the location is kept secret to protect their clients."

"You thinking Mrs. Drayton was one of her clients?" Nate winced. "Did they talk to each in the bookstore?"

I thought back. "No, but I came into the store a minute or so after Mrs. Drayton. They could've exchanged pleasantries. But she didn't so much as flash a smile in Mrs. Hathaway's direction on her way out the door. Then again, she is still grieving."

"They live, what—a couple blocks from each other South of Broad? They have to be acquaintances at a minimum."

"Agreed. But it's a huge leap from acquaintances to confidants, further still to Anne Frances Drayton being Tess Hathaway's client. If Mrs. Drayton was abused—and we surely haven't proven that— she may have been considering leaving her husband and moving to a shelter. But bottom line, she hadn't left her home."

"I wonder how easy that would've been for her," said Nate. "As a practical matter. Abused spouses often have less personal freedom than most folks."

"Could be she was caught in the act of trying to leave or was maybe trying to work out the details of leaving. We need to know how much access to their considerable resources she actually had. If she had an escape plan, maybe that plan went sideways and her husband wound up dead. But she wasn't the one driving the car. So, there was an accomplice. Unless Tess Hathaway is more like her sister than it appears, I don't see her behind the wheel. It's suspicious, Tess having a connection to Poppy and her being in the bookshop when Anne Frances was there. But that's all it is."

"Let's back up here." Nate stood and crossed the room to the case board. "Our possible narratives of the crime are, number one, Poppy hit Phillip Drayton by accident and is afraid to tell the truth. Number two, she hit him on purpose and is either A, Mrs. Drayton's accomplice, or B, deranged and imagines herself a vigilante protector." He created a numbered list as he spoke.

"Possibility number three," said Nate, "is that an unknown subject hit him accidentally and fled. And four would be that an unknown subject hit him on purpose and fled, with options A and B for either Mrs. Drayton's accomplice or someone trying to protect her, and C for motives unknown."

We both stared at the list and mulled it for a few moments.

1. Poppy: accidentally hit Phillip Drayton
2. Poppy: intentionally hit Philip Drayton
    a. Mrs. Drayton's accomplice
    b. Vigilante: protecting Mrs. Drayton
3. Unknown Subject: accidentally hit Phillip Drayton and fled
4. Unknown Subject: intentionally hit Phillip Drayton and fled
    a. Mrs. Drayton's accomplice
    b. Vigilante: protecting Mrs. Drayton
    c. Unknown motives

"Looking at it logically, all laid out like that," I said, "it seems that we're missing an unlikely possibility, but a possibility nevertheless. Poppy could have killed him for unknown motives."

Colleen popped in with a puff of blue smoke. She adored theatrics. "Except I told you that Poppy didn't kill him."

"Yes, you did," I said. "But we need to look at this analytically. And your input is what we refer to as unverifiable facts. It's part of our process. We need to look at this from every angle or we might miss something."

"You're wasting time," she said.

"Lookit," I said. "Our chart is not symmetrical. We can't prove that two C is not a possibility, so we need two C on the board."

Colleen bray-snorted exuberantly. "You are so anal-retentive it's ridiculous."

Nate added 2 C to the chart: Poppy—unknown motive.

"The really interesting thing about this case is how Drayton got the injuries that didn't kill him," said Nate.

"A Taser, pepper spray, and a puncture wound—that could've been caused by any of a long list of things, but in combination with the other two items, I'm betting on one of those tactical pens. I have one myself in my purse. These are all items women carry to protect themselves."

"You thinking he attacked someone who fought back, but not his wife?" asked Nate.

"It's possible he abused other women in his life." I dug all ten fingers into my hair, blew out a long breath. "We need a lot more information on Phillip Drayton. The man is dead through an odd set of circumstances. He's not here to defend himself."

"Fair point," said Nate. "But we need to ascertain whether or not he did, in fact, abuse his wife. It goes to motive."

"By all means, we do," I said. "But we need to consider all the possibilities. What about his blog? People have killed over bad restaurant reviews before. I'll profile Phillip Drayton next. Any number of people could've had all manner of motives to kill him. Then I'll tackle Anne Frances and Poppy Oliver."

"When is the funeral service?" asked Nate.

I googled "Phillip Drayton Charleston, SC". The first hit was his obituary. "The service is at St. Michael's Church. Tuesday morning at eleven, interment following at Magnolia Cemetery. The family is receiving friends Monday evening from six to eight at J. Henry Stuhr's downtown chapel."

"We need to be at all three places," said Nate.

"I'll come if I can," said Colleen. "But I'm pretty busy right now."

"Who are you harassing into running for the Devlin seat on town council?" I asked. Colleen's primary mission was protecting our island home from overdevelopment. The most compelling reason was the difficulty of evacuating, given that the island could only be reached by boat, and the ferry had limited capacity. An open seat on town council was a priority for her. Some island residents were vulnerable to the lucrative nature of real estate development on our pristine island.

"It's tricky," said Colleen. "Calista would be perfect, but it will take a lot of persuading people to vote for someone who's only lived here a few years. I have a few other ideas in my back pocket. You just focus on Poppy and let me worry about the town council."

"We could really use you to read minds at the funeral," I said. "Everyone who knew Philip Drayton will be there. It's a gold mine of potential information. That said, I don't want you to get in trouble." There were strict rules about what Colleen could and could not get involved in. She'd been known to push the boundaries.

"Like I said, I'll come if I can," she said. "But don't waste your time investigating Poppy. The timing is critical here."

"Why?" I asked. "I mean, to be sure we have a sense of urgency. We don't want Poppy to end up in jail. That would be horrible for someone as innocent as she seems to be. But what else do you know?"

"Another life is in danger," said Colleen.

"Whose?" I asked.

"I don't know," she said. "That's all I've been given."

I squinted at her. "Why are you being given hints about this case? It has absolutely nothing to do with your mission."

"Duty calls." She started to fade.

"Wait—dammit, Colleen," I said. "Did you put someone up to hiring us through Rutledge and Radcliffe? Who is our client?"

She disappeared with a theatrical *pouf*.

From the corner of my eye, I saw a news alert on my phone. Tropical storm Jack had formed in the Atlantic. Panic rose in my chest. I closed my eyes, took a deep breath, tamped it down.

"You all right?" asked Nate.

"Fine." I reached for a smile.

"What's wrong?"

I shook my head. "Another storm."

Nate studied me. Concern, love, and bemusement wrestled on his face. "We've either got to find a way to ease your fears, or we need to relocate inland. These nightmares of yours—I worry you're not getting enough rest."

"You know I can't leave here," I said. "This place owns me."

"What am I going to do with you?" he asked.

"We'll get to that later." I teased him with a smile. "Right now, I need to get to work on Phillip Drayton. He's the first piece of the puzzle."

Nate shook his head in surrender, put the dry erase marker back in its tray, and moved back to the sofa. "I'll search property records for all of them."

I started an electronic profile for Phillip Drayton, pulling together information from public records, several private subscription databases, the scant information in his obituary, and what Sonny had told me.

Phillip Michael Drayton was born March 23, 1973 at Medical University of South Carolina to parents Charlotte Ann Bull and Phillip Michael Drayton, Senior. Both parents were Charleston natives, their names indicating I could spend days tracing their heritage and, while interesting, it was likely irrelevant. They were both deceased.

Phillip attended Porter-Gaud private school and then Duke University. He had no criminal record, and no civil actions had been filed against him. He owned his home on Murray Boulevard through a family trust, as well as property in Naples, Florida and

Southampton, New York. None of the property was mortgaged.

He'd been publicly recognized for sizable charitable contributions made through The Drayton Foundation. He and Mrs. Drayton enjoyed a comfortable lifestyle. No software or database I had access to would give me banking information or the details of his investment accounts or tax returns. There were limits to the information I could gather electronically. But everything I could find indicated that whatever Phillip Drayton's problems had been, they weren't financial in nature. Anne Frances Drayton was the only other beneficiary of the family trust, and she now controlled The Drayton Foundation.

Phillip's blog, *Charleston Feasts & Yarns,* was interesting. Along with weekly restaurant reviews, he posted historical anecdotes and notices of upcoming cultural events he found intriguing. From skimming his blog, I couldn't see angry restauranteurs coming after him. Then again, there were hundreds of reviews here and it would take days to read them all, but from what I'd seen of the most recent, if he'd ever eaten at a restaurant he didn't find superb, he didn't blog about it.

Phillip seemed to enjoy having his photo taken with chefs, and every one of those featured was smiling. Still, I needed help going through the reviews. I couldn't discount someone taking revenge for a bad writeup from two years ago that had led to a restaurant's demise. Interesting that Phillip's highly photogenic wife wasn't in any of the photos, nor was she mentioned in the blog posts I read.

I logged on to Facebook and searched for Phillip Drayton. His security settings must have been set to public, because I could browse his friend list and, it appeared, everything he'd ever posted—and he'd posted a lot. There were links to his blog posts, photos of him with restauranteurs, chefs, and local celebrities. I scrolled past two with Bill Murray.

There were occasional photos with his wife—at charity events and on holidays. I studied the photos of Anne Frances Drayton. She looked happy. They both did. But appearances were often deceiving. Like the blog, a thorough search of Facebook would be time consuming. I set that aside for later.

Next, as was my custom, I created profiles for everyone closest to Phillip and worked my way out. The software I used made easy work of tracking family connections, automatically populating information on close relatives. Sadly, Phillip had few of those. I found the brother Sonny had mentioned, Daniel John Drayton. Phillip had married only once, five years ago, and had no children. I started with his wife.

Anne Frances Carlisle was born on May 5, 1976 in Chicago. Her parents still lived at the same address and she had a brother in an adjacent zip code. Nothing I found suggested she'd attended college. The first address records I located aside from her current address and the one on her birth certificate was in Naples, Florida, where she lived from 1995 until she married Phillip Drayton in June of 2010. She'd worked as an interior decorator. Was that how they'd met?

An announcement in the *Naples Daily News* said that the couple had married in a private ceremony at The Inn on 5th, and then left for an extended honeymoon trip to Europe. No attendants' names were listed. It was a low-key wedding for someone with Phillip Drayton's means, especially given that it was a first marriage for both of them.

I couldn't find any evidence that Anne Frances had worked after they returned from their honeymoon and settled into Phillip's Charleston home. So, she gave up her career, but based on what Poppy had said about her being at home every day, she didn't seem to have thrown herself into the Charleston social scene. She had no criminal record and no civil actions against her. And no Facebook profile. Anne Frances Drayton had a small electronic footprint. Sonny had said Phillip's brother suspected she had something to do with his death. Why?

Daniel John Drayton was two years younger than Phillip and had attended the same schools. He, likewise, had no criminal or civil actions and had inherited wealth which he seemingly managed well. If he'd had a motive to kill his brother, it didn't appear to be money, even if he hadn't known that Anne Frances inherited everything. I'd need to learn much more about him than was available in databases.

I did a preliminary search for distant Drayton and Hall relatives. Second and third cousins were scattered across California, in the Atlanta area, and in Vermont. It was virtually inconceivable that any of those folks were involved in Phillip's death. Still, I made a note.

Next, I turned my attention to Poppy Jayne Oliver. She was born on Valentine's Day in 1981, at MUSC. Her father was in the Army and died in a training accident at Fort Irwin in California when she was only two. Her mother, the former Jayne Smith, had died of breast cancer in 2008. Poppy was the only child of two only children. Both sets of grandparents were deceased. How sad for anyone to be that completely alone in this world. I said a prayer of thanks for each and every member of my gloriously dysfunctional family.

I wondered how long Poppy's mother had been sick. Nothing I found indicated she'd gone to college. Had she been taking care of her mother? They'd lived in a quiet West Ashley neighborhood. I remembered Poppy saying that she'd had to sell the house to pay the medical bills. She'd gone to work for the postal service twelve years ago. Before that, she'd held a variety of jobs at businesses ranging from restaurants to retail shops to a grocery store. Nothing vaguely suspicious popped up in Poppy's background—not even a traffic ticket.

I sighed long and loud. "All of these people have uneventful timelines. We need to talk to Mrs. Drayton, and to Daniel, the brother. Find out what's not a matter of record. Why he's suspicious of her. But with the visitation tomorrow and the funeral Tuesday, I don't want to intrude on these folks' grief."

"Probably better we don't introduce ourselves as investigators until after the funeral anyway," said Nate.

I noodled that over. "Plus, whoever is responsible for Phillip Drayton's death, they're already worried about the police. As soon as they find out private investigators are also snooping around, they'll get even more skittish. We need them to relax and get careless. The more they have to worry about, the more careful they'll be."

"So, you think we should put off interviewing the widow and the brother for a few days?"

"That feels right," I said. "This whole case is unconventional—we don't even know who our client is. Perhaps our approach should be upside down as well. The first thing we typically do is talk to everyone involved. Let's don't interview anyone just yet—don't let them know we're investigators. Let's watch them all for a few days and see what happens."

Nate thought for a few moments. "That could work. At least until we find out who hired us and what they know."

"Want to go to the visitation as Tommy and Suzanne?" My middle name was Suzanne. Nate's was Thomas. We often used our alter egos, Tommy and Suzanne, for situations requiring a pretext, along with Mamma's maiden name—Moore.

"That works," said Nate.

"I think we should be married."

Nate tilted his head from left to right, considering. "Okay. Tommy and Suzanne with a twist. What's our connection to Drayton?"

"Seriously? No one is going to ask us that. If they do, I'll be suddenly overcome with grief and you'll have to take me home. If we try to fake something, we run the risk of tripping up."

"Okay," said Nate, "but you'd best go in disguise. Then you can still interview the wife and the brother later on."

"Fine by me. I love playing dress-up."

"Do you now?" His drawl was low, husky, suggested all manner of things.

My breath caught in my throat and my heart rate picked up. His blue eyes twinkled with warmth and mischief. I made a few promises with mine. Then I stood and sashayed out of the room.

He caught me before I reached the stairs, wrapped long, tanned, strong arms around me and kissed me on the back of the neck. Then, real low, he said, "You have some intriguing possibilities in your closet. I confess to a particular fondness for the black lace. I'll open a bottle of wine and be right up."

I smiled as I climbed the stairs. I was a lucky, lucky woman.

# NINE

Monday morning, after our run and breakfast, I headed back into Charleston. Nate's project for the day was to dig deeper into Phillip Drayton's life—his friends, his blog, and his social media presence. I was off to check in with Sonny and then Poppy before running surveillance on Tess Hathaway.

It was a sad truth that the people closest to Poppy were the people on her mail route. That included 327 homes and forty businesses. In theory, any of them could've been our client. But we had to start somewhere. The conversation I'd overheard between Tess and Aida Butler, where Aida's primary concern was her reputation and Tess referred to Poppy as "Our Poppy," convinced me Tess Hathaway was the logical place to start. My instincts said she was our client, and my instincts typically served me well. I wanted to know what our client knew. I met Sonny for coffee first thing at Kudu on Vanderhorst.

It was early yet and still bearable, so we sat in the courtyard. I admired the artsy flourish on my mocha, inhaled deeply, savoring the blend of coffee and chocolate, then took the first sip. Sonny washed down a bite of ham and cheese croissant with coffee, then said, "So, what do you have?"

I raised both eyebrows, widened my eyes. "Virtually nothing. For several reasons, we've elected not to interview anyone directly just yet. We want to observe them for a few days."

"Good luck with that," said Sonny. "The wife has barely left the house. I followed her to the funeral home and to the church to make arrangements."

"Any friends come by?" I asked.

"A few neighbors, couple other women brought casseroles and whatnot," he said. "But no one stayed longer than five-ten minutes."

"She seems very isolated," I said. "Her only family is in the Chicago area. A brother, parents. It's sad none of them have come down to be with her."

"Not everyone is as close to their family as you are."

"I know that's true. I just feel bad for her," I said. "From a practical standpoint, it doesn't appear that she has family close enough that they would kill to protect her."

"You mean if her husband was abusing her."

"If he was, right," I said. "And if she has local friends who would defend her to the death, they're staying clear of her right now."

"Looks that way." Sonny had a great poker face.

"I dug into her background last night," I said.

He raised his eyebrows, looked away, and picked up his coffee.

Had he found something there I'd missed? Sonny had access to certain types of information I didn't. "Her electronic footprint is awfully small," I said. "Have you run across anything that makes you suspicious of her aside from the fact that she's the spouse?"

Sonny gave me a sour look.

I knew it. He knew something he hadn't planned to volunteer just yet, but he wouldn't lie to me either.

"This probably doesn't mean anything," he said.

"What doesn't?"

"She popped up in a report as a witness in a drug case. Apparently ran with a rough crowd as a teenager—before she left Chicago. She was a known associate of Lucious Calvin Carter, a drug kingpin. Back then he was more a rising star in the drug and gang world. He's got a long rap sheet and a reputation for violence."

I stared at him. "That was an awfully long time ago. Did she have a juvenile record? Did she testify against him?"

"No, she didn't have a record. And the case wasn't against Lucious, it was one of his underlings. She did not testify. The defendant never made it to trial. He was killed in a hit and run accident."

"Wait, Sonny. You don't think—"

"No, I don't think Anne Frances Drayton is a serial hit and runner. I told you. I know she didn't drive the car that hit her husband. It's just—" He seemed to be searching for a word.

"Intriguing," I said.

"Yeah, intriguing."

I mulled that for a few minutes. It could be irrelevant. Everyone had baggage. Some of us had heavier bags than others. "She's certainly turned her life around. She lived in Naples for fifteen years after she left Chicago—no criminal record. She must've been running with a classier crowd or she would've never met Phillip Drayton, much less married him."

Sonny shrugged. "I told you. It probably doesn't mean anything."

I tucked that away to think about more later. "Hey, I wanted to ask you: when you came to her door Thursday night, how long did it take her to answer?"

"Less than five minutes. Why?"

"If the doorbell woke her right up, she didn't miss anything else that went down in her house."

"That's a fact."

"What was Drayton wearing?" Poppy had told me, but I was leading Sonny somewhere.

"Khakis. A golf shirt. Loafers, no socks. No raingear."

"So, what's your theory? I mean, what *was* he doing outside in that torrential rainstorm?"

Sonny took a long sip of coffee, rolled his lips in and out.

"Honestly, I have no idea. It could've been anything. Maybe he saw someone in distress. Maybe he took a wild hair to walk in the rain—people do that. We may never know what he was doing outside. But your client and her car were there, and her car has a dent in the fender. She is also overly involved in the lives of the people on her mail route. Could be she was lying in wait, watching the house. Might've done that for a long time, waiting for an opportunity. Maybe in her mind, she thought she was saving Mrs. Drayton from further abuse and possible death. That's one of several possibilities I'm working."

"But then why would Poppy get out of her car? Why stop at all?"

"I don't know that—yet."

"Sonny, you know I have a lot of respect for you. Hell, you're family. But I think you're reading this one wrong."

"Noted."

"What about the cars street-parked along Lenwood that night?"

"What about them?"

"Did you run the tags?"

"Of course I did. Every one of them belonged to someone who lives on Lenwood."

I shrugged. "Just dotting my i's."

"Yeah, well. Let me know when you're all done."

"Has forensics finished with Poppy's car?"

"Not yet."

"But clearly they haven't found any trace evidence—fibers, blood, anything that ties Poppy's car to Phillip Drayton— or you would've already arrested her."

"There are more tests they can run."

"Let me know when you're all done."

\*    \*    \*

If you know the route of any given mail carrier, it wasn't hard to track them down. Fortunately, the routes are posted online. I was certain there was some scientific method or other as to how the routes were drawn, but it evaded me. Many of them included non-contiguous blocks and partial blocks. I picked Poppy's out easily based on the few stops I knew were on it. I had no way of knowing where she'd start her route, so I drove the streets until I saw a mail truck parked on Hasell, between Meeting and King. I snagged a metered spot half a block away, locked the car, and scanned the street for Poppy as I made my way to her truck.

I didn't have to wait long. As Poppy approached, the wary look on her face came into focus. "Fancy meeting you here." She put her mail cart in the truck.

"Hey, Poppy," I said. "You doin' okay today? I have some bottled water in the car if you need it."

"I'm good. Just, you know, have to get the mail delivered." She looked at a spot over my shoulder, gave me a little half smile. "Is everything okay?"

"I'm so sorry to bother you while you're working. But something's come up, and I wondered, how well do you know Tess Hathaway?"

Poppy blinked, looked directly at me. "Mrs. Hathaway? She lives across from White Point Garden."

"Right. How well do you know her?"

"Not well. She's usually not there when I deliver the mail. I mean, she's a nice lady. Why are you asking me about her?" Poppy sounded vaguely protective.

Strains of music wafted across the street. Classical. I didn't know the piece, but it was lovely, soothing. I glanced towards it. A grey Honda Accord rolled slowly by with the windows rolled down. The woman behind the wheel stared in our direction, either at me or at Poppy, it was hard to tell. She was maybe in her mid-thirties with long, straight, pale blonde hair that extended below the window line. My eyes met hers and she jerked her head towards her windshield, then slammed on brakes as she nearly rear-ended the car in front of her. What was her deal? It was probably nothing, but I made a note of the tag number. Where had I seen a grey Honda recently? I thought for a moment. The woman parked along the Lower Battery, staring across the water. But there must be hundreds of grey Honda Accords in Charleston County, not to mention the daily influx of tourists.

Poppy cleared her throat.

"I'm so sorry. I'm just running through the list of neighbors, trying to get a feel for folks." I gave her a reassuring smile.

She shrugged. "There's not much I can tell you about Mrs. Hathaway to be honest. I know her to speak to her. That's about it."

I squinted, recalled again how Tess Hathaway had referred to her as "our Poppy." "When you say you know her to speak to her, do you mean you say 'hello,' or wave at her if you see her, or do you know the names of her pets?"

"Zelda." Poppy smiled. "Mrs. Hathaway has a mixed breed. Zelda looks like a Goldendoodle, but she's a shelter pet. Mrs. Hathaway says she's not sure what all is in there. Zelda's a sweetheart. She loves baby carrots."

Carrots. Zelda and the goats. I was going to have to start carrying raw carrots in case I needed to sweet talk an animal. "So you do know her? Mrs. Hathaway, I mean."

"Sure, I know her. Just not as well as some of the folks on my route, I guess. I'm not sure what you want to know." Poppy's forehead creased.

"That's it for now," I said. "I'll let you get back to work."

"You have my cell phone number, right?" she asked.

"Yes, of course. I'm sorry again to have bothered you." I understood she was curious why I hadn't just called to ask her that question. But non-verbal communication was key in my business. I didn't want to just hear the answer to a question. Whenever possible, I needed to see how people reacted. Poppy knew Mrs. Hathaway well enough.

"No worries." Poppy climbed in her truck. "Call me if you have any more questions."

"Sure thing." I smiled and waved.

Poppy was loyal, and she took her job responsibilities seriously. I liked her more each time I spoke with her.

It was nearly ten o'clock. Surveilling Tess Hathaway was next on my to-do list. She might be at home, but then again, she might have gone out for the morning. I decided to drop by Zelda's Fine Resale on King Street to check it out. It was doubtful that Tess would be there. She very likely had staff to run the store. But I might learn something useful there. I parked in a metered spot half a block away.

It was a few doors up from the Society Street intersection, just past Anne's. The three-story brick and masonry building featured large storefront windows. I could only imagine what the rent must be. Bells chimed as I pushed open the door.

"Good morning," Tess Hathaway herself called from behind the cash wrap desk. "Welcome to Zelda's."

"Good morning." I returned her smile.

"Everything is ten percent off today." Her voice was polished. Something about her called to mind the current queen of England, but she was quite a bit younger. "Let me know if I can help you find something."

"Thanks," I said. "I think I'll just browse."

"Very well then." She turned back to a conversation in progress with a black woman in nurse's scrubs.

The sales floor was well organized and attractively laid out. Wide swaths of gleaming hardwood floors were visible between the racks. Someone who knew ladies' retail apparel had designed the floor set. Four women browsed in different sections of the store. I skimmed through dresses. They had some cute things from top designers and the prices weren't bad. But I wasn't there to shop.

I worked my way towards the register, pretending to check out the merchandise. When I got close enough to overhear Tess's conversation, I picked a blouse from the rack and examined its seams.

"Don't you worry yourself one little bit about it. I'll take care of it." The nurse had a gentle voice, sweet.

"You're very kind, my dear," said Tess. "With Jenny ill, I'll need to be here all day today, probably tomorrow as well. I don't know what I'd do without you."

"I'll let you know how it goes," said the nurse.

"Please do." Tess turned to a woman who approached the desk with an armful of clothes. "I'm so happy you found some things that you can use."

"Bye now." The nurse headed towards the door.

There was nothing to be gained by hanging out in the store all afternoon unless I wanted to confront Tess and ask her if she was my client. I wasn't ready to do that just yet. I went with my gut and followed the nurse out the door.

She turned left and walked south on King Street with a purpose. She didn't window shop or meander. I was glad I had on my walking shoes. She crossed Market Street, then turned left, walking down the right-hand sidewalk. A block later, she crossed Meeting, and continued along South Market, weaving in and out of groups of meandering tourists.

When she reached the corner of South Market and East Bay, I figured we'd go right or left, where most of the foot traffic was headed. Across East Bay sat the Customs House, and beyond that a massive cruise ship was docked in the Cooper River. We crossed East Bay and headed towards the Carnival Ecstasy.

Because she'd seen me in the resale shop and I had no

opportunity to change my appearance, I hung back, but kept her in sight. I was beginning to think I was tagging along on her daily exercise stroll. Then, she turned right on Concord. My antennae went up. Surely not.

Bless Pat, if the nurse didn't walk into Buxton Books. *Damnation.* I didn't dare follow her inside. Was this the errand she was running for Tess, or did she simply want a book to read? I passed the door, stopped in front of the window to the left of it, and peeked inside.

She scooted straight over to the display of *The Ghosts of Charleston.* I crossed Cumberland, slipped out of my overblouse, and tied the arms around my waist. Then I pulled a clip out of my purse and twisted my hair into a knot. It was the best I could do to look different than I had in the resale shop. I pulled out my tourist map and waited on the corner. Less than five minutes later, the nurse came out of the bookshop empty handed and turned right on Cumberland.

I stayed on the opposite side of the street and a few steps back. She crossed East Bay and followed Cumberland to Meeting Street, then turned left and walked a block to Queen Street, where she turned right. One block later she crossed King Street, then turned right and headed north. Was she headed back to the resale shop or taking a self-guided walking tour of Charleston?

Half a block up King Street, directly across from the Charleston Library Society, the nurse abruptly veered left. She was headed through the back entrance to the Unitarian Graveyard. I paused at the wrought iron gate set between brick columns. If you weren't looking for it, you might miss it, sitting as it did in the midst of Charleston's busiest shopping district. Slate plaques set into the brick columns announced that the Unitarian Church in Charleston was founded in 1787 and informed visitors that it was one of the oldest Unitarian churches in the United States, and the oldest in the South.

I passed through the gate and followed the nurse down the shaded path. After a few feet, the slate gave way to a concrete walkway lined with planting beds filled with deep green, glossy-leaved plants that might have been a cousin to hostas. Immediately to my left was a tall brick building, and on the right a garden wall. I hung back. If the nurse spotted me on the path, she might make me for a tourist. She might not glean that I was following her. But whatever she was up to, she might abort it.

The plants in the beds lining the walk were now a mix of palms, ferns, and shrubs, some flowering, others not. It was a lush haven inside the city. The temperature dropped and the noise from the busy shopping district behind me faded like someone had turned down the volume on the world. I continued down the walk and passed through another iron gate and into the Unitarian graveyard.

As I walked inside, I was struck with the recognition that I was on hallowed ground. Of course, I knew that—it was a church graveyard. But the knowledge washed over me just the same. This particular graveyard had always fascinated me, not only because it was haunted. It was wild and lush, dotted with palm trees, crepe myrtles, and live oaks. Spanish moss dripped low from tree branches to the tops of the gravestones.

The pathways were maintained, but everything else was God's secret garden, and only he tended it. Owing to their philosophy that this was the way their dead wanted it, the Unitarians let flowers, vines, and all manner of foliage grow wild over the graves. Even inside the wrought iron gates of family plots, the graveyard was a riot of nature. The air was dense, more humid even than normal for Charleston in August. I caught a whiff of perfume, felt someone brush by me.

I turned, but no one was there. My skin prickled, from the base of my spine, all the way up to my neck. Owing to my first-hand experience with the departed, perhaps I was more sensitive to their presence. Or perhaps my imagination was in overdrive. Either way, this sacred place was both beautiful and spooky, even in broad daylight.

I walked a few steps down the brick pathway, then turned right, scanning for the nurse. I couldn't see her, but the graveyard was so dense with foliage, she could be a few feet away from me. Where had she gone?

Taking care to step lightly, I followed a dirt path towards the center of the graveyard. A few steps later, I heard voices. I crouched behind a headstone.

A woman's voice. She spoke rapid-fire in a language I didn't understand. Spanish?

"Now, Sofia, honey, you know I don't understand a word you say when you talk to me in Spanish." The sweet-voiced nurse spoke slowly, in a soothing tone.

"I *said*, what are we going to do with all of this shit that has hit the fan?" The woman spoke with a Spanish accent, her words heavy with worry.

"I told you, Tess has everything under control."

"How? How can she possibly have *this* under control?"

"We just need to trust her and trust God," said the nurse. "Everything's going to be all right. We're doing The Lord's work. He's going to look after us, you'll see."

"Jacynthe Grimes. Are you seriously telling me that you think The Good Lord approves of this...this *debacle*?" She said something else in Spanish under her breath.

"I grant you this is bad. Real bad. It weighs heavy on my heart too. But the Lord does work in mysterious ways," said the nurse—Jacynthe. "He will set everything to rights in his own time, in this world or the next. I am at peace with whatever happens. You just settle yourself down. Stop fretting, now, you hear me? Have faith in God's grace. Stress is so bad for you. It can cause all kinds of health problems, you know."

"You are off duty, Nurse Grimes."

"I'm just trying to look after you. You can't do for others if you're sick yourself," said Jacynthe.

"Fine. I will try not to worry. Thank you for coming."

"Any time," said Jacynthe. "Listen, can you stop by the bookshop tomorrow morning? Tess is tied up at the store and I'm working a double shift. I can take Wednesday, I'm the guide for one of the tours. I think we're going to hear from the Paxton girl soon. She's ready."

"Surely. Am I to take her home with me?"

"Yes, for the time being. Tess said she'll have room at Moultrie Street soon."

"All right. I'll take care of it. Bye now."

"Bye sweetie," said Jacynthe.

I watched for movement through the trees. I had no way of knowing which path the women would take out of the graveyard. Jacynthe would likely go back the way she'd come in. The most likely reason they'd be meeting in a graveyard was that they didn't want to be seen together. I now knew Jacynthe's name, what she looked like, that she was a nurse, and that she was a tour guide for some of the tours out of Buxton Books. I wanted to get a look at Sofia. Stealthily, I crept towards the front of the graveyard, which faced Archdale Street.

As I approached the circular brick walkway at the front of the graveyard, a tall, slender, Latina woman with glossy, tortoise shell brown curls that hung past her shoulders passed through the gate and went left on Archdale. That had to be her. I gave her some space but kept her in sight and followed her down the narrow sidewalk. At Queen Street, she turned left. Less than a block later she crossed the street and went into the parking garage at 93 Queen.

I hovered underneath a tree between two park benches, tapped the camera icon on my phone, and then pretended to talk on it. A few minutes later, a white Porsche 911 Carrera exited the garage and turned left. It was her. I hoped she had on her sunscreen, because it was August in the Lowcountry and the top to that convertible was down. Damnation. My car was parked all the way back on George Street near King. I snapped a picture of her license plate as she drove away.

Had Jacynthe gone back to the resale store? For lack of a better idea, and because I had to go past it to get to my car, I headed back there. I walked in the opposite direction from the one the woman in the Carrera had taken, towards King Street, then turned left and covered the five blocks back to the resale shop at a fast stride. The bells welcomed me inside again.

"Well, hello," said Tess. "Welcome back."

"Hello." I smiled.

"Did you decide on something?" she asked.

"Not yet." I returned to the rack of dresses, surveyed the room. Tess appeared to be alone.

"Did you know that one hundred percent of our proceeds go to support shelters for women and children who are victims of domestic abuse?" she asked.

"I did know that, yes."

I continued browsing but could feel her looking at me. Was she suspicious? I had been there twice that day, but surely customers did that occasionally.

"Dear, is everything all right?" she asked.

I looked up from a navy tailored dress. Kind eyes radiated empathy and concern.

Oh. Of course. She thought perhaps I was looking for help.

"Yes." I lowered my eyes, shifted my weight from one foot to the other like maybe I was nervous. "I'm fine." I studied the navy dress, then slid the hanger sideways to see the next one on the rack.

An entirely new twist for Tommy and Suzanne formed in my head.

# TEN

J. Henry Stuhr's downtown chapel sat on the corner of Calhoun and Smith. At five after six, Nate and I drove past the red brick building with white columns and pulled into the parking lot. It was packed. Nate pulled the Explorer into the last available spot.

"Merry, I have to go. I've got work to tend to." We'd been on the phone ever since Nate and I had left the house. We were both worried about our parents. "Let's talk tomorrow." We said our goodbyes and I ended the call.

"Apparently Phillip Drayton was quite popular," said Nate. "I still think we need a cover story."

"All right, fine. But if we're going to that much trouble, let's go through the receiving line. What is the least verifiable connection we could possibly have? Did you go to school with him at Duke?" I asked.

Nate winced. "It's not perfect. His brother went to Duke too. But I'm betting they didn't know every single one of each other's friends. Plus, that's been a while. Local connections are hardest. Too many people in the room who might think they should know us if we knew Phillip from one of his charities or some such thing. Let's go with Duke."

"Okay, but did I know him there too?"

"Yeah, but you went to Meredith College in Raleigh. You and I were dating, and you met him through me."

"Okay, but that means if one of us is overcome with emotion, it should be you," I said.

"Hey, I have a sensitive side," he said. "Let's do this."

He climbed out of the Explorer, walked around the back, opened my door for me, and offered me his hand. "You do make a lovely brunette, but I much prefer your natural shade."

"Thank you, Sweetheart." There was just nothing quite as appealing as a gentleman, especially one who willfully ignored the every-six-weeks highlight appointments required to maintain my "natural" multi-toned blonde. In addition to the brunette bob wig, I wore brown contact lenses and a navy skirt suit that had belonged to Gram. It wasn't dowdy—just much more conservative than my wardrobe. A navy and yellow scarf worn in a double loop close to my neck, and much heavier makeup than I typically wore completed the disguise.

"Her car is the last one in the row closest to the building." I slipped a GPS tracker from my purse. "Silver Lexus."

"Roger that."

We walked towards the side entrance to the building hand in hand. Others moved from the parking lot towards the chapel, some two by two, some alone, and some in small huddles. As we walked between Anne Frances's car and the one beside it, I paused.

"I need to fix the strap on my sandal." I made sure my voice projected.

Nate stood behind me, shielding me from the view of anyone walking in the direction of the building, which was everyone at that hour. I leaned down and attached the GPS tracker to the back-driver's side wheel well of the Lexus, then stood and smoothed my skirt. If Anne Frances was slipping out of the house while Sonny wasn't watching, we'd know.

"All set?" asked Nate.

"I need to take these shoes in to the shop. This strap is loose."

We proceeded towards the building. Nate held the door for me and then two ladies behind us. I waited for him at the top of a short stack of steps. A video display at the end of the hall announced that the family of Phillip Drayton would be in room C, the second room on our left. A line of folks waiting to pay their respects to the widow snaked all the way out into the hall. We moved to the back of the line.

As the line moved forward, we entered the first of three connecting parlor rooms, which formed an L-shape. Each one was more crowded than the next. Traditional furnishings, wingbacks, sofas, and arm chairs, dotted the rooms. Forty-five minutes later, we were in the third room with the deceased. Thankfully, the casket on the far right between the United States and South Carolina flags was closed. In front of a pair of burgundy wingbacks with floral throw pillows, Mrs. Drayton and her brother-in-law stoically accepted condolences. If there was tension between them, they hid it well.

When our turn in front of the widow came, Nate held out his hand to her. "Mrs. Drayton, I'm Thomas Moore. This is my wife, Suzanne. We knew Phillip back in college. I'm so terribly sorry for your loss."

She was striking, in a black sheath with a long-sleeved cardigan, her hair pulled back to a bun at the base of her neck, with little makeup. Her large grey eyes, delicate features, and porcelain skin made her look incredibly vulnerable. "Thank you so much for coming."

Her tone had the ring of sincerity. She turned to me and offered me her left hand. Nate still held her right. "It was so good of you to make the trip. I know Phillip would appreciate it. Thank you, truly."

"By all means," I said. "We're just in shock. Is there anything at all we could do to ease your burden? We'll be in town for a few days. At Charleston Place. Please call if you think of anything." Naturally, I knew the odds of her doing such a thing were roughly the same as her riding an elephant down King Street. She didn't know us from Adam's house cat. But these were the things we said in situations where words were entirely inadequate.

"Thank you for your kindness. I will." She nodded and looked past me to the next person in line.

We moved on to the brother. This was my first look at Daniel Drayton in person. He was not at all what I expected. His brown hair was long and wavy, covering his ears and touching his collar in back. His mustache didn't reach his goatee and he wore a soul patch. It might have been that combination, or it could have been the drunken slur of his voice that brought to mind Johnny Depp in his Captain Jack Sparrow role.

Nate introduced us, repeating what he'd said to the widow.

"Of course. Tommy? My God, man—what's the matter with you? What's with the 'Mr. Drayton' rubbish?" Daniel pulled Nate into a hug and slapped him on the back. "Good of you to come."

Perhaps Daniel Drayton had so many friends in college they all ran together in his memory. Or perhaps he drank a great deal then, or now, or both. "We weren't sure you'd remember us," I said. "It's been such a long time."

"Too long," said Daniel, too loudly. "Why'd it take you two so long to get to Charleston for Heaven's sake? S'not the other side of the planet, you know. Where are you staying?" He still held Nate in a half embrace, his right hand holding on to Nate's, his left on Nate's shoulder.

"Charleston Place," I said. "Please call if there's anything we can do."

"It's a damn shame," said Nate. "I can't tell you how sorry we are."

Daniel's face fell, like he'd suddenly remembered why he was there. "It's a damn disgrace. Phillip was all the family I had left. Let's get a drink after. Come by the house, would you? You know where it's at, right? Tradd Street. Number forty-one."

"Thank you so much for your hospitality," said Nate. "But I'm afraid we have a previous commitment this evening."

I resisted the urge to elbow my husband. It would be tricky if Daniel reminisced too much, but alcohol was the universal lubricant for tongues. We could learn a great deal.

"Tomorrow then," said Daniel. "You can't turn a bloke down on the day his only brother is buried, can you now?"

"Certainly, we'll be there," I said.

"Eight o'clock-ish," said Daniel.

Nate extricated himself, patted him on the shoulder. "See you then, brother."

We waded through the clusters of people who'd stopped partway out of the room to chat with someone they knew, and into the adjoining room. It was way too full of people. Claustrophobia spurred me to make a quick exit. I tamped it down. Through the crowd, I spotted an empty yellow upholstered chair in the corner. From there, one could see everyone coming and going.

"Tommy," I said a bit louder than necessary, "I think I need to sit for just a moment. My head is simply pounding."

"Of course." Nate put an arm at the small of my back and escorted me to the chair, murmuring "excuse me's" as we negotiated our way through the crowd.

I settled into the chair and Nate hovered beside me. No one paid us the slightest bit of attention. The line of people continued moving from the room to our right, through the room where I sat, and into the next room. Slowly, I scanned the room, searching faces. On my third pass around the assembly of well-dressed Charlestonians, I saw her.

Across from me, behind a pair of portly older gentlemen, a voluptuous redhead hovered alone just outside the doorway to the chamber where the casket was. She appeared to be in her early to mid-thirties. Her eyes and nose were red and moist. She twisted a wad of Kleenex with both hands. Whoever she was, she cared deeply for Phillip Drayton.

I was formulating a pretext to go talk to her when the line

moved up and Poppy Oliver stepped into the room. What in the name of common sense was she doing here?

I looked at Nate. He was wondering the exact same thing. She'd never seen him before and I was in disguise, so we weren't in danger of blowing our cover. But why on earth would she come to family visitation?

"Because the people on her route are all the family she has." Colleen popped in, perched on the back of the sofa, with her ankles crossed between two elderly women. She wore a shimmery white dress and must have read my mind—knew I'd made note of it.

"I know mortals who were close to Phillip Drayton are in mourning, and I get it," she said. "But I keep telling you, passing from this world to the next is not the tragedy you people think it is."

*Try again to read Mrs. Drayton's mind—the brother too.* I put a hand on Nate's arm and he leaned down. "Keep an eye on Poppy," I said. "I need to talk to the redhead."

He nodded.

I stood and crossed the room. "Pardon me," I said. "Do you know where the ladies' room is?"

She nodded. "Take a left out this door, then go to the end of the hall and make a right. It's not too far down on the left."

"I'm so sorry to be a bother," I said. "But I'm not feeling at all well. Could you come with me? I'd ask my husband, but, well, it is the ladies' room."

"Sure." Concern crossed her face. She took my arm and helped me make my way into the hall. "Are you feeling faint?"

"I am. I don't know what's gotten into me."

"Have you eaten today?" She led me down the hall.

"Not much," I said.

"I haven't eaten in a couple of days," she said.

"Did you know Phillip well?" I asked.

"You could say that," she said.

"We were friends in college," I said. "I haven't seen him in years, to tell you the truth. I think maybe I'm coming down with something."

"Right in here." She opened the door and we stepped into a small lounge.

I moved to a small settee on the right and dropped into it. "I'm so sorry to trouble you. Thank you so much. I'm Suzanne Moore, by the way."

"Mallory. Mallory Lucas."

"So, you were close to Phillip?" I smeared sympathy all over my face.

She teared up, nodded.

"I'm so sorry," I said. "How stupid of me. I apologize for prying."

"It's all right. I shouldn't have come here." Tears rolled down her cheeks.

"Why would you say that?" I asked. "That's why they have these things—for those left behind. Phillip, as they say, is in a better place."

"I believe that's true," she said. "He wasn't perfect. But he had a good heart."

"I remember him that way," I said. "It's just so tragic. And they haven't even caught the person responsible. At least that's the last we heard. Is there any news?" I hoped to hear her theories. Typically, folks shared those easily.

"Not that I've heard," she said. "But it wouldn't surprise me in the least to find out that—that—" She inhaled deeply, wiped her eyes with the back of her index finger. "I should go. Are you all right? Do you want me to get you some water or anything?"

*Finish the sentence already. What*? "I'll be fine," I said. "Thank you again."

She nodded. "Good bye, then." She opened the door and stepped into the hall.

Just as the door swung closed, a man said, "Mallory, love.

There you are." Daniel Drayton's voice.

"Daniel." She sobbed.

I waited five seconds, then opened the door. Mallory and Daniel were locked in an embrace. He rubbed her back as she cried. I couldn't see her face, but his eyes were squeezed closed.

I slipped past them and down the hall as discreetly and quickly as I could. Clearly, they knew each other quite well. I made my way back to parlor C, which had only gotten more crowded. Nate chatted with a gentleman in a bow tie who appeared to be a spry ninety-something. Poppy had evidently made her way into the room where Anne Frances was receiving. A feeling of foreboding washed over me. How would Anne Frances react to Poppy? She'd been friendly to her, but that was before the accident. Did Anne Frances hold Poppy responsible for Phillip's death?

I wended my way back through the crowd and into the middle room, stretching to see over the tops of heads. Someone brushed by me and said, "Excuse me."

I turned to see a woman with very long, straight blonde hair walking away from me. Was that the woman from the Honda on Hasell Street? Something about her tickled my natural curiosity. I was torn between following her and tracking down Poppy. I needed to see about Poppy. I moved to the far side of the entryway to the casket room. Poppy stepped in front of Anne Frances. They embraced each other warmly.

Neither of them cried.

From Daniel Drayton's chair, Colleen raised two open palms. "Still can't read the wife. But Poppy has a clear conscience."

# ELEVEN

I spent the trip home from Charleston on the phone with Mamma. Nate got out of the car and went into the lounge on the ferry. I rolled down the windows, put Mamma on speaker, and removed the wig, which was making my scalp itch something fierce. I fluffed my hair, sanitized the fool out of my hands, and took out the contacts while Mamma alternately vented about Merry running off to get married, Blake's revolving-door of girlfriends, and the mess that had not yet been cleaned up in her backyard.

It was nearly ten before Nate and I made it home. We were famished, and it was far too late to cook. I pulled the leftover Chinese food out of the refrigerator while Nate opened a bottle of pinot noir. We sat at the island in the kitchen and caught each other up on the day as we passed the cartons back and forth.

I told Nate what Sonny had told me about Anne Frances Drayton's history with a drug kingpin in Chicago.

He stopped, his glass halfway to his lips, and narrowed his eyes. "On the surface, that sounds compelling. But when you take into account how long ago it was and what her life is like now, it's hard to see how that would figure in."

"I agree, especially after seeing her tonight. It's like she lives in another world now. But still, I'm going to dig into this Lucious Carter character when I get a chance. See if I find another connection to her. Just dot my i's. Another thing that strikes me, though, is would a woman strong enough to extricate herself from the drug and gang culture allow herself to be a victim of abuse?

Doesn't seem the right personality type to me."

"Nope," said Nate. "That doesn't fit."

I told him about Poppy's protective reaction to Tess Hathaway, the nurse in the resale shop, her visit to the bookstore, the trip to the graveyard, and the gorgeous Latina named Sofia in the Porsche.

"How do you know she's Latina?" asked Nate.

"She speaks Spanish—she could be from Spain, of course. But of the twenty-one countries in the world where Spanish is the official language, most of them are in Latin America, and that's closer, so I'm going with that for now." I took a bite of sesame chicken.

"Sounds reasonable. I didn't mean to get you all riled up."

"I'm not riled up."

"You sound riled up. Maybe you should finish eating first, and then finish telling me about your day. You have a tendency to get cranky when your blood sugar drops."

I raised an eyebrow at him, swallowed a bite of spring roll. "I can multi-task. I've got the nurse's full name and Sofia's license plate. I'll profile them first thing tomorrow. But it looks to me like they're working with Tess. Helping abused women. Somehow, they're sending messages to each other through the bookshop."

"Seems a bit elaborate," said Nate. "Why not just text?"

"An over-abundance of caution? I don't know. Yet. Oh, and there's another woman. Pale blonde in an old Honda. She may or may not be involved, but I saw her twice today and possibly once on Saturday, which provokes my suspicious nature. I also have her tag number. Did you find anything useful on our victim?"

"I picked a handful of folks I could connect to him through the Drayton Foundation, and a few social media friends. Called them up. Told them I was doing a piece on Phillip for *Charleston Magazine*. No one had a bad word to say about him, though that doesn't surprise me. People rarely speak ill of the dead, especially to a reporter. That said, my general impression is that Phillip

Drayton was cheerfully dedicated to the enjoyment of life—feasting, fine wines, friends. A good-time Charlie, as it were. And he generously supported a long list of local charities."

"Interesting. Big turnout tonight at the funeral home too. Anyone offer anything about Anne Frances?"

"A few of them called her quiet, reserved. Made observations as to how she was not as outgoing as her husband. A couple of them remarked that she wasn't *from here*, and they had no idea who her people were."

"Naturally." I sipped my pinot noir. Knowing who one's people were was of paramount importance in our world. It was about history, connections, or lack thereof.

"But they all gave the impression they thought the marriage was happy. I asked specific questions. A man's friends would never volunteer to a reporter that they suspected him of wife abuse. But at least a few of them would hesitate to tell me that he was happily married. There would be hedging. Didn't happen. Even the ones who questioned her heritage said the Draytons were in love with one another."

"So if he abused her, he hid it well from his friends. And undoubtedly, he would. If all abusive men were ill-tempered, wore wife-beater t-shirts, and stayed drunk, fewer women would marry them to begin with."

Nate chewed thoughtfully, tilted his head towards his shoulder, cocked an eyebrow in an expression that conceded the point.

"What about the blog?" I asked.

"I think Phillip Drayton enjoyed eating out at restaurants, liked the attention he got as a reviewer. For what it's worth, the restaurant folks I spoke with told me that Mrs. Drayton came with her husband to dine. Guess she just didn't want to be a part of the blog. I read through a ridiculous number of his stellar dining experiences. Then I asked Blake if Nell could help us out."

"She'll love you for that." Nell Cooper was Blake's dispatcher/office manager. She kept him and his office in order, but Stella Maris was a sleepy town and most days she filled her hours browsing the Internet.

"I told her she could pick her favorite restaurant and I'd get her and Bill a gift certificate," said Nate.

"That just might keep you on her good side, but it's going to be expensive. What about Facebook?"

Nate shook his head. "Nothing useful. I did finish the property records search. That was the most interesting part of my day."

"Pass me the lo mein, would you? What'd you find?"

"Tess Hathaway owns the property on South Battery outright—well, through a private trust. Zelda's Safe House—the foundation—owns no property. However, Mrs. Hathaway, through an impressively intricate web of corporations, owns eight different homes throughout Charleston County, plus the building on King Street that houses the resale shop."

"Rental properties?" I asked.

"You'd think, but no. There's not a single rental listing for any of the properties. And one of them is on Moultrie Street."

"Where Jacynthe said Tess was going to send the new girl. Instead of a single shelter, she's stashing the women in a network of houses," I said. "Smart."

"Looks that way to me. Makes sense she'd have a nurse involved. I imagine some of them come in injured."

I swallowed a bite of beef fried rice. "I wonder what the woman in the Porsche brings to the table?"

"The question is," said Nate, "did Anne Frances Drayton reach out to them? I mean, yeah, we can connect Poppy to Tess, and Poppy to Anne Frances Drayton. But Tess to Anne Frances? That's another story altogether. The coincidental bookstore visit is awfully thin. We could spend a lot of time figuring out the details of how these women operate, but is it connected to our case or not? And I think we need to know that before we waste time investigating these good women who are 'doing the Lord's work.'"

I squinched up my face. "They were all worked up about something. That conversation in the graveyard—I'm thinking Phillip Drayton's death is the debacle weighing heavy on their hearts. They may not be responsible, but they know something."

"Maybe," said Nate. "But we need more. A lot more."

"I have a plan for that."

"Okay."

"I'm thinking Tommy is abusive," I said.

Nate chewed thoughtfully.

"Going undercover with these women would not be dangerous." I preempted his typical first response to my working undercover.

"Perhaps not," said Nate. "That may be the quickest way to suss out what's going on with them, but they're not going to talk to you about another client."

"No, they won't," I said. "We need serious leverage. Let's sleep on that. Hey, did you check on Anne Frances?"

"During the ferry ride. She left the funeral home at eight fifteen and went straight home." We had apps on our phones that followed the tracker in real time and made a record of everywhere it went.

"Will you cover the funeral?" I asked. "The interment is trickier—could be only family. Maybe watch from a distance? Jacynthe went to the bookstore today around 11:15. She asked Sofia to stop by there tomorrow. I don't know when she'll show up, but I want to see what she does."

"You are a stubborn wench," said Nate. "I grant you that whatever these women are up to, it's intriguing. But I state again, for the record, we have not established a connection between their shenanigans for a good cause and our deceased man-about-town."

I shrugged, gave him a grin. "I gotta go with my gut."

"As you wish."

"My second three favorite words."

"But tomorrow evening, since you so graciously accepted his invitation, we need to go to Daniel Drayton's for a drink." Nate shook his head. "That's risky, Slugger. If he figures out we're not who we claim to be, no tellin' how he'll react. We don't know yet that he didn't have a motive to kill his brother."

"Speaking of which...the curvaceous redhead at the funeral home?" I asked.

"Yeah. You find out anything from her?"

"Her name is Mallory Lucas. She alluded to suspicions but didn't tell me what they were. But, after she left me in the ladies' room, I saw her in the hall with Daniel. They were comforting each other in a very cuddly manner. I need to dig into her background with the Draytons. But what I want to know from Daniel Drayton is why he suspects Anne Frances. Surely he'll tell two old college friends all about it."

Nate drained his glass. "I'll clear this up. Get yourself ready for bed. We've got a big day ahead of us tomorrow."

I stood and kissed him on the back of the neck before heading upstairs. He knew my nighttime routine took ten times longer than his.

That night I had the dream again—the one where a Category 5 hurricane is closing in on Stella Maris. The ferry has sunk, and Nate and I are rushing to escape by boat with two children when a giant wave washes him overboard.

I woke up in tears and reached out for Nate. He was breathing steadily beside me, oblivious. I was glad I hadn't woken him, as I often did. From his bed in a corner of the room, Rhett, who was wide awake, gave me a worried look.

Colleen faded in, sat on the corner of the bed.

Rhett made a soft noise, raised his head in greeting. His tongue hung out in a sloppy grin.

Colleen rubbed my leg. "Go back to sleep," she said. "You're safe and so is Nate. We'll talk tomorrow."

# TWELVE

The next morning, I skipped my run. I had work to do before heading into Charleston. I made a strong pot of coffee, poured myself a cup, kissed Nate, and ruffled Rhett's fur as they went out the door. Rhett snuffled his disapproval.

I settled in at the computer and started a profile for Jacynthe Grimes. She was a widow, age 48, with three grown children and a three-bedroom ranch on Sheridan Road in West Ashley. She had no criminal record, however, when her husband was alive, she'd gotten a protective order against him. That explained why she wanted to help victims of abuse. She'd been one herself.

I found her on Facebook—one more person who should really tighten her security settings. Most people had no idea what all strangers could find out about them on social media. She was an ER nurse at Medical University of South Carolina and sang in the choir at her church. Her posts were mostly church activities, inspirational memes, and photos of her two grandbabies. I searched her friends list but found no one connected to our case. Jacynthe Grimes appeared to be a good-hearted, sweet-natured grandmother who loved her church.

Mallory Lucas—the curvy redhead last seen in the arms of Daniel Drayton—was next on my agenda. She was a native Charlestonian who'd attended Porter Gaud with the Draytons, one year behind Daniel. She'd studied Art History at Furman and was currently employed by the Gibbes Museum of Art. She had no criminal background or civil complaints. Her top-floor condo at

One Vendue Range had set her back close to two million dollars. Mallory had never been married.

Her Facebook profile was filled with pictures of her having a good time at this event or that. She attended lots of parties. Both Drayton brothers appeared in photos with her, some group shots, some just the three of them, and a few of her with one or the other of them. None of them indicated a romance, but everyone's body language certainly suggested they were all plenty comfortable with one another.

The thing I couldn't get out of my mind was Mallory saying that she shouldn't have come to the visitation. She'd known Phillip Drayton most of her life. The only reason she'd say such a thing was a guilty conscience. The question was, what was she feeling guilty about? Was it an unrequited love, an affair, or something much worse?

Next, I pulled up the photo of the Porsche's license plate, opened a subscription database, and queried the tag number. Interesting. The car was registered to SCS, LLC. I opened another database and searched for the company. Sofia Catalina Sanchez. The brunette with interesting highlights driving the Porsche.

Ms. Sanchez, age 50, unlike most everyone else in this case, had a colorful history. A native of Colombia, she'd arrived in Charleston with her maternal grandmother in 1981, when she was sixteen. Her background had holes. I couldn't tell where her parents were now or in 1981, but her father was Colombian. Sofia apparently had dual citizenship because her mother was a US citizen.

She'd attended public schools. I couldn't find any evidence she'd gone to college. She'd been arrested a few times for lewd behavior and once for assaulting a gentleman with a stiletto. Her story was that he refused to pay her for a personal dance in the private room of the strip club where she worked. She'd also been sued for alienation of affection by a wife who claimed her husband expected her to dance like Sofia. The arrest records were all 25 or more years old.

Sofia married Hugh Conrad in 1999, and I could find no record of a divorce. But there was no mention of him in any of her data aside from the marriage license. I did a quick search for him. Apparently, he lived a quiet life these days. Neither of them seemed to have social media accounts, or if they did, they were under pseudonyms.

I dug into real property records. Through SCS, LLC, Sofia owned close to a hundred acres and a home worth five million dollars on Ashley River Road—paid cash for it in 2000. I pulled up a map. Good grief, it was just past Middleton Plantation. Where had a former stripper—I assumed she'd changed professions—come by that kind of money? If Hugh Conrad was her sugar daddy, wouldn't his name be on the property as well?

Like the widow Drayton, it appeared Sofia Sanchez had done well for herself in Act Two.

It was nearly seven o'clock and I needed to be in Charleston by the time the bookshop opened. I set Sofia aside and turned my attention to the blonde who kept turning up. First, I ran the Honda's tag. The car belonged to Robert Williams. The address was on Darlington Avenue in Charleston. That was in Wagener Terrace, a neighborhood between the Ashley River and Rutledge Avenue, north of Hampton Park, popular with families and young professionals. That hadn't been Robert driving the Honda.

A quick check showed that he was married to Emma Claire Baker Williams. I googled her and found her corporate profile on the Ridgetech website. She was a software developer. Her Facebook profile hadn't been updated in months, but other people tagged her in posts. She and Robert had two children, a boy and a girl. I gleaned from some of the posts and comments that Robert had a serious illness. Emma had a short list of Facebook friends, none of them were pertinent to our case in a way I'd uncovered thus far.

Unsure if or how any of these women were connected to Phillip Drayton's death, to be thorough, I printed their photos and added them to the case board. I'd dig into them all further as soon as I had a chance.

I grabbed a quick shower, dressed, and packed a few surveillance essentials—a small cooler with bottled water, Cheerwine, and a turkey sandwich, Dove Dark Chocolate Promises, mixed nuts, and pretzels. Then I grabbed a dress, a pair of matching sandals, and the brunette wig, so I wouldn't have to come home to change before we went to Daniel Drayton's house. These days, everything else I might need—Clorox wipes, Lysol spray, extra hand sanitizer, garbage bags, a change of clothes, various hats, sunglasses, et cetera, plus all my toys, everything from my camera to eavesdropping equipment—was stored in the back of one of our cars.

I picked up the cooler and my garment bag and stopped by my office where Nate, dressed in a suit for the funeral, studied the updates I'd made to our case board.

"You heading out?" asked Nate.

"Yeah. What are you going to do after the graveside service? You coming home until time to head over to Drayton's?"

"Nah. No sense in that. Think I'll check in with Sonny. Maybe check on Poppy. Wanna grab dinner before? I'd rather not eat at ten o'clock again tonight."

"Sounds good. Poogan's Porch? I was craving their mac and cheese just yesterday."

"Six thirty? That should give us time to eat a leisurely dinner and still arrive at Drayton's by eight-ish."

"Perfect."


There's a single parking meter on the west side of Concord Street between the Customs House and Buxton Books, which sits on the corner. At 9:25 in the morning, I had no trouble scoring the spot. For my purposes that day, it was perfect. Since I was essentially lying in wait rather than following anyone, there wasn't a need for me to hide. I fed the meter with my handy City of Charleston Smart Card and went inside the bookshop. I wanted a copy of *The Ghosts of Charleston* for myself, see what all the fuss was about.

No other customers were in the store and I'd never seen the young woman working the register that morning, whose name tag claimed she was Christine. Nevertheless, I paid with cash and took my book back out to the car. I flipped open the book and skimmed the table of contents. Being familiar with spirits in general, and the ones that haunted Charleston in particular, I smiled in recognition at some of the tales recounted in the book. Perhaps we'd see Zoe Saint Amand that very evening at Poogan's Porch.

I set the book aside. The thing about surveillance is you really can't read or otherwise entertain yourself, or you might miss the thing you're waiting to see. I decided to skip getting out the Nikon camera. As close as I was to the bookstore, my iPhone would serve my purposes well.

Surveillance time was, however, good for pondering. I needed to connect the dots between our merry band of altruists and Anne Frances Drayton. And then what? Say she had been in touch with them? I didn't think for a moment that two grandmas and an ex-stripper had run Phillip Drayton over. There was zero evidence they were violent. Well, aside from the stiletto incident.

On the other hand, two of them were widows, one a documented victim of abuse, and the third—where was Hugh Conrad? I pulled out my iPad, held the screen so that the top of it was lined up with the door to the bookstore, and searched harder for Sofia Sanchez's husband. Originally from Nashville, Conrad had moved to Charleston in the nineties and been quite successful in real estate development. He was thirteen years older than Sofia. There was no record of his death, but no record of him living for the last fifteen years either.

From the time I got back to the car until eleven fifteen, fourteen women—four pairs and two groups of three—went in and out of the bookshop. I snapped photos of each, but they all seemed carefree, and they all came out with bags indicating they'd purchased something.

At eleven thirty, a couple rounded the corner from Cumberland. She looked to be in her early to mid-thirties, he was maybe a little older. They held hands, but he had a sour look on his face. She was talking, looking up at him. I took their picture. He leaned down, said something in her ear. There was a threat on his face. She paled. He opened the door for her and they walked inside the bookstore. I climbed out of the car and followed them.

She browsed the display to the left inside the door. He hovered. I crossed the room, stood on the far side of the oblong table, and pretended interest in a thriller. She moved to her right, past the double window to the bookshelf in the corner. He was close on her heels. Something was off about him. It was clear he had no interest in reading. But it was more than that. It was like he was guarding her, but neither I nor Christine were threatening in the slightest.

After a moment, she moved on to the display of *The Ghosts of Charleston*. She picked up a copy and flipped through the pages. A bookmark fell out and landed on the table in front of her. She picked it up, slipped it back inside the book, and returned it to the middle of the display.

"You finding anything?" The man's voice was impatient.

"Can I have this one?" She picked up a copy of *The Ghosts of Charleston*, this one from the end of the row of books.

"Fine," he said. "Let's get it and get out of here."

She took the book to the cash wrap desk and the man handed Christine a credit card.

"Did you find everything you were looking for?" she asked.

The woman smiled. "Yes, thank you."

Christine rang her sale and handed her a bag with her book. "I hope you enjoy that."

"Thanks." The woman smiled tightly.

The man put an arm around her waist and hurried her out of the store.

"He was intense," said Christine when the door closed behind them.

I raised my eyebrows in an expression that said, *Boy Howdy.*

I crossed the room to the display of *The Ghosts of Charleston* and picked up the book that the woman had replaced in the middle of the display. "I was thinking I might like another copy of this, for a friend."

"We sell a lot of those as gifts. Locals buy them for visiting friends. A few of them are in here every week. Everyone loves a good ghost story."

I opened the book to the bookmarked page. It was between page sixty and page sixty-one. I'd half expected an SOS note to fall out, but there was just the bookmark. "Come to think of it, she may already have it. I'll have to check."

"Well, you can be sure we'll always have that one in stock." Christine smiled.

"Precisely what I was thinking." I put the book back exactly where the woman had left it, said goodbye to Christine, and returned to my car.

It was 11:30, and breakfast that morning had been skimpy—a slice of whole wheat toast with peanut butter. I pulled out my turkey sandwich and a Cheerwine. Had the young woman in the bookshop left a message for Sofia to find? On page sixty of the ghost book, there was a photo of the white Charleston single house at 76 Meeting Street, which now served as the rectory for St. Michael's Church. The same St. Michael's Church where Phillip Drayton's funeral was now underway.

The house hadn't always been the church's rectory. The church purchased it in the early 1940s. Before that, the house had been, according to local legend, well and truly haunted. Apparently, the Episcopalians had chased off the ghosts. But what had it to do with our case? Or was that simply a random page where the young woman had stuck the bookmark?

I finished the sandwich and munched on some pretzels. Then, for the next two hours, I continued searching for a more current record of Hugh Conrad, to no avail. At 1:45, a limousine pulled to the curb in a no parking zone across the street from the bookstore. A very large, solid looking man with close-cropped brown hair and dark sunglasses got out of the passenger side and opened the backdoor. Sofia Sanchez emerged.

The burly guy closed the car door, scanned the area. She said something to him, then looked both ways and crossed the street. He waited by the back car door but continued to survey his surroundings. No doubt he was hired security, and he had made note of me. The driver, who I could not see through the tinted window, could also see me.

Sofia entered the bookshop and returned five minutes later with a bag. Her stalwart companion opened the car door and she slid inside. A moment later, the limo pulled away from the curb. I started the car. Shit, shit, *shit*. I'd have to make a U-turn to follow them. The security team would make me in less than a New York minute.

In my rearview mirror, I watched as the limo made a left on North Market. Were they headed over to 76 Meeting Street now? The hearse would've been parked on Meeting Street in front of the church, in the turn lane, the family cars behind it. That could've stretched all the way back to St. Michael's Alley, which separated the house from the graveyard, but they'd surely left by now. It was nearly two o'clock. I pulled forward and made a right on Cumberland. Maybe the light would catch them at North Market and East Bay.

As I stopped at the corner of Cumberland and East Bay, I craned my neck right. I rolled forward, looking. There. They made a left on East Bay. I continued on Cumberland, crossing in front of them, then made a left on State. For the moment, I was riding parallel to them, one block over. If they were headed back to Sofia's home on Ashley River Road, they'd turn right on Broad Street and take that until it turned into Lockwood, then cross over the Ashley River Bridge.

If they were headed to 76 Meeting Street, they would make a scant half-block detour along the way. I zipped ahead on State Street, crossed Queen, and made a right on Broad. There was far more tourist traffic on East Bay, which would slow the limo down. They should still be behind me. I turned left on Church, then made a right and rolled slowly down St. Michael's Alley. Fortunately, no one pulled in behind me. I crept down the narrow lane, barely wide enough for my car. To my right, a narrow sidewalk's width away, were the front doors to historic houses. On my left, small patches of grass and parking courts offered a bit of a buffer to the homes beyond.

As I neared the end of the alley, the brick courtyard wall of St. Michael's graveyard was immediately on my right and 76 Meeting Street to my left, with Meeting Street directly in front of me. I glanced in my rearview mirror. Still no one behind me. This was the narrowest part of the alley. Claustrophobia squeezed at my chest. Deep breaths. Deeeep breaths.

If I rolled forward, I'd be sitting in the middle of the sidewalk, which was what you had to do in order to see to turn onto Meeting Street. But I wasn't ready to turn just yet. If they were coming here, the limo should be closing in. I needed to see what went down. Across Meeting, in front of the post office might've been a better vantage point, but the odds of snagging a parking space at that exact moment weren't great.

Being in that alley was like having blinders on. I could only see what happened right in front of me. The view was too narrow. I would have to take a chance on getting a parking spot across the street. I inched forward, looked right, then left for pedestrians.

Approaching on my left, walking up Meeting towards Broad, came the couple from the bookshop, hand-in-hand. The limo rolled gradually up behind them. The young woman looked up at the man and said something, a warm smile and a look that asked "pretty please" on her face. She handed him her phone. He cut his eyes upward in a quick eye roll, then nodded and took the phone. She moved in front of one of the colorful, overflowing window boxes on 76 Meeting. The man held the phone to take her picture. She was talking to him as the limo pulled close to the curb in the no-parking zone right behind him.

The front passenger door opened, bumping the man. He yelled, spun on the burly guy as he climbed out of the car. Burly guy was way bigger. The man appeared to think about his next move.

While he was preoccupied, the driver's side passenger door opened, and the woman darted around the back of the car. Just before she ducked into the car, she hollered, "I'm leaving you of my own free will. Don't come looking for me."

He roared with rage, lunged in her direction.

Both doors closed, and the limo rolled away.

He ran a few steps, pounded the trunk. I snapped a photo of the tag, though I was positive who it was registered to.

The man stood in the middle of Meeting Street, with two raised fists, red-faced. "Arrrrrrrrr. You *bitch*. Wait 'til I get my hands on you."

The limo turned left on Broad Street.

The apoplectic man braced himself, his hands on his knees, panting. He might've been foaming at the mouth.

I honked my horn at him. He was in my way.

He spun on me like a wild man.

I turned right out of the alley and followed the limo. He moved out of my way at the last possible moment.

I was reasonably certain where the limo was headed, so I didn't try to catch it. Sofia had asked, and Jacynthe had answered in the affirmative. They were taking the woman to Sofia's house for the time being. I took a leisurely drive out Ashley River Road. Once you're out of the city, it's a scenic trip—two lanes, lined with a dense stand of trees dripping Spanish moss.

Along the way, I called Sonny to give him some context just in case a man reported his wife kidnapped near St. Michael's Church at two o'clock that afternoon. Okay, I didn't give him nearly as much context as he wanted. I left out everything right up to the woman stating that she was getting into the car of her own free will and that she didn't want her husband to come looking for her.

"Is this connected in any way to the Phillip Drayton case?" he asked.

"I'm not certain yet." This was the absolute truth.

"How did you come to be sitting in St. Michael's Alley at the exact right moment to witness a woman leaving her husband in such a dramatic manner?"

"Pure luck." There was a certain amount of truth in that statement.

"What are you not telling me?"

"Sonny, I have to go now. I just didn't want you to call out the cavalry if this man says his wife was kidnapped. She wasn't. Talk soon." I ended the call before he could cuss me.

Just past the entrance to Middleton Place, I slowed.

Then I drove another mile, and the only road I saw was an unmarked dirt road. When I got to Ashley River Drive, I turned around. The dirt road must've been Sofia's driveway. I eased past it again, scanning the trees for security cameras.

Bingo. I didn't dare linger in the area. I headed back to Charleston. The woman in the limo was likely safer than she'd been in a long while.

It was twenty minutes past three when I made it back to the city. I pulled into the first metered parking spot I found on Broad Street, just past Legare, across from the Cathedral of St. John the Baptist. I needed a place to change and freshen up. Charleston had a plethora of lovely inns and luxurious hotels, but typically, for business, Nate and I would grab a room at the Hampton Inn if we needed one. We were scrupulous when spending a client's money. A quick rate check showed that The Mills House—conveniently located on the corner of Meeting and Queen, across the street and a block away from the recent non-abduction on Meeting, and also across Queen Street from Poogan's Porch—had a better rate that night. I booked a room.

I drove another two blocks down Broad and turned left on Meeting Street. Moments later, I came to a stop at the light directly in front of the pink hotel with creamy trim and a frilly wrought iron balcony on the second floor. I turned left on Queen and parked in the garage behind the hotel. Along with my garment bag and the tote that doubled as my purse, I grabbed the overnight bag I kept in the car and checked in, leaving a key at the desk for Nate.

All of the rooms in the Mills House were redone a few years back, and they were lovely. Mine was done in cerulean blue, cream, and taupe, and overlooked Meeting Street. It had a lovely view of the city. In the cool quiet, I took a deep breath, texted Nate to let him know where I was, then pulled out my laptop and settled in at the desk to dot an i.

I opened the hotspot on my phone and connected it to my laptop. This was far more secure than any hotel's Wi-Fi. Then I logged into the database where I could access vehicle registration. The limo's tag did not come back to SCS, LLC, as I'd suspected, but rather to The Planter's Club. That rang a faint bell. I'd heard rumors about a private, upscale club in an old plantation house. Was that what Sofia was up to these days? Was she behind The

Planter's Club?

I pondered that for a moment. James Huger would know. If it went on in Charleston, was a secret, and a bit risqué, James knew about it. He had old Charleston money, and the connections that came with it. He was also a devoted husband and father, and a philanthropist. I'd first met James the year before while working a case involving a high-class bordello. On a delicate matter, I'd kept information not relevant to my case, but potentially damaging to his reputation, confidential. His friendship had proven quite helpful on a couple of occasions since. When he'd given me his cell phone number, he'd told me to call him any time for any reason. I made a point not to abuse the privilege.

"Liz Talbot." I could hear the smile in his voice when he answered.

"How are you, Mr. Huger?"

He chuckled. "My dear, if you have this number, we're on a first name basis, as I am quite sure you are aware."

"How are you, James?"

"I am well, thank you for asking. To what do I owe the pleasure?"

"I'm working on the Phillip Drayton case."

"Phillip? I thought that was an accident."

"That remains to be seen," I said. "There are several loose ends that need to be tied up."

"How may I be of assistance?"

While I had him on the phone, I might as well ask. "Did you know him?"

"Well, certainly. Phillip and I were in the same class at Porter Gaud. I knew him most of his life. Hell, I was a pall bearer at his funeral this afternoon."

"Oh no, I'm so sorry for your loss. I had no idea."

"Beatrice and I were out of town. We missed the visitation, I'm afraid. Nevertheless. To be frank, we haven't been close since we left for college. But lifelong ties are special. His brother, Daniel, asked if I would serve, and of course I was honored."

"Do you know his wife?" I asked.

"Not well. She seems very nice. A little quiet. We saw them socially several times a year."

"Forgive me for asking, but were you aware of any marital problems?"

"Not at all. As I said, Phillip and I hadn't been close in many years, but that kind of thing tends to make its way onto the gossip circuit."

"If someone suggested that he perhaps abused her, what would you think about that?" I asked.

"Well, I would hate to believe such a thing about Phillip. It's not at all consistent with the man I thought I knew. There again, no one really knows what goes on between two people aside from those two individuals, do they?"

Coming from him, that was a loaded statement if ever there was one. I inhaled long and slow. "Certainly, you're right. The other thing...the main thing, actually, is what can you tell me about The Planter's Club?"

"On the record, nothing, naturally," he said.

"Understood."

"Lovely club, in a restored plantation out past Middleton. Very private. You have to be a member, or a guest of a member. One doesn't drive there, ever. You'd never get past the gate. You have to be picked up and dropped off by their private limousine service."

"How does one become a member?" I asked.

"One must be nominated by a member, then approved. Then one is invited to join. The initial dues are substantial."

"What's it like?"

"Hmm, well, the first floor is a series of lounges and dining rooms. Very tastefully appointed. They have the best chefs, top shelf liquor, an excellent wine list. Early in the evening, there's piano music in the main lounge. The music wafts through the dining rooms. Later, a lounge singer or two perform. As the evening wears on, things become a bit more spirited. There's a floor show."

"What sort of floor show?"

"Musical numbers, dancing, occasionally comedy routines."

I chose my words carefully. "We're not talking Lawrence Welk here, are we?"

He laughed. "Most assuredly not."

"Nudity?"

"A bit, but tastefully done. It's not a strip club."

"So that's the first floor. What goes on upstairs?" I asked.

"That's the owner's private residence."

"Members don't go up there...for privacy?"

"Not at all. My dear, some of Charleston's leading citizens are members of this club. There are no lap dances. I take my wife there. Many men do."

"What do you know about the owner?"

"Ahh, the charming Ms. Sanchez. She grew up rough, had a rocky start. Straightened herself out. Married money. She enjoys playing the hostess. Occasionally she performs herself."

"Performs?"

"She sings. Lovely voice. Would you and your husband like to go as my guests? See for yourself?"

"I thought you'd never ask."

"I'll make the arrangements. I'll text you a password and a phone number. You call whenever you'd like to go and ask for a car. Give them your name and the password and they'll pick you up, then bring you home when you're ready. Oh, they don't accept payment of any sort during the evening, and for goodness sake, don't try to tip anyone. It's all on my account. Don't give it a thought."

"What's the attire?"

"Creative black tie. Wear a floor-length dress, my dear. Most of the ladies do. Your husband should wear a tuxedo, but many of the gentlemen get artsy with their ties and cummerbunds, if he's so inclined."

"Thank you so much. I really appreciate your help."

"Happy to assist. I predict you'll have a lovely time. Is there anything else?"

"One last thing. Does Ms. Sanchez's husband work with her at the club?"

"Hugh? No. To be frank, I've never met anyone who cared for Hugh. Boorish man. He retired years ago. Used to be in real estate. They have a home in Honduras. Hugh loves to scuba dive. I can't recall the last time anyone mentioned him coming back to Charleston."

"Ah, well, that explains it." It seemed an odd arrangement, but as far as I knew, Hugh Conrad had no bearing on the case I was hired to work. "But it does make me wonder about something else."

"What's that, my dear?"

"Sofia has clearly turned her life around, but her people are not well-connected. She married money, but it's brand new money, made by a guy from Nashville who no one likes."

Amusement crept into his voice. "You're wondering how a club owned by someone from off is all the rage with the Old Charleston set, for whom one's history is sacred?"

"From off" was the way Charlestonians referred to folks born anywhere else, but now residing in Charleston. "Exactly."

"Tess Hathaway is Sofia's dear friend. I'm sure you must know Tess is a Rivers."

"But how did Sofia become such good friends with Mrs. Hathaway?" I asked. "How would their paths have ever crossed?"

"Charity work, I'm told. Sofia is heavily involved in Tess's foundation—Zelda's Safe House."

"And that explains that. Thank you again."

We said our goodbyes and I hopped in the shower. It had been a long day already, and I needed my wits about me for the charade awaiting us after dinner.

# THIRTEEN

Charleston is blessed with so many wonderful culinary experiences. Often on date night, Nate and I try one of the newer restaurants that have sprung up over the last few years. But Poogan's Porch is one of a few restaurants that is nearly as familiar as Mamma's dining room. Housed in a charming yellow Victorian built in 1888, it feels like home. The menu, heavy on Southern comfort food artfully prepared, never disappoints.

We were seated in the far corner of the back dining room, next to a wall of windows overlooking the courtyard. Nate took a quick look at the wine list while the waiter filled our water glasses.

"We'd like a bottle of the Sass Willamette Valley Pinot Noir," said Nate. "And if you would, go ahead and get us some of the mac and cheese, fried green tomatoes, and ribs and pickles started."

When the waiter stepped away, I said, "Thank you for not making me choose between the mac and cheese and the fried green tomatoes." Nate loved the ribs.

"You said you were famished. When your wife is famished, a smart man feeds her as expeditiously as possible, preferably with her favorite foods."

"You are a very smart man."

"You know we'll never eat all of that and our entrees."

"I very well could tonight." I studied my menu. "I think I'll have the filet mignon, but with asparagus instead of the broccolini."

Nate grinned. "You're going to eat the steak and the blue cheese and ricotta dumplings."

"I might get to some of the asparagus," I said.

The waiter returned with our wine and went through the presentation efficiently. When he'd filled our glasses and moved away, Nate raised his glass. "To the prettiest lady I know."

"You are too kind, sir."

"Nonsense. I'm simply making an observation."

We both sipped our wine.

"Yum," I said.

"Hard to beat a Willamette Valley pinot noir," said Nate. "You'll never believe who one of Phillip Drayton's pall bearers was."

I smiled sweetly, tilted my head. "James Huger?"

He drew his eyebrows together, looked around. "Where is she?"

"Colleen? I haven't seen her today, which is odd, come to think of it. She promised me we'd talk." I mentally pushed the dream away with both hands.

"How did you know about Huger?"

"I actually spoke with him this afternoon." I brought Nate up to speed on the couple at the bookshop, the episode with the limo, The Planter's Club, and our invitation to visit.

"So, these women, they communicate via bookmark," said Nate.

"Exactly."

"Why use a bookshop at all? Why not have women pop into the resale shop on King Street and leave a message they need help?"

"My guess is because it's common knowledge that proceeds from that store support victims of domestic violence. Often those victims have limited freedom. If their abusers saw them going into that store, that could make it harder to escape."

"Okay, so they leave a bookmark in a specific book that is guaranteed to always be in stock. And that tells these women what?"

"It's a request for pickup. Like manually ordering a rescue

Uber. They communicate locations that way. I'm not sure about the time. The woman on Meeting Street was picked up at two o'clock, but Jacynthe and Sofia met at the Unitarian graveyard around eleven a.m."

We both mulled that for a moment. A server delivered our appetizers. I slid the ribs over to Nate and left the mac and cheese and fried green tomatoes in the middle of the table. Then I scooped some of each onto my small plate. I savored the first bite of smoked gouda, country ham, and pasta. "Ummm." I closed my eyes.

"You sure you don't want some of the ribs?" asked Nate.

"No, thank you. I'm eating strategically."

The waiter returned to take our dinner order.

Nate said, "The lady would like the filet mignon, medium rare. Please substitute asparagus for the broccolini. And I'd like the pan roasted scallops."

"Very good," said the waiter. "I'll get those started."

"Slugger, I hate to keep flogging this poor horse, but we still haven't tied Anne Frances Drayton to Tess Hathaway and her...associates. Do you really think it's worth our time to investigate this club?"

"Honestly, I'm convinced Tess Hathaway is our client. Poppy has a very limited support system. Tess's conversation with Poppy's landlord, Aida Butler, proves she's looking out for Poppy."

"I'd agree that's likely," said Nate. "But I don't think it necessarily follows that Anne Frances was one of her clients—that Mrs. Hathaway knows anything whatsoever about what actually happened to Phillip Drayton. I think it's just like Fraser and Eli told us—she wants to help her friend, Poppy, who's in trouble. I think it's as simple as that."

"You don't think she was the woman who made the second call to 911. From the burner phone? The woman Sonny described as regal? A local matron whose extracurricular actives explain why a woman in her position would have a burner phone to begin with?"

Nate winced. "I'll grant you it's possible. But we have no evidence to support that theory."

"Agreed. Which is why we need to keep investigating these women until we have enough on them that they have no choice but to tell us everything they know. I think they're smart enough that there is no evidence. We have to make them talk."

"That's a tall order," said Nate. "My impression is, women dedicated to a cause like that, it will take a lot to get them to violate a confidence, endanger their operation."

I sighed. "I have no desire to endanger their operation. They're clearly providing a service to women who need help." I sliced off a bite of fried green tomato.

"But what if, in the process of solving our case, we uncover information that incriminates one or more of these women? It's possible one of them accidentally hit Phillip Drayton, panicked and left the scene. Are you going to be able to live with it if the unintended consequence of solving this case is that one of these women providing a necessary service to the vulnerable ends up in jail?"

I sighed, pondered that. "I pray we don't end up there. But I think we have to follow the evidence wherever it leads—to the truth, no matter how painful. We know Tess Hathaway has good attorneys and knows how to use them."

"That's a fact."

After we'd eaten half of our appetizers, I put down my fork. "I want to be able to enjoy my steak."

"What say I ask the waiter to box these up? You may feel peckish later."

I smiled. "Indeed, I might."

Nate signaled the waiter, and in short order the appetizers were cleared, and our entrees arrived. After we'd each had a bite of our own food and each other's, Nate asked, "You talk to your mamma today?"

"I called her this morning while I was on the ferry. She was on a tear about the goats."

"But the goats are gone. They're someone else's problem now."

"She's still dealing with the aftermath. Apparently in addition to the considerable issues in the backyard, and the neighbors' yards, the goats feasted on Mamma's hostas, among other things in the front yard."

Nate swirled the wine in his glass, watched it. "I hope you don't feel neglected."

"Neglected? In what way?" I squinted at him, gave him a little grin over the top of my wine glass.

"I don't go to the same extravagant lengths to get your attention that you're accustomed to observing your daddy employ in order to keep your mamma's."

"Oh please. You do an excellent job of keeping my attention, and you well know it. And if you ever bring home farm animals, I won't hesitate to send you straight over to Merry's house."

"Noted." He forked a bite of scallops, grinned at me. A wayward lock of hair had curled onto his forehead, the way it often did right before he got it cut.

I resisted the urge to brush it back, just for the pleasure of touching him. I rather liked that blond curl, and if I called attention to it, he'd make sure to have his hair cut the next day.

We ate inside our own little bubble for a few moments. Neither of us said anything, but the electric current that flowed between us was a palpable thing. My heart raced, my breathing went shallow.

After a few minutes he said, "It's a shame we have work to do yet this evening. I can think of much better ways to pass the time."

I smiled. "As can I."

The waiter refilled our wine glasses, asked if he could get us anything.

"We're good, thank you." Nate didn't take his eyes off me. "I was serious about taking some time off. Once we wrap this case up, let's get away for a while. We can go to Greenville, or anywhere you like."

"Greenville maybe," I said. "But I don't think we should spend the money on a vacation right now. There's too much we need to do at home." I wouldn't trade our beach house for anything. But upkeep on oceanfront property was expensive, especially when the home was more than fifty years old.

"Greenville then," said Nate. "It'll be a little cooler there, maybe."

I knew what he was thinking. Maybe I'd sleep better away from the coast. "Anything else interesting happen at the funeral?" I asked. "Besides James Huger being a pall bearer?"

"Mallory—the redhead from last night—was demonstrably upset."

"Was Daniel comforting her?"

"Not at all," said Nate. "She steered well clear of the family. The thin blonde woman, long straight hair, you put her picture on the board this morning along with Jacynthe's, Mallory's, and Sofia's. She was at the funeral."

"Emma Williams. The woman in the older Honda. Software developer. I'm not sure what her connection to any of this is. Could be she simply knew Phillip somehow, could be a number of ways. The only odd thing was the first—possibly second—time I saw her, she was staring at Poppy and me out the window of her car."

Nate shrugged. "Poppy have her hair up in those pigtails?"

I grinned, nodded. "Yeah. She did. It could be as simple as that. Any of Anne Frances's family turn up at the funeral?"

"If they did, they didn't sit with her in the church, or accompany her and Daniel to the gravesite. Very small crowd there. The minister, the pall bearers, Anne Frances, and Daniel."

"How did they act towards each other?" I asked. "Anne Frances and Daniel?"

"They were civil, I'd say. Certainly not leaning on each other for comfort or anything like that. About the same as at the funeral home."

I sipped my wine. "Do you think she knows that he told Sonny he suspects her of killing his brother? Surely if there's that much animosity between them she isn't oblivious to it."

"I'd say at least she knows he suspects her. She's likely thinking if he hasn't told the police that he will at some point."

"Speaking of Sonny, did you talk to him today?" I asked.

"Yeah, he came to the funeral. We watched the graveside service together from my car. Parked a safe distance away at Magnolia and used the binoculars."

"He have anything new?"

"No, and I'm afraid he's going to go with the simplest explanation if another one doesn't surface soon. The simplest thing being that Poppy hit Phillip Drayton by accident due to poor visibility and then she was afraid to admit it. I'm not saying he believes that. I think he suspects Poppy of something much more sinister, but realizes he may be unable to prove it."

"Do you get the sense he's going to arrest her soon?"

Nate rolled his lips in and out. "He isn't exploring alternative theories. Forensics has nearly exhausted what they can do with the car. He's close. I asked him for more time."

"What did he say?"

"Because he doesn't see Poppy as a danger to others, or a flight risk, and because I assured him we were keeping a close eye on her, he agreed to one week, but he was very clear that would be the end of it."

"Good thing we work well under pressure."

# FOURTEEN

We popped back into the hotel after dinner. Suzanne had been a brown-eyed brunette Monday night at the funeral home. I skipped the extra layer of makeup and the wardrobe change. Daniel Drayton had clearly been drinking when we met him. Besides, few men paid that much attention to the style details of a woman, especially given the circumstances.

Number Forty-Two Tradd Street was situated between Meeting and Church. It was only a few blocks from the hotel, so we walked.

"It's purely too hot out here for this wig," I said.

"I would imagine," said Nate. "Perhaps we'll feel like a swim when we get back to the hotel. That will cool us off."

"That sounds heavenly. I think I have a suit in the car."

"Let's hope so. I doubt you can get away with skinny dipping in that pool, as much as I would enjoy that."

The pool at the Mills House was on the second-floor deck, surrounded by guest rooms with porches overlooking the water.

As we approached the lovely Georgian brick town home with black shutters, Nate said, "I didn't have a chance to speak to Daniel at the funeral, but he may have noticed me. If he did, he noticed you weren't there."

"I had a migraine, but I'm feeling better now."

"All right then. Show time." Nate kissed me and rang the bell.

"Coming." Daniel called from inside the house.

The double doors swung open. He wore a black shirt, sleeves

rolled up, with a richly hued brocade vest, and jeans. In mid-sip of his drink, he finished, then raised his glass higher in greeting. "Great then. So glad you could come."

He stepped back, opened the doors wider. "Come in, come in. Hot as hell out there. What can I get you to drink?"

We stepped inside, and he closed the doors behind us. The house was quiet. No snippets of conversation floated into the entryway from another room. Did I just assume there would be other guests?

"Let's head back to the keeping room, shall we? S'cooler back there. Closer to the liquor too." Off the foyer to our left was the dining room. He led us through it, across wide plank pine floors. "Watch your step here."

We stepped down into the kitchen, which had exposed brick walls. The house was clearly quite old, but it had been completely modernized. To our left was a nook with several sets of glass doors leading to a courtyard.

"You have a lovely home," I said.

"S' great, isn't it? Built before the Revolutionary War. No one knows exactly when. Would you like to see it? We could take a tour."

"Thank you, maybe later," I said. "To be honest, I had a migraine earlier. The heat outside must've gotten to me."

"Horrible. And the bloody humidity. You just about have to be a fish to go outside. Here, please sit down." He pointed to a sitting area at the far end of the kitchen. "I'm having bourbon, but I haven't found that it's particularly helpful with a headache, to be perfectly honest. What can I get you?"

"I think I'll start with club soda if you have it. Just until I'm hydrated a bit." I sat on the far end of the sofa facing the fireplace. An upholstered bench in front of it served as an ottoman.

Daniel looked at Nate, lifted his chin.

"Bourbon sounds great," said Nate. "Rocks, please."

Daniel walked between the bench and the fireplace to a wet bar beyond it. Nate sat beside me on the sofa, leaving Daniel his choice of matching leather chairs on opposite sides of the sofa.

"D'you remember the night Phillip got stopped on the way back from Raleigh?" asked Daniel.

Nate didn't miss a beat. "Which time?"

Daniel roared with laughter. "Right. Of course. Senior year. Funny thing was, he hadn't been drinking at all. The rest of us were drunk as Cooter Brown. Car smelled like a brewery. Phillip thought it would be fun to act as if he were drunk, too."

"I remember it well." Nate shook his head, laughed. "I was a junior, by the way."

"And I was a sophomore. It was Phillip's senior year. Thought that cop would blow a gasket when Phillip passed the breathalyzer. D'you remember what he said?"

"Phillip, or the cop?" Nate laughed.

Daniel howled, handed us our drinks. "Phillip said, I can try again if you'd like."

We all laughed, sipped our drinks. Daniel dropped into the chair closest to the wet bar. "Suzy, you let me know when you're ready for something stronger. Vodka, I believe, is your drink."

I offered him my sunniest smile. "I cannot believe you remember that."

"Hey, I may have killed a few brain cells since college, but I remember the important things, like what beautiful women like to drink." He toasted the sentiment.

Nate raised his glass. "Hear, hear."

"Daniel," I said, "I'm terribly sorry to have missed the service. I declare those migraines lay me low. I understand it was quite touching. Please forgive me."

"Nothing to forgive, Suzy," he said. "Phillip wouldn't have wanted you to be out in that awful heat not feeling well. He was a gentleman, my brother, above all else."

Was he really? I honestly wanted to believe that, not the least because we could erase several possibilities from our case board if Phillip were not in fact a man who abused his wife.

"Hear, hear." Nate raised his glass. He and Daniel drank.

"I surely remember him that way," I said. "His poor wife. She must be positively devastated. I can't even imagine." I shook my head.

Daniel made a noise. It was something akin to "Hannnff." Clearly, he intended it as a scoff.

I paused, my glass partway to my lips, looked at him.

His face was a mask of rage. "You don't know my sister-in-law, do you?"

"Why, no," I said. "We only met her Monday night."

"No." Nate shook his head.

"Ha," said Daniel. "You're better off for it. She's a cold bitch, that one. Phillip worshipped her. It was obvious from the beginning she married him for his money."

"Oh no," I said. "You don't mean it."

"Hell, I don't," said Daniel. "I told the police. They're looking into it. I'd bet my last nickel she killed him."

"It's always the wife," said Nate.

Daniel nodded, pointed to Nate with the hand holding the highball glass as his proof. "Exactly right."

"Would she have run over him with her car?" I asked. "Is she that cold-blooded?"

"Oh, she's cold-blooded all right," said Daniel. "But calculating as well. She wouldn't get her hands dirty, oh no. Not that one. She'd have used her wiles. Gotten someone to do it for her."

"Do you think she was having an affair?" asked Nate.

"I know she was," said Daniel. "Phillip told me."

I wondered what the statistics were on that. If she were abused, how likely was it that she had the personal freedom to conduct an extramarital affair? Wouldn't a woman bold enough to cheat leave a man who hurt her? Were those two things mutually exclusive or did the affair trigger the abuse? "That's horrible," I said. "Did you tell the police who she was having an affair with?"

"Don't know who it was." Daniel drained his glass. "Phillip didn't know. But he said he knew for certain she was seeing someone." He stood, looked at Nate. "Another?"

Nate nodded, handed Daniel his glass.

"Did he tell you how he knew that?" I asked. "That would probably help the police, any detail, wouldn't you think?"

Daniel had his back to us, filled the glasses. "It was odd. He wouldn't say how he knew. I had the impression something was really bothering him. Aside from his wife being unfaithful, I mean. Something about the whole thing had him shook up."

"Well, I certainly hope the police catch her and whoever her accomplice is," I said.

Daniel handed Nate his glass, then returned to the leather chair.

"How did he meet her, anyway?" asked Nate. "You can tell to hear her talk she's not from here. I know he didn't date her in school."

"Naples. Remember the house in Naples?" asked Daniel.

Nate laughed. "I do."

"Phillip went down to make arrangements to have it redecorated. Some tart he'd been dating told him it needed updating. He dumped the tart but decided maybe she was right. I thought it was perfect just the way it was."

"I'd have to agree with you," said Nate.

Daniel gave him an odd look. "Did you ever go there? I don't recall that. I know Phillip and I talked a lot about spending holidays there."

"Once." Nate nodded. "We snuck down just him and me. We were supposed to be studying for finals."

"Bastards, both of you, to go without me." Daniel still wore a slightly confused face. He shook his head as if to clear it.

"So, Phillip met Anne Frances there?" I asked. "In Naples?"

"She was the bloody interior decorator," said Daniel. "He barely dated her ten minutes. Insisted she was the love of his life. His soul mate, if you can imagine that."

We both waited for him to go on.

"Beautiful woman, I'll give her that." Daniel looked at his glass. "Seemed nice enough at first. Made a good show of being affectionate. But there was always something off."

"What do you mean?" I asked.

"Most beautiful women want a big wedding. Phillip—he loved throwing a party better than anything. Well, until he met her. I guess he loved her more. But he wanted to have a huge wedding, invite the whole town. She wouldn't have any of it. In the end, he said it wouldn't be fair to her because we knew a lot of people and she'd have a terribly small guest list. Everyone would sit on the groom's side of the church. Poor form to embarrass the bride. So, they got married quietly in Naples. I was a witness, and there was a girlfriend of hers. What was her name? Sasha something. It was a sad little affair."

"But Phillip was happy, right?" asked Nate.

"I've never seen him so happy in my entire life." Daniel studied his glass, looked perplexed. "Phillip wasn't stupid. Hard to believe he was taken in by her."

"Did you try to talk him out of marrying her?" I asked.

Daniel screwed up his face. "You knew Phillip. He was pig-headed as they come. But no, I'm sorry to say. I really didn't. I figured he was a big boy. Who was I, after all, to give him advice? He could make his own decisions. I figured maybe I had it wrong. Maybe it would work out. If not, it would cost him a great deal of money before it was over. I did tell him to get a prenup. Wouldn't hear of it. Said it would be an insult to her—to their love. I should've tried to talk him out of it. I never dreamed it would cost him his life. It's my fault he's dead."

"Come on now," said Nate. "It's not your fault. That's crazy talk."

"Most beautiful women like to have their pictures taken," said Daniel. "Happy to strike a pose for the camera. Not this one. You'd think she was from one of those cultures where they believe the camera steals your soul or some rot. Pathologically averse to having her picture taken."

I mulled that. She had avoided being in the photos on the blog, for sure. But there were photos of her and Phillip online—charity events and the like—though they were scarce compared to those of Phillip by himself.

"I felt really bad for poor Mallory today," said Nate. "Is she coming by tonight?"

"Mallory?" Daniel's face changed subtly, softened. He looked at his glass. "No, I don't think so." He took a long drink.

"She went to high school with y'all, right?" I asked.

"S' right," said Daniel. "We knew her from the time she was in kindergarten. I was in first grade, Phillip in third. I think she loved my brother from that point on."

"She's a beautiful girl," said Nate.

"Isn't she?" said Daniel. "I can't imagine why Phillip never thought so. Well, that's not fair. He was a red-blooded man, after all. He had to see she was beautiful, didn't he?"

"Undoubtedly, he did," said Nate.

"Said he thought of her as a sister," said Daniel. "But I'm not so sure."

"What do you mean?" I asked.

"If you're not getting love at home..." Daniel gave me a knowing look over the rim of his glass. "Sometimes you take it where you can find it. Couldn't blame him."

"You think Phillip and Mallory..." I sipped my club soda.

"Could be," said Daniel. "Poor Mallory. She wanted so badly to be Mrs. Phillip Drayton. I don't think she ever got over it. Still single." He drained his glass again, then rose to refill it. He looked at Nate.

"I'm good."

"Suzy, you ready for a vodka tonic?" asked Daniel.

"Why not?"

"Exactly." Daniel slurred the word. "Why the hell not?"

He returned in a moment and handed me a glass.

"Thank you." I set the club soda down and pretended a sip of the vodka. "Were any of your sister-in-law's family in town for the service?"

Daniel made his signature noise again. "They couldn't be bothered. Of course, we've never met any of those people."

"Really?" I asked. "She and Phillip were married for more than five years. They never came to Charleston?"

"Not once. Oh, she went to Chicago once or twice a year to see them. Said they didn't fly, her parents. You'd think the brother would at least get on a plane. I don't know who's in worse shape, me—I have no family left at all—or the ice queen. She has family, but they clearly want nothing to do with her. Maybe they're just as cold as she is."

"It's all so very sad," I said.

"Tommy, you remember Chandler Manigault, don't you? He was the same year as you at Duke."

"Of course," said Nate.

"Old family friend," said Daniel. "He and Vivian, his wife—d'you know her?" Daniel pivoted his head to me.

"Yes, I think so." I looked at Nate, as if he might confirm such a thing.

"Vivian, yes. Lovely girl," said Nate.

An odd look crossed Daniel's face. "They were out of town and missed the reception at Stuhr's. Spoke to him briefly this morning. They're coming by. Should've already been here, come to think of it." The crease in his forehead deepened.

Was Vivian not a lovely girl at all? Was a memory surfacing that was at odds with something about our appearance or our story?

I set down the vodka tonic and rubbed my temples.

"Darling, are you all right?" asked Nate.

"I'm afraid the vodka wasn't the best idea," I said.

"The headache is back?" asked Nate.

"I'm afraid so."

Nate stood, set down his glass. "Daniel, I'm afraid we'll need to continue this another time."

"Right." Daniel climbed unsteadily out of his chair. "Terribly sorry. Probably my fault. Shouldn't've given her the drink."

"Not at all," I said. "I should've known better. Thank you for your hospitality. I would like to come back when we can see the house."

"Of course," said Daniel. "Anytime. You have my number, right?"

"You know, I don't think I do," said Nate.

"I've had the same cell number since I was twelve." Daniel screwed up his face.

"Me too, but I'm afraid I've had quite a few new cell phones since college," said Nate. "My number may be the same, but I've lost all my contacts at least twice—before everything was in the cloud."

"I know what you mean," said Daniel. "Happened to me too. Here." He grabbed his phone from a table in the foyer. "Give me your number and I'll text you mine."

Nate recited his number and they completed the exchange.

Daniel opened the door to see us out. "Do call me now. We'll see the house and maybe go to dinner. Maybe Chandler and Vivian can come as well. Have you been to FIG?"

"Love it," I said. "Let's plan on it."

"Good night, love." Daniel hugged me bye. "Tommy." He clasped Nate's hand then pulled him into a hug.

Nate clapped him on the back and we waved as we walked away.

When we turned the corner at Meeting Street, Nate said, "Who do you suppose are the real people he thinks we are?"

"I have no idea. I mean, clearly he remembers a couple that he and Phillip ran around with in college, and whoever it was, they didn't show up for the funeral."

"I feel bad for the guy," said Nate.

"Yeah, me too," I said. "But I wonder..."

"What?"

"I think Daniel is in love with Mallory."

# FIFTEEN

We took the first ferry back to Stella Maris the next morning. Rhett greeted us at the bottom of the front porch steps at 7:00 a.m. Nate went on inside while I petted and babied Rhett for a few minutes, then gave him a treat. "Let me change and we'll go for our run, all right boy?"

He barked his consent.

I hurried up the steps and through the front door, climbed the stairs, and dashed down the hall to our bedroom. From the bathroom came the sound of Nate enthusiastically singing "Cheeseburger in Paradise." When I stuck my head in, he was tying his shoes. I stepped into our walk-in closet to get my running clothes. Rhett was waiting for us downstairs.

As much as I wished things were different and Nate and I could start a family of our own, I knew that would mean a career change for me. There was no way I could keep the schedule I did with children. It was bad enough I didn't give Rhett nearly the attention I would've liked.

He never went without, mind you. For times when we were gone overnight, or got tied up, the automatic feeder and filtered water reservoir in the mudroom saw that he had what he needed. And the doggie doors on the walk-thru into the garage and at the door leading into the mudroom at the top of the steps made sure that he could come and go as he pleased. If we were out of town more than one night, Blake or Merry came by. But there was no substitute for interaction with me and Nate, and I was hyper-aware of that.

Children would be a whole nother thing. My mind turned again to the recurring nightmare, the two children Nate and I carried with us as we ran from the storm. The boy was about five, the girl maybe three. She was named Emma Rae—for my grandmother. I wasn't able to have children. Merry and I both had aggressive cases of endometriosis leading to hysterectomies a few years back. But Nate and I could surely adopt. Colleen had told me not to take the dream literally. But was I meant to have children? Even if they might die with us in a horrific storm?

A shimmery, gold-flecked cloud appeared with me in the closet. After a moment, Colleen appeared. "You cannot live your life in fear."

"I don't know how not to be afraid of what you've shown me—all that you've told me." I shook my head. "Giant storms, earthquakes, tsunamis—good grief, Colleen. Of course I'm afraid."

"You know I'm still learning this job, right?"

"Seems to me like you're getting pretty good at it," I said. "But I wish you'd be a bit more forthcoming at times. For example, who—"

"Later." She sent tiny golden sparks flying from her fingertips to shush me.

It worked. I sat on the tufted stool in the closet.

Colleen said, "You know my primary job is protecting the people on this island—keeping the population to a level that can be safely evacuated in case of emergency."

I nodded.

She lowered her eyes. "Well, maybe I went overboard with that dream. With some of the things I've told you."

"What do you mean?"

"I planted that image of one of several alternate scenarios in your subconscious to make sure I had your attention—to make sure you understood on a personal level why we have to control development on Stella Maris. The consequences of letting the population rise are catastrophic. But I never meant for that to be a recurring nightmare. Once it was in your mind, well...I can't erase it from your subconscious. And now, normal summer tropical activity is about to give you a nervous breakdown."

"But I thought we needed to prepare for a major storm."

"We do. We need to stay prepared. Because there will always be storms and natural disasters. The things we can control—like population, supplies, storm shutters, building codes—those things we need to focus on, and for that, I need your help along with the rest of the town council. I have to keep the town council one that cares more about people than money."

"I understand all that, but—"

"You have to let go of what you can't control," said Colleen. "No one—not one living soul on this planet is guaranteed that they'll spend tomorrow here. Sure, some will pass through a storm from this world to the next. Some will travel via car accident, or illness. Focus on shining the light wherever you can and let God worry about the big picture. You cannot live in fear. Fear is the first step down a dark path. You are meant to walk in the light."

"The children..."

"That's your decision. Yours and Nate's. It always has been, and always will be. There's no right or wrong answer."

"But if we adopt children, and then they suffer because of it."

Colleen gave me a sad smile. "This world is a beautiful, magical place. But it's also imperfect. There will always be suffering. You can't choose not to love because bad things happen. You can't cover the people you love in bubble wrap and keep them safe. Adopt children if you want children. Or give that love somewhere else. But stop living in fear. There is no fear in love. Love drives out fear."

A silvery aura appeared around her and she faded away.

I inhaled slowly, exhaled. For a few moments, I sat there, just breathing. Finally, I pulled on my running clothes and headed downstairs.

We ran our five miles and played Frisbee with Rhett on the beach. I felt lighter than I had in a long while. Then we went inside and got cleaned up. I fixed us each a glass of Cheerwine and met Nate in my office. We both settled into the sofa and sipped as we reviewed the possible narratives on the case board.

1. Poppy: accidentally hit Phillip Drayton
2. Poppy: intentionally hit Philip Drayton
   a. Mrs. Drayton's accomplice
   b. Vigilante: protecting Mrs. Drayton
   c. Unknown motives
3. Unknown Subject: accidentally hit Phillip Drayton and fled
4. Unknown Subject: intentionally hit Phillip Drayton and fled
   a. Mrs. Drayton's accomplice
   b. Vigilante: protecting Mrs. Drayton
   c. Unknown motives

"I think we have a few additional possibilities." I walked to the case board and picked up a marker.

"Yep." Nate rubbed his forehead. "I wish we could eliminate some."

"Honestly, I think we can eliminate Poppy altogether."

"I just don't think we're there yet."

"We need to check in with her," I said. "I know she's nervous. Maybe I'll do that afterwhile."

"All right. So, Mallory Lucas was in love with Phillip Drayton. I say that makes her a suspect."

I sighed. "Agreed." I added Mallory Lucas to the list of possible suspects, with a motive of jealousy. "We need to find out where she was on the night Phillip was killed. And what she drives."

Nate sat on the sofa, picked up his laptop. A few minutes later her said, "An Audi S5 Cabriolet convertible. Red."

"Hard to confuse that with a white SUV. But she could've rented one."

"Agreed. And I agree with you. Daniel Drayton is in love with Mallory, which gives him a motive to kill his brother, especially given he suspected they were having an affair."

"Yep," I said. "He thought his brother was treating her badly, should have married her instead of Anne Frances. So, he's mad at him—it's clear he loved his brother—but he thinks Mallory deserves to be treated better." I added Daniel Drayton to the board, also with a motive of jealousy.

Nate said, "If you're going in to check on Poppy, why don't I run down Mallory's alibi?

"How are you going to play that?" I asked.

"Trickery. I texted our buddy Daniel a link to an article on a boutique bourbon I think he might like. Embedded in that link is that handy little piece of code that allows us to do fun things with his cell phone."

A smile crept up my face. "Perfect." We could now turn Daniel's phone into a listening device and access anything stored on it, including his contacts.

"I'm going to call Mallory," said Nate, "identify myself as an associate of Detective Ravenel's. I will absolutely *not* state that I'm his partner or a member of the Charleston Police Department. If she draws that conclusion, well..." He shrugged. "Anyway, I'll ask her to meet me, someplace public. I'm going to tell her that Anne Frances used her as an alibi."

"Nice. You're going to need a disguise. She saw you at the funeral home. And you can't discount that we might have the occasion to see Daniel again, and she'll be there."

"I'm aware. You're not the only one who can go incognito, you know."

I made a face. "Are you putting that black gel stuff in your hair?"

"It'll wash right out."

"It better. We've got Wednesday night dinner at Mamma and Daddy's tonight."

Nate rubbed his face with his hands, didn't say a word.

"Speaking of Sonny," I said, "he may have checked Daniel's alibi. Maybe check with him on that?"

"Will do."

I headed back into Charleston on the 11:00 a.m. ferry to track down Poppy. Nate would take the noon trip across the water. We avoided being seen together in costume unless we were both disguised. We lived in a small town—people could get the wrong idea.

Once on the lower part of the peninsula, where most of Poppy's route was, I did a grid search for her. I found her truck parked under the shade of a live oak tree near Washington Square, on Chalmers Street, a picturesque cobblestone lane that ran between State and Meeting.

She was looking down and jumped when I knocked on the window. She raised and lowered her shoulders in a sigh and rolled down the window. "Liz. You scared me. Did you lose my phone number?"

"No, I'm so sorry, Poppy, but I needed to show you something. You hanging in there?"

"I'm okay." She smiled. "I'm the one who's sorry. You're trying to help me, and I snapped at you. I was just having my lunch and reading a little bit. What did you need to show me?"

I pulled out my phone, opened my camera roll, and scrolled to the photos of Jacynthe, Sofia, Emma, and Mallory. "I know you know Mrs. Hathaway. But do you know any of these ladies? None of them are on your route."

She laid down her sandwich on a paper towel and took my phone. She showed me Jacynthe's photo. "I don't know her, but I've seen her before. I'm not sure where. Wait, she's a tour guide. She leads the ghost tours at Buxton Books sometimes. A few of the others, I think. She's a sweet lady."

"Okay. If you think of anywhere else you might've seen her, let me know."

She swiped to the next photo. Sofia. "Her I don't think I've ever seen before."

"What about the next one?"

Poppy swiped again, to Emma's photo. Poppy bit her bottom lip. "I've seen her several times recently, but we've never spoken."

"Where did you see her?"

"On Monday, when you and I were talking and she drove by with the windows down."

"Right."

"She did that again yesterday. Rode by slow and looked at me like that. On Murray. It's weird."

Yes, it was. Very weird. "Is that it?" I asked.

"And at the funeral home. She was there. Also, the funeral."

"Anywhere else?"

She winced. "I don't think so."

"Swipe once more."

Poppy stared at Mallory Lucas. "Oh yeah. Her, I've definitely seen."

"At the funeral home and the funeral?"

"There too, but I think she stalked Mr. Drayton."

"Stalked him?"

"I like to come to White Point Garden in late afternoons, if the weather's nice and it's not too crowded. I ride my bike down, put out a quilt, watch the boats, watch the sunset. It's lovely. This woman, she liked to watch Mr. Drayton. Several times, when I was riding my bike to the park or home, I noticed her parked along the Lower Battery, watching for him to come home."

"How did you know that's what she was doing?" I asked.

"It's like she wanted him to see her. She'd wait 'til he pulled in the driveway. Watch him drive inside the garage, then leave."

"Did you ever see her waiting for him to leave? Follow him?"

"No. She just watched him come home. Well, that's all I saw, anyway. The Draytons had enough problems. They didn't need that...that...whatever she was up to."

"What kind of car was she in?"

"A red convertible."

"Did you tell Detective Ravenel about this?" I asked.

"Yes, but he didn't seem very interested. I think he's made up his mind."

I was very much afraid she was right. "I'm sorry to keep you from your lunch. Please, eat."

She took a bite of her sandwich.

"What kind is it?"

She swallowed, sipped her water. "Peanut butter."

"I love PB and Js."

"I was out of the J. I need to get to the store. Just peanut butter today."

"Dinner will taste good tonight," I said.

She chuckled. "I live alone. It's hot. I'm not cooking tonight. Dinner will be a bowl of cereal."

I thought about the platters and bowls filled with home cooked food that would be waiting on me at Mamma's house that evening. Then I watched her take another bite of that peanut butter sandwich and wash it down with water that was very likely tepid at best.

"Poppy, do you like country fried steak with gravy?" I asked.

"Oh man, I love that stuff. I haven't had it since..." She looked down. "That was my mother's specialty."

I swallowed hard. "Will you do something for me?"

"Sure, what do you need?"

"You haven't met my husband, Nate—he's my partner, too. I

want you to tell him about Mallory Lucas. Do you think you could
come to our house this evening and do that, maybe help us
brainstorm a few things? It would really be a big help." Of course, I
didn't need her to tell Nate this story—I could tell him just fine. But
I didn't know Poppy that well. She'd likely consider a dinner
invitation to my parents' house odd.

"I guess..."

"Listen, it will be kind of a pain because we live on Stella
Maris. You'll have to take the ferry—" I stopped. Poppy didn't have
a car. "Never mind. What time will you get home from work today?"

"Five, if I'm lucky."

"I'll pick you up then," I said. "And by no means should you
eat cereal. In fact, don't eat anything else today. I'd stop eating now
if I were you."

She knit her brow. "Okay."

# SIXTEEN

Despite the advice I'd given Poppy about not eating before dinner, I was sorely tempted to head over to Closed for Business on King Street. I craved a spicy chicken sandwich and some gravy fries. Sometimes tricky cases made me crave food that was not necessarily healthy, but surely tasty. I curbed my urges, saved my calories for Mamma's gravy, and popped into Verde a couple blocks farther down King for a quick salad.

I put my earbuds in and called Mamma as I munched on my Southern Harvest salad.

"Hello?" I could hear the stress in her voice. Besides, she had caller ID just like most everyone else. She knew exactly who was calling before she picked up the phone. The fact that she pretended she didn't know it was me was a tell.

"Hey, Mamma. Is everything all right?"

"Peachy keen," she said in a voice that let me know everything was far from all right. "I hope you aren't calling to tell me you and Nate can't make it for dinner. I've thawed five pounds of cubed steak."

"No, we'll be there."

She drew a ragged breath. "Well, good then. What can I do for you?"

"I was wondering if it would be all right if I brought a guest?" I bit my lip. This was an inexcusable breach of etiquette—asking Poppy before checking with Mamma. I don't know what had come over me.

"Liz darlin', I'm sure you know this is not a good time for company in our house." I could feel her struggle. It was against Mamma's nature to be inhospitable. "Who is it?"

I sighed. "A client. I wouldn't ask, but the poor girl has no family whatsoever. I just watched her eat a peanut butter sandwich for lunch in her mail truck, and she's planning on having cold cereal for dinner. I feel bad for her."

"You are exactly like your father, you know that." It was her turn to sigh.

"What? Where did that come from?"

"Do you know who is riding some sort of tractor around my backyard right this very minute?"

"Oh no."

"Yes, exactly. It's Ray Kennedy. Your daddy's cousin Ponder is spreading mulch."

"Mulch. That sounds like progress," I said.

"Well, you'll see it for yourself this evening. You might as well bring your friend. I can't abide the thought of someone having cold cereal for dinner. Your sister does that. She thinks I don't know it. Drives me batty. I have a cake in the oven. I'll see you at six o'clock."

"Thank you, Mamma. I appreciate it." As we said our goodbyes I couldn't help thinking that having company might be the only thing that saved us all that evening. There was a limit to how much any of us would act out in front of guests.

While I had my phone out, I pulled up the tracking app to see if Anne Frances had decided to leave the house. I really wasn't expecting she would—she'd just buried her husband the day before. No matter what their relationship had been, she was probably emotionally exhausted, and from all indications she didn't go out much under normal circumstances.

I stared at the display for a moment. There was a blue blinking dot where I was, and a red blinking dot where Anne Frances

Drayton's car was. My dot was stationary. Hers was not. She was on Ashley Avenue, between Tradd and Broad. Was she headed back to the bookstore?

She turned left on Broad. Where was she going?

I tapped Nate's photo in my favorites list, stuck my phone in the outside pocket of my cross-body bag, and cleared my place. Then I was out the door.

Nate wasn't answering.

I opened the Find My Friends app. Nate was at Market Pavilion Hotel. Was that where he'd met Mallory?

I texted him: *AFD on the move.*

Then I dashed down King Street to my car, climbed in, and put my iPhone on the magnetic disc that held it in place so I could see the screen. The red blinking dot was on Highway 17, halfway over the Ashley River. I double tapped the dot. This would route directions from me to my target. I started the car and pulled into traffic.

Following the directions the British woman with impeccable enunciation gave me, I took King Street to Broad. At the stoplight, I was behind a UPS truck and a Prius. I willed the light to change. Anne Frances was on Folly Road. I watched the dot blinking along the line. Finally, the UPS truck turned right and the Prius crossed Broad. I turned right and urged the UPS driver to go faster. After an eternity, he turned right on Logan.

I zipped ahead as fast as traffic would allow, grateful when the outbound lane of Broad Street split into two lanes, just before Rutledge. I passed the Malibu in front of me and sped up, flirted with a speeding ticket. It wouldn't be my first.

I followed Broad until it turned into Lockwood, then turned left on 17 South and crossed the Ashley River. Anne Frances was on Maybank Highway, headed towards Johns Island. I wouldn't be able to catch her without driving recklessly. But wherever she was headed, I wouldn't be far behind her.

I followed the voice directions, kept my eyes on the road, and glanced occasionally at the screen. By the time I crossed the Stono River, Anne Frances was on Bohicket Road. Was she going to Kiawah or Seabrook?

Forty-five minutes after I left the peninsula, I followed Anne Frances onto Kiawah Island Parkway, just as her blinking dot came to a stop at The Sanctuary at Kiawah Island. This could be anything from a lunch date with a girlfriend, to an afternoon at the spa, to a romantic rendezvous. Daniel had said Phillip suspected—no, he was certain—Anne Frances was having an affair. Was her lover her accomplice?

I found her Lexus in the parking lot. If only I had a tracker in her purse. I took my phone off the magnet.

I'd missed a text from Nate: *I see you. Done here. Want me to join you?*

I called him. "I'm still thinking about how to find her. She could be anywhere. No telling how long she plans to stay. Could be the afternoon or the week. What'd you find out from Mallory?"

"She has no alibi. She stayed in that night. It was so nasty out she curled up in front of the TV."

"Hmm, I wonder how long her condo building saves security footage."

"Ahead of you there. They still have it saved digitally. They're happy to share it as soon as law enforcement shows up with a subpoena."

"I wonder how secure that server is," I said.

"My plan is to impress you with my investigative and technical prowess by scaling that particular wall," said Nate. "That's next on my agenda. Mallory was unsettled enough by my interview that she called Daniel as soon as she was in her car."

"How do you know that?" I asked.

"Well, I watched her walk back to her car. As soon as she started the engine, she was issuing voice commands. I could see her lips moving. She could've been singing, I guess. But she wasn't. Remember the code I installed on Daniel's phone?"

"I do."

"I activated the feature that turns his phone into a listening device. I couldn't hear her end of the conversation, of course, but from his end, I could tell she was upset and he was comforting her. Clearly, she repeated the story I told her about Anne Frances using her as an alibi. He's beyond pissed about that—more convinced than ever that she killed his brother. Has a call in to Sonny. I need to give him a heads up. And Daniel plans to further comfort Mallory over dinner this evening at seven."

"Interesting. We should eavesdrop on that as well. Can you record it? We'll be at Mamma and Daddy's house."

"Sure thing. I'll set it up before we leave."

I told him what Poppy had said about Mallory stalking Phillip.

"Seems she had an obsession with him at the very least," said Nate.

"What did Sonny say about Daniel?"

"He likewise has no alibi."

"Damnation. I just wish we could eliminate one suspect. Just one."

"I feel your frustration. Want me to head your way? We can beat the bushes over there together. I can hack into the security footage later."

"I have a better idea." I smiled at him through the phone.

I heard him smile back. "Now why didn't I think of that?"

"It's that black mess in your hair."

"You'll watch to see if she heads home?"

"Yeah. I'll monitor the app in case she leaves. Poppy's already delivered her mail for today. Unless the lawn service or some such shows up, you should have the place to yourself."

"Roger that."

"But be out by four. You need to be on the four thirty ferry home to get cleaned up for dinner."

"I'll set an alarm," said Nate.

"Oh, and Poppy's coming with us."

"With us where?"

"To Mamma and Daddy's for dinner."

"Are you sure that's a good idea?"

"Of course not," I said. "But maybe she'll be a calming influence."

He blew out a long breath. "See you at the house."

Enough time had passed that Anne Frances had checked in if she planned to. I called the hotel and asked for her room.

"One moment please," said the operator.

The phone rang twice.

"Hello." A man's voice.

Hell's bells. "Yes, good afternoon, sir. I'm calling to confirm your room service order."

He chuckled. "Damn, you folks are good. I haven't placed one yet. But since I've got you on the line, send us up a bottle of your best champagne and some strawberries."

"Right away sir. Two flutes?"

"That'll be plenty." He hung up the phone.

Holy shit.

Phillip Drayton had been right. There was no way his widow had met someone and gotten close enough to share afternoon champagne and strawberries with them in the just over twenty-four hours since she'd buried her husband. She had been having an affair. I needed to know with whom.

I'd never been inside The Sanctuary at Kiawah before—had no idea what the layout was like. But Google knew. I pulled up a satellite view. Damnation. The hotel was a huge complex consisting of three main wings, with various restaurants and amenities tacked on.

When the champagne and strawberries didn't arrive, Anne

Frances or her friend would call to inquire about it. He or she would be disgruntled, so the hotel would rush to get the order filled. How long did I have to figure out which kitchen room service was sent up from? I pulled up the website.

The Ocean Room was the fine dining option on-site, and it wasn't open in the afternoon. I'd start with Jasmine Porch, the full-service restaurant onsite. I hopped out of the car and jogged partway down the path in the direction of the hotel lobby, then slowed. If I knew what room they were in, what would that buy me?

What I needed was the name of whoever she was with and a photo. A photo of them together would be even better. There was no way to take photos, even with the Nikon and a long lens, inside any of the rooms on this property during the middle of the afternoon without attracting the attention of management.

I decided to pass some time sitting in the impeccably decorated lobby. It was two o'clock. If Anne Frances and her paramour were only here for a couple of hours, I could wait them out. Otherwise, I'd need a plan B. I opened the app just to verify her car was still parked outside—it was.

If I were her, I'd make my secret lover leave by one of several paths around the property that didn't go through the lobby. I'd've made him park half a mile away and walk down the beach. Anne Frances struck me as a smart lady. The question was, how smart was her side guy?

From my spot in a comfortable arm chair flanking a sofa, I could alternate looking right out the front entrance, and left across a wide lawn flanked by walkways. For two hours, I watched people come and go—couples, families, golfers—a random sample of folks relaxing and enjoying the gorgeous surroundings.

At almost straight up four o'clock, just as I was about to formulate a quick plan B, Anne Frances Drayton walked out the front door of the hotel by herself. Dammit. I was hoping she'd be careless. I glanced out the window across the lawn. No sign of a man walking down a path by himself.

I texted Nate: *She's leaving.*

When I looked up from my phone, a mid-to-late thirties guy ambled into the lobby in the general direction of the front door. Maybe just shy of six feet tall, he had sun-streaked medium brown hair, a beard that was scruffy in the way some women found attractive, a mustache, and muscles and a tan that were both well-tended. He wore khaki shorts and a long-sleeve button-down with the sleeves rolled up. If he wasn't someone's boy toy, he was auditioning for the part.

He watched something in the general direction of Anne Frances Drayton's retreating derrière. When he walked out the front door, I rose and followed. He headed down the path to the left of the trees in front of the hotel, towards the lot opposite the one I'd parked in, then sauntered across the parking lot to a blue Ford Fusion that might not've been the first one ever made, but it sure looked like it. I held my phone down as I passed behind it and snapped a photo of the plate. He backed out of the space and drove past me on his way out.

I pretended to be texting with my thumbs, held the phone just below chest height, and got a photo of him in profile. It was the best I could do without attracting his attention. I couldn't care less about that if he hadn't spent the afternoon with Anne Frances Drayton. But I knew in my gut he had done exactly that.

# SEVENTEEN

Poppy and I swung by the house, parked my car, and hopped in with Nate.

"Poppy, this is my husband and partner, Nate. Nate, this is Poppy." I checked his hair, making sure there wasn't a trace of the black gel.

Nate raised an eyebrow at me, then did a double take on Poppy. She looked quite a bit different this evening. Her rich brown hair was loose and hung below her shoulders, and her bangs were swept to the side. She wore a lovely yellow sundress and sandals. She'd added perhaps a touch of mascara and lip gloss. She was lovely.

They both said their nice-to-meet yous and whatnot. There wasn't much time for us to talk before we rolled into Mamma and Daddy's driveway.

I inhaled deeply, then slowly exhaled and turned to Poppy, who was in the backseat. "My family may be a little...animated...this evening. There's a pool going in the backyard, and it's created a lot of stress. But, they're nice people, really, and I promise the food will be good."

"They're harmless," said Nate.

"Okay." Her face creased, and she smiled a little smile. "But I thought you wanted to talk about the redhead and Mr. Drayton."

"We'll get to that later," I said. "But we all have to eat, right?"

"Sounds great." She reached for her door handle, looked at me for a sign I was getting out of the car.

"Okay then," I said.

We opened the doors and climbed out of the Explorer.

"What a beautiful home," said Poppy. "Did you grow up here?"

"Yes, I did." I grabbed Nate's hand, and we walked up the steps.

He opened the door and held it for both of us.

"Mamma," I called out as we walked down the entry hall.

"In the kitchen."

Oh, thank you, Sweet Lord. Maybe things would be back to normal. She sounded calm.

A loud squeal came from the den.

Nate and I looked at each other, then dashed down the hall and into the den. I didn't want to look.

"Hey, Tootie. Nate." Daddy stood. "Who's this you have with you?"

I looked past Daddy to Kinky, who was back in her bed. Chumley sat in his customary place by Daddy's chair, oddly disinterested. I stared at the pig.

"Liz?" said Daddy.

I looked up at him. I might've had a crazed expression on my face.

Poppy held out her hand. "Hey, I'm Poppy Oliver."

"Frank Talbot. Nice to meet you. What can I get you to drink?"

"Oh, I'm good right now, thank you," said Poppy. "What a cute pig. What happened to her leg?"

"She is, isn't she?" Daddy said. "Pretty little pig. She took a fall. But she'll be fine, soon as the cast comes off."

"Daddy?" I gave him a look that said, *What the hell?*

"Oh." Daddy winced, gestured with the hand that wasn't holding a high ball glass. "Kinky didn't take to the man's other pig after all. He brought her back this afternoon. Nate, pour yourself some bourbon."

"I think I will." Nate moved to the wet bar.

"How's Mamma?" I asked.

"Your Mamma's in the kitchen," Daddy said, like maybe I was Not Quite Right.

"I know *where* she is." I spun on my heels and walked across the hall. "Mamma?"

She stood in front of the stove, stirring gravy, like she'd done thousands of times before. "Liz darlin', ask your daddy to open some wine for dinner. Maybe a blend tonight. Do you know what your guest likes to drink?"

"Mamma, Kinky—"

She smiled brightly. Was she medicated? "Sweetheart, I know that infernal pig is back. I was here when the gentlemen who came on Sunday returned her. They brought the goats back, too. Did you know that?"

"Why on earth would they do such a thing?" The vague alarm that had been building in my stomach rose in my throat.

"It seems the woman in Folly Beach didn't have any takers for goat yoga, whatever on God's green earth that's all about. But right now, we have a guest for dinner. And this family is going to hold it together until after she leaves. Now. Please, ask your daddy to open a nice red blend." She nodded at me, round-eyed.

"Hey everybody," Merry called.

I stepped into the hallway, met her eyes. Joe and Blake were right behind her calling out hellos.

Merry stopped short. "What's wrong?"

Joe and Blake ran into her, then both apologized. They all looked at me expectantly.

"Pig," I said softly. "Goats."

"What?" Merry squinched up her face

Kinky squealed again.

"Oh no," said Blake. He stood there a split second, then slid behind Merry and Joe and went into the den. "Dad, what in the—"

I crossed the hall in two steps. "Blake," I said, "this is my friend Poppy Oliver. Poppy, this is my brother Blake. Merry, you and Joe come meet Poppy."

They stepped into the den, and everyone said hey and all that.

I took a steadying breath. "Daddy, Mamma asked if you would please open a nice red blend for dinner."

"Sure thing." Daddy moved towards the wet bar, pulled two bottles of wine out of the adjacent wine rack. "Maybe better open three."

I suppressed the urge to ask for tequila. "Poppy, come meet Mamma."

Poppy followed me into the kitchen.

"Mamma," I said, "this is Poppy. Poppy, this is my mamma, Carolyn Talbot."

Mamma put the wooden spoon in the spoon rest and moved around the island to get a better look at Poppy. "It's lovely to meet you, dear. I'm so happy you could join us this evening. I'm afraid things are a bit disheveled here tonight. I hope you'll forgive us."

"My goodness," said Poppy. "You cannot be serious. It's so nice of you to have me. You have such a lovely home, and dinner smells amazing."

"Oh, it's nothing fancy," said Mamma. "Just a simple weeknight dinner."

Poppy took in the stove and counter behind Mamma. Her eyes widened.

Mamma moved back to the stove. "Liz, honey, would you set the table? Ask Merry to come put things in serving dishes."

"What can I do to help?" asked Poppy.

"Thank you, honey," said Mamma. "But we have this down to a routine."

I called Merry, then moved to the sink to wash my hands. I lathered them for two minutes, then rinsed thoroughly. Then I applied a thick coat of sanitizer. From the corner of my eye, I watched Mamma roll her eyes.

When I turned around, Poppy seemed to be trying to swallow a smile. She was looking out the backdoor. My eyes followed hers. Daddy's cousin Ponder held all three goats on leashes. Two of them had twisted around him in opposite directions, while the third strained to run away. In the background, Ray Kennedy struggled to prop panels of plywood over the top of Chumley's compound. The good news was I could see Chumley's compound from the house again, because the piles of dirt were gone. The backyard was vastly improved since Sunday, but still had a long way to go. The goats would not be a help.

"The pool is coming along, Mamma," I said.

"Umm," Mamma said.

Poppy said, "I'll help you set the table. Let me just wash my hands." She began repeating the process exactly as I had done it.

When Poppy reached for the sanitizer, Mamma said, "If you like that stuff, help yourself. But please don't feel obliged. It's not a household custom."

"Oh." Poppy took a small squirt, rubbed her hands together.

"Are Ray and Ponder staying for dinner?" I asked.

"I've already fed them," said Mamma. "Ray doesn't eat after four o'clock anymore. Some newfangled health kick he's on. An array of pills and tonics are involved, of course. Ponder ate with him so he wouldn't have to eat alone."

I walked towards the dining room and Poppy followed. In short order we had Mamma's mahogany dining room table set for eight. Merry brought in the steak and gravy and set it on a trivet next to the vase of blue hydrangeas in the center of the table. Then she carried in mashed potatoes, fried squash, butter peas, green bean casserole, sliced tomatoes, fried apples, and biscuits. There wasn't enough room, and tomatoes and the apples had to go on the sideboard.

Poppy said, "I haven't seen this much food at the same time

since I was little and my mother would take me to pot luck suppers at church."

"This is how Mamma expresses her love," I said. "She feeds us all silly."

"Frank," Mamma called. "Y'all come on now. Dinner's getting cold."

Nate carried two bottles of Radius red blend and worked one on to each end of the table. Blake set a third directly in front of his place. Joe and Daddy filed in behind them. We all sat in our customary places, with Poppy on the other side of Nate, next to Daddy, and across from Blake.

Mamma offered Merry and me her hands and said grace. After she finished, she sat there for a moment with her eyes closed, squeezing my hand, and I guessed from Merry's expression, hers too.

Merry and I looked at each other for a long moment.

Daddy passed the steak and gravy to Poppy. "Here you go."

Mamma finally let go of my hand. She served herself some butter peas and passed them to Merry. For the next few moments, we passed food, fixed plates, and complimented the cook, who was very quiet. Daddy kept stealing glances at her, then looking back at his plate. What on earth was he planning to do with those animals?

"Poppy, are you originally from this area?" Mamma asked.

"Yes ma'am," said Poppy. "I grew up in West Ashley."

"I've always loved the established neighborhoods in that part of town," said Mamma. "Do you still live there?"

"No, I live downtown now," said Poppy.

"Wow," said Merry. "That must be nice."

"It is," said Poppy. "I love it."

"Do you have family nearby?" asked Mamma.

Mamma was off her game, and understandably. I had told her Poppy didn't have family, hadn't I? I gave Mamma a warning look—one she normally would have understood immediately.

"No," said Poppy. She cleared her throat gently. "I...my family is gone."

"Where'd they move to?" asked Blake.

"No," said Poppy. "I mean, they've all passed away."

Blake looked stricken. "I...I'm so sorry."

Poppy shook her head slightly, sipped her wine. "No, it's fine. Really. How could you have known. And, I mean, it wasn't recent. I really like this wine. It's great. I don't drink wine very often. But I like this. A lot." She sipped some more.

"It is good," I said. "Daddy, I hope you stocked up on this."

"Hmm? Oh, yeah. There's more if we need it," said Daddy.

"Mamma, those hydrangeas are gorgeous," I said.

"They are lovely, aren't they?" she said. "They're All Summer Beauties."

Everyone seemed to be struggling to find safe topics of conversation. There were so many places we dared not go, especially in front of company. The table was quieter than usual. Finally, my brother had all of that he could handle.

"So, Dad, what's the plan?" he asked.

"What plan?" asked Daddy.

"For the goats, the pig," said Blake.

"Well, I don't know." Daddy moved food around on his plate. "They just got here a little while ago. Ray and Ponder are settling the goats in for tonight, so they don't bother the neighbors. Kinky, she's fine."

Mamma set down her water glass a little harder than normal.

"Why can't the goats go back wherever they came from?" I asked.

"It's a farm over on Johns Island," said Daddy. "They have a no return policy."

"As should we." Mamma's voice was coated in saccharine.

"Is Chumley all right?" asked Merry. "He seems awfully quiet."

"Oh," said Daddy. "I gave him some Valium."

Everyone but Poppy looked at Mamma, and we were all thinking the exact same thing. She'd had Valium too. And it would wear off, for both Chumley and Mamma.

Nate said, "Surely there's another petting zoo somewhere around that would love to have them."

Poppy said, "What about the one at Magnolia Plantation? Or, there's one that brings pets around to children's birthday parties."

"That's a fine idea," said Daddy. "Two fine ideas. I'll call them both tomorrow."

Joe said, "I'm sure there are others. We'll find a place for them. Don't you worry Mamma C."

Merry looked vaguely unhappy but resigned.

Mamma made note. "Perhaps you'd like to keep them with you until permanent arrangements are made."

"No," said Merry. "I'd just get attached."

We all continued eating and complimenting the food. My Mamma's steak and gravy really is decadent. But things were still abnormally quiet.

Blake tried again. "Did y'all see where there's another storm in the Atlantic? Leroy. Some of the models have it headed our way. We need to keep an eye on this one."

My stomach clenched. I put down my fork and picked up my water glass.

*You cannot live your life in fear.* Colleen's words echoed in my brain. I took a deep breath, tried to chase the tension from my body.

Nate looked at me, cut his eyes at Blake.

Blake gave him a quizzical look, shrugged. Then he tried another track. "Poppy, what do you do for a living?"

"I'm a mail carrier," she said.

"Oh my goodness." Merry put a bite of food together and pretended she hadn't witnessed the scene at Taste between Poppy and Sonny. "That's a hard job, especially in this heat."

An odd look crossed Blake's face. He and Sonny spoke several times a week. He'd probably heard Sonny's take on Poppy Oliver.

"It's not so bad," said Poppy. "Actually, I like my job most days. I get to be outside, talk to people. Get to know some of the people on my route."

Blake opened his mouth to speak.

Loud noises I couldn't identify came from the direction of the kitchen, bumps and bangs. We all looked in that direction.

"*Frank*," Ray Kennedy's voice was urgent.

Then we heard the bleeting.

"Oh, dear Heaven," said Mamma. "Is that—"

Three goats bleeting.

In the kitchen.

Kinky squealed urgently.

Chumley gave a medicated, half-hearted howl.

"Cuz," called Ponder. "*Cuz*. We need you in the kitchen. Come quick."

"I'm coming," called Daddy. "Liz, you girls take your mother over to your house for a while, would you?"

"Cuz, I'm *real* sorry," Ponder called.

The goats trotted down the hall and into the dining room.

Everything happened at once.

One of the goats hopped up on the dining table.

Water and wine glasses toppled.

The sound of crunching glass and hoofs on mahogany filled the room.

Daddy cursed and the rest of us gasped and slid our chairs back.

With one foot in the mashed potato bowl, the goat on the table commenced munching on the hydrangeas.

Mamma's eyes got huge. She leaned back as far as she could, then stumbled to stand, backed up, and gave a soft cry.

The other two goats were under the table bleeting their heads off.

"Where's the rest of the Valium?" I asked.

"Powder room medicine cabinet," Daddy said over his shoulder as he stepped into the foyer.

Blake lunged for the goat on the table.

I grabbed Mamma's arm. "Come with me. Merry, medicine cabinet."

"Got it." She dashed across the dining room.

I swiveled my head to make sure Poppy was following me.

"Come on little fellow." She reached down and picked up one of the goats. "Let's get you back outside."

"Poppy, I'll wait for you in the car," I said.

"Be right there," she said in the softest, gentlest tone.

Blake stared at her with an expression I couldn't read. But he didn't look happy.

I gentled Mamma outside and into the Explorer. Merry brought the Valium, a bottle of water, and two unopened bottles of wine. After a few minutes, Poppy climbed into the back with Mamma.

"The goats are all outside. The men are going to clean everything up, good as new," said Poppy, in the same voice she'd used on the goats.

Mamma said, "Franklin Talbot has never cleaned a solitary thing his entire life."

Poppy took her hand. "Nate and Blake and Joe are going to help. And the other two gentlemen."

Mamma clasped Poppy's hand in both of hers. Tears filled her eyes. "I'm positively mortified."

"Why?" asked Poppy.

"You're our guest," said Mamma. "And wildlife ate hydrangeas on my dining room table."

"Mrs. Talbot," said Poppy, "this is the best meal and the best time I've had in ages."

"Please, sugar," said Mamma, "call me Carolyn. Merry, I'd like two of the little yellow pills please."

# EIGHTEEN

Nate, Rhett, and I all missed our run Thursday morning. Mamma was in the guest room—the yellow one that had been mine before I moved into Gram's old room. Merry had gone back to the house and packed Mamma an overnight bag. Blake dropped Nate off the night before just in time for him to take Poppy home and get back on the last ferry.

I came downstairs at six thirty, an hour and a half later than usual. Halfway down the stairs I smelled bacon and coffee. When I walked into the kitchen, Mamma said, "Good morning, Sunshine."

She was flipping blueberry pancakes. I might have groaned. Not that her pancakes aren't good—they're legendary.

Nate handed me a cup of coffee. "Sit."

I sat at the bar. "Have you heard from Blake this morning?"

"Yeah," said Nate. "He and Nell are calling around to find someone to take the animals. The goats are incarcerated until they get that worked out."

"So, the plywood on Chumley's quarters—that worked?" I scrunched my face at Nate.

"Ah, no," said Nate. "The goats are in the actual jail. Blake has them."

"At least they are out of my house." Mamma smiled, slid two plates of pancakes and bacon onto the table by the window. "Elizabeth, stop twisting up your face that way. I've told you a million times that causes wrinkles. Come eat your breakfast."

We moved to the table. I looked at Nate.

"Resistance is futile," he said. "We'll run an extra mile tomorrow."

Mamma went back to the stove and made herself a plate with one small pancake and one slice of bacon. Then she joined us at the table. "I was thinking I could air out some of the rooms upstairs you don't use very often—change the sheets on the beds. Give them a thorough cleaning."

"Mamma, that's not necessary, really. Please. Just relax until things are straightened out at home. Why don't you sit in the sunroom and read? I'm so sorry, but Nate and I have to work today, or we'd do something fun. Plus, Nate's headed back over to help Daddy as soon as we get caught up."

"It's better I keep busy," she said.

I knew then she would cook us lunch and dinner if we didn't stop her. My metabolism couldn't stand up to a full day of Mamma's cooking anymore. "I have a great idea. What about that spa day?"

"Hmm. I don't know. I can take care of you children while you work."

Nate said, "I think a spa day sounds like a fine idea. When's the last time you've taken some time for yourself, Carolyn?"

Mamma made a skeptical face.

"I'll make the call," I said. "Merry hasn't left to go to work yet. She can drop you off. You can spend the day getting pampered, and hopefully, by the time you get home, your house will be set to rights."

By eight o'clock, Mamma was on her way to Charleston, and Nate and I were settled into the sofa in the office with more coffee. Rhett walked around the room a few times, then laid down on his cushion in the corner.

"Tell me," I said, "before I positively pop from curiosity. What did you find at the Drayton house?"

"For starters, thirteen separate sets of emergency room

discharge papers for Anne Frances, all local, all since they've been married. Radial fractures, multiple contusions, general pain in her torso with no discernible cause. Textbook abuse."

"Oh, that poor woman." I closed my eyes, unaware until that moment how much I'd been hoping to find that Poppy was mistaken and the Draytons had been happily married.

"There's more," said Nate.

"What?"

"The first time she went to the ER, and in all but four cases, the nurse's name on the discharge papers is Jacynthe Grimes."

"That's how she got involved with them," I said. "Of course. That's how they find women who need help. Jacynthe can't report the abuse without the patient's consent due to HIPAA laws. So, she tells them if they need help to reach out to her, Tess, or Sofia."

"Looks like you were right. Probably because victims of abuse are often controlled, like the woman you saw Tuesday, they set up a system for them to communicate when they're ready to leave their abusers."

"It's really a clever setup if you think about it," I said. "Anything else in the house?"

"I scanned some bank statements we need to go through," said Nate. "I uploaded them to the case file. There were several joint accounts, and those records were in the study with brokerage accounts, tax records, all that—my guess is it was Phillip's study. Masculine decor. Nothing that was specifically hers. But she does have one credit card that's in her name alone, and one bank account. Those records were in the bottom drawer of her dressing table. They're the ones I scanned."

"Sonny's been through all that. He said there was nothing suspicious there," I said.

"We have more information now," said Nate. "We should take another look."

"You're right. It's all about context. Anything else?"

"No, not at the house," said Nate. "But I did listen to the recording from Mallory and Daniel's dinner conversation before you got up."

"And?"

"Short version for now. They ate at his home, alone. Apparently, someone cooks for him. Anyway, the chef left before Mallory arrived. Mallory was still upset about being interviewed again. Daniel was indignant on her behalf that she'd been asked for an alibi, but curious why she thought she had anything to worry about. He didn't come right out and ask her if she and Phillip were having an affair, but he tread pretty close to it."

"What did she say?"

"That she'd had a crush on Phillip for a long time, but he'd never shown her the slightest bit of attention that wasn't strictly platonic. She confessed to following him, sometimes sitting in her car waiting just to get a look at him. She's worried the police have found out about that and see it as a sign of her guilt."

"And they have. Poppy told Sonny that Mallory was stalking Phillip," I said. "But they weren't having an affair?"

"Not if she was telling Daniel the truth. He bought it anyway. Seemed very happy with that development, though not quite so pleased to hear the depths of Mallory's obsession with his brother. He rallied quickly, I'll give him that much. It's pretty clear he plans to redirect her attention to him."

"Are you going to make a run at her building's security camera footage this morning?"

"Yes, to eliminate her," said Nate. "But I think if either of them did it, it was him. Now you—did you get a look at who Anne Frances met at Kiawah?"

"I think so." I explained my deductive reasoning to Nate. "I'm going to look him up, see what I can find on him. Maybe he's the guy and maybe he's not. But the only reason you drive forty-five minutes out of town for a two-hour hotel stay is if you're doing something you're not supposed to be doing with *someone*." I moved to my desk and turned on the computer.

Rhett looked at me glumly from the corner.

I sighed, gave him a rueful look.

Nate said, "Soon as I get inside this server we'll play some Frisbee, okay boy?"

Rhett huffed. He stood and sashayed out the door, as if to let us know he wasn't waiting for either of us.

"We need another dog," I said. "He's by himself too much."

"Maybe," said Nate. "But no goats and no pigs. Not that there's anything wrong with either. We just don't live on a farm."

He searched my gaze from across the room. Sometimes I wondered if he was looking for signs I was developing my daddy's strain of insanity.

I flashed him an eye roll and went to work.

The Fusion's plate came back to Ryan Sutton, age thirty-five. The address was for a condo at Folly Beach. I created a profile for him, looking for connections to Anne Frances. The first one popped up fast. He was originally from Chicago and had attended the same public schools as Anne Frances. He'd moved to Los Angeles when he was seventeen and lived there for thirteen years. He had a background in modeling and was a member of the Screen Actors Guild. His work history was spotty, with occasional, short-term stints in the restaurant industry.

But in late 2010, he relocated to Charleston and paid $350,000 cash for the condo. It was small, just over 500 square feet. But it was oceanfront and not cheap real estate. Where had he come by that kind of money? I couldn't find a local work history. Either what he did for a living now was illegal, or he was paid under the table, or he had some other means of support.

It was a bit unusual for someone who lived on the beach at Folly to be a guest at The Sanctuary, one island over, where rooms started at $500 a night. Maybe someone would do that for a wedding or a special anniversary. But Ryan Sutton had left alone at the exact same time Anne Frances did the same. That, along with the fact that he was originally from the same place as Anne Frances and relocated to Charleston not long after she returned from her honeymoon, made me nearly certain he was the man I'd taken a room service order from the day before.

Was he also a murderer?

I ran a criminal background check. He had a handful of misdemeanors from California—traffic violations, assault, drug possession—but it didn't appear he'd ever stayed in jail longer than a weekend. Did he have a juvenile record? I had no way to access that information.

I turned to social media but couldn't find a Facebook profile for Ryan. I couldn't look for him in Anne Frances's account, because she didn't have one either. We'd have to dig further into Ryan Sutton the old-fashioned way. I knew where he lived and what he drove, I just needed to find him and put a tracker on his car so we'd know when it was safe to check out his condo.

I set Ryan aside for a moment and pulled up the images Nate had scanned of Anne Frances's credit card and bank account statements. She shopped online a good bit, which was consistent with her pattern of shying away from leaving the house. I skimmed for other patterns and spotted one right off.

"Did you look at these statements at all?" I asked.

Nate looked up. "No. I just scanned images and flipped pages. Tried to get as much data as I could. Why?"

"She's been going to The Sanctuary at Kiawah every Wednesday since November of 2010. The amounts are relatively consistent, going up over time—about what room and tax would be with maybe a hundred dollars in room service charges. If I hadn't called the room she checked into, I'd think these were spa charges."

"That's probably what she told her husband she was doing—going to the spa."

"And if Sonny asked her about it, I bet that's what she told him too," I said. "This makes my head spin."

"What do you mean?"

"We've established that she's a strong woman—she got herself off a bad path, moved to Naples, started a business. But she was married to a guy who beat her. She stayed with him and cheated on him with this guy from a past she'd put behind her. She knew him when *she* was in high school. He's four years younger than her. That means nothing now, but when she was a senior, he wasn't even *in* high school yet."

"So, they most likely weren't sweethearts way back," said Nate.

"I've seen stranger things, but I'd say almost definitely not. Girls that age, especially girls as pretty as she surely was, date older guys, not ones whose voices are still changing."

"They might be having an affair now, but passion for her didn't inspire him to move all the way across the country," said Nate.

"This case has too many moving parts." I rubbed my temples. "I still don't want to talk to Anne Frances yet. I think it's to our advantage that she doesn't know we're watching. I want to talk to someone—anyone—who knows Anne Frances Drayton. She's such a private person. It's hard to find anyone who knows her better than Poppy, for goodness sake. Except for Daniel Drayton, who's obviously biased."

"Hmm." Nate had gone back to his hacking project.

I pulled up the profile I'd done on Anne Frances Carlisle Drayton and scrolled to her marriage certificate. "Sasha Alvarez."

"Who?" asked Nate.

"The other witness on the marriage certificate. Daniel said she was Anne Frances's girlfriend. The wedding was private. I thought perhaps she worked at the inn where they got married, or with the officiant."

I started a profile on Sasha Alvarez. She was also from Chicago, was the same age as Anne Frances, and had attended the same schools. Sasha had moved to Naples around the same time as Anne Frances. She'd worked as a hairdresser. Her last job and lease history ended abruptly in June of 2010. Sweet reason, it was as if she'd left the wedding and disappeared. I widened my search, scanned for a death certificate and found one in Los Angeles County, California, dated August 11, 2010. The address on the death certificate was in West Covina, California, an LA suburb. She wasn't visiting—she'd moved there. Sasha had died of a drug overdose while Anne Frances was still on her honeymoon.

I mulled that. Why had Sasha left Naples when Anne Frances got married? Why Los Angeles? What, if any, was her connection to Ryan Sutton? I needed to talk to someone who knew all these people from Chicago.

I pulled up the copy of Anne Frances's birth certificate. The software I used had populated information about her parents and brother—the folks from the Chicago area who didn't fly—along with their address. I pondered a pretext for a moment while I looked for a landline phone number. When I found it, I dialed her mother.

"Mrs. Carlisle?" I asked.

Across the room, Nate looked up from his laptop.

"Yes, who's calling?"

"I'm with the high school reunion committee. We're trying to get current contact information for Anne Frances, and I wondered if you could help me. We're hoping for a good turnout."

"Anne Frances?" The woman sounded horribly sad and a bit confused. "I wish I could help you. We haven't seen her since the year after she graduated."

*What?* My antennae went up. "I'm terribly sorry, ma'am. We had on our paperwork that she was still in the area."

"No, I'm afraid not. Last time we saw her she was with Nikki Parks and the Alvarez girl. The three of them left town together. Talked about Hollywood, but who knows. If you find her, I hope you'll ask her to call home. It's been a long time, and my husband isn't in good health."

"Yes ma'am. I surely will." I ended the call.

"You're not going to believe this." I told Nate what Anne Frances's mother had said.

"Explains why they didn't come for the funeral," said Nate. "Who's Anne Frances been visiting in Chicago?"

"What kind of person doesn't talk to their parents for twenty years?"

I searched our primary background database for Nikki Parks. In addition to her birth certificate, I found a couple drug related arrests in the Chicago area from 1995. She would've been eighteen. But there was nothing after that. If she'd left town with Anne Frances, she should've shown up in Naples, like Sasha.

"Something is not right here," I said.

"But what?" asked Nate. "Maybe it should be a crime to ignore your parents, but it isn't."

"There's more to it. There has to be."

I searched every place I knew to look for Nikki Parks. Her parents had passed away when she was seventeen, a few months apart. She didn't have any siblings. Unlike Sasha, there was no death certificate on file for Nikki—at least not one I'd been able to find.

I was beginning to reconsider talking to Anne Frances. But what did any of this have to do with Phillip Drayton's death? Maybe nothing at all.

I opened the GPS tracking app on my Mac. What was the widow Drayton up to today?

Hell's bells. Anne Frances was parked in front of the bookshop, which didn't open for another thirty minutes.

Was she there to signal for a pickup? Why? Phillip couldn't hurt her anymore.

Did she suspect Tess knew something about Phillip's death? Was she doing her own sleuthing?

"Got it," said Nate.

"The security footage?"

"I've got Mallory coming into the garage at 5:10 and back out again at 8:45. And she's home again at 11:25."

"*Damnation.* That gives her plenty of time to swap cars, hit Phillip, and trade cars again."

"It would've been nice to be able to eliminate one of them," said Nate. "But just because she left her condo doesn't mean she killed Drayton. If Mallory were homicidally inclined, I don't see her going after her soul mate. She'd've gone after Anne Frances."

"You're probably right, but why lie about being at home?"

Nate said, "My guess is she's nervous. Sonny must've asked Mallory questions that made her squirm after Poppy told him about the stalking."

"Maybe Mallory was somewhere she shouldn't've been that very night. Hell, that could've been her on the burner phone— maybe she was parked over there staring at the house and saw the whole thing go down. Nah, that doesn't feel right. She probably would've chased down the car that hit Phillip." I stood, grabbed my purse.

"Where you headed?"

"I need to get to Charleston. Anne Frances is back at the bookshop."

"You want me to come with you?" He looked hopeful.

"I've got this," I said. "You've got your hands full with Daddy."

He closed his eyes, nodded. "But I'm going to keep my promise to Rhett first."

# NINETEEN

It was eleven o'clock before I made it to Buxton Books. According to the GPS, Anne Frances was parked in the Visitors Center parking garage on the corner of Meeting and Mary. What was she doing there?

Christine was working in the bookstore again that morning. "Did you find out your friend didn't have the book?"

"As a matter of fact, yes. I may have a couple of friends who need a copy." I walked straight over to the secretary with the display of *The Ghosts of Charleston.* Nine copies were on the shelf, spine out. I picked up the book in the middle.

The bookmark was between pages eighty-eight and eighty-nine. "The Haunt of the Dock Street Theatre." I put the book back where it had been, in the middle of the row, and picked up a copy from another stack. Then I made my purchase and returned to my car.

Anne Frances, or at least her car, was still at the Visitor's Center garage. The last pickup I'd witnessed had been at two o'clock. With no indication otherwise, I would assume today's would be the same. I had nearly three hours to wait. It would be cooler inside a parking garage, out of the direct sunlight. I pulled into the garage across Cumberland. Once I was settled, I took my iPad out of my tote and continued my deep dive into Ryan Sutton's background. What had he been doing for the last five years? How did he support himself?

My phone played a few bars of "Carry on Wayward Son" by

Kansas. Blake's ringtone. "Hey Big Brother, what's up?"

He sighed heavily. "Mom called me this morning. On her way into Charleston to go to the spa, she said."

"You have no idea what a blessing that is."

"I probably do," he said. "But she told me to go by the house and make a platter of leftovers for that woman you brought to dinner last night. I have no idea where she lives. Don't know her phone number. And I've got a platter full of steak and gravy."

"I'll share her contact with you when we hang up," I said. "She'll be grateful for that food."

"What's going on with all that?"

"All what?"

"I know Sonny thinks she ran into that guy," he said. "What do you and Nate think?"

I felt my forehead creasing. "We respectfully disagree."

"Yeah, I don't see it either," he said. "I better go. I need to get rid of all this food so I can get back to work."

I shook my head, shared Poppy's contact information with Blake while giving him an odd look he couldn't appreciate, and returned my attention to Ryan Sutton.

Periodically glancing at the red blinking dot that told me Anne Frances was still parked in the same place, I checked vehicle registrations for anything other than the Fusion. Bingo. Ryan Sutton owned a 2001 white Ford Econoline E-350 Super Duty van. Why?

Could a white van be mistaken for a white SUV in the rain?

I googled images of the van. It was awfully large, but it was possible someone might mistake it for an SUV in a deluge.

When I looked at the GPS app at one fifteen, Anne Frances was on the move. She was headed down Meeting Street. I put my phone on the magnet, started the Escape, and exited the garage. I wanted to be in position near Dock Street Theatre before she arrived. I zipped over to Church Street—this section was one-way running north. I pulled to the curb across the street from the Dock Street Theatre, a few car lengths before the entrance.

While I watched on the screen, Anne Frances turned off Meeting onto Cumberland. Halfway down the block, just across from the Powder Magazine, she turned into the Cumberland Street garage. She was a block and a half away from me.

At ten minutes 'til two, she walked around the bend in Church Street that accommodates St. Philip's Church. In a cream-colored pantsuit, she carried an overnight bag and a purse. She checked her watch, slowed her gait. In the rearview mirror, I watched for a limo. What was she up to and why?

Anne Frances crossed Queen Street and climbed the two steps to shelter in the shade of the historic theatre's second story verandah. I glanced from her to the rearview mirror and back.

At precisely two o'clock, Tess Hathaway's Cadillac pulled to the curb directly in front of the theatre. Anne Frances put her things in the back seat, looked up and down the street, then climbed into the car. The Cadillac pulled back into traffic. I let a car between us, then followed.

I followed them all the way back out to the Planter's Club on Ashley River Road, then I headed home. The only way I could get past the dirt road entrance was in one of the club's limousines.

On the ferry ride back to Stella Maris, Poppy called me.

"I thought you'd want to know," she said. "That blonde woman—the one you showed me the photo of? She turned up on my route again today. Same thing. She just drove by slowly and looked at me. It's just so weird."

"It is that." What in the name of reason was that all about?

"Please tell your mother thank you for the food."

I could hear the smile in her voice.

# TWENTY

As it turned out, The Planter's Club had no availability for Friday evening, but could accommodate us on Saturday. We spent all of Friday holed up in our situation room hashing through all the bits and pieces of information we had accumulated about our upside-down case. At lunchtime, I went to the kitchen to forage for lunch and found a glass dish full of homemade pimento cheese Mamma must've left for us. When on earth had she had time to make that?

I put together a tray of sandwiches and glasses of Cheerwine and carried it back into my office. We sat on the sofa with our feet propped up, munched, and studied our revised case board, which lamentably kept growing.

1. Poppy: accidentally hit Phillip Drayton
2. Poppy: intentionally hit Philip Drayton
   a. Mrs. Drayton's accomplice
   b. Vigilante: protecting Mrs. Drayton
   c. Unknown motives
3. Unknown Subject: accidentally hit Phillip Drayton and fled
   a. Emma Williams?
4. Unknown Subject: intentionally hit Phillip Drayton and fled
   a. Mrs. Drayton's accomplice: Ryan Sutton?
   b. Vigilante: protecting Mrs. Drayton. Limo driver? Tess? Jacynthe? Sofia? Emma?
   c. Unknown motives
5. Mallory Lucas: jealousy

6. Daniel Drayton: jealousy
7. Ryan Sutton: money/jealousy

"The thing is," I said, "it's impossible to prove a negative. Just because we can't prove Poppy didn't conspire with Anne Frances Drayton doesn't mean she did. I see that as too farfetched to even still have on the board."

"I can see I was giving the two of you way too much credit." Blake stood in the doorway between the foyer and my office. He gestured dramatically at our case board, his face pinched into a scowl. He was clearly agitated.

"I didn't hear you come in." I scrunched up my face. "What are you talking about? Are you hungry? There's pimento cheese in the kitchen."

"That goofy woman did not kill anybody," said Blake.

"She's not goofy," I said. "What's wrong with you?"

He massaged the back of his neck with one hand and continued gesticulating his scorn at our case board with the other. "How can you possibly think a woman gentle enough to coax those goats from hell outside would intentionally run over a man for any reason?"

"We don't actually think that," said Nate.

"But it's right there in black and white." Blake muttered something under his breath. "And Sonny. I think he's actually going to arrest her." His voice rose. My brother was as angry as I'd seen him in a while.

"Blake," I said. "When did you talk to Sonny?"

"Few minutes ago." Disgust contorted his face.

Alarm rose in my chest. "You think he plans to arrest Poppy today?"

"No, no," said Blake. "He said he agreed to wait. But I know Sonny. He thinks he's got this figured out. He does not. I thought maybe y'all did. I can see I was wrong about that."

"Lookit," I said. "This is a complicated mess of a case. But we do have some things figured out. We do *not* think Poppy hit Phillip Drayton, either accidentally or on purpose. But what I really want to know is why are you so worked up?"

"I'm not worked up," said Blake, in a tone that demonstrated exactly how worked up he was. "It's just, that girl is so...so...innocent. It bothers me. She trusts people too much. She thinks everyone has good intentions. It's gotten her into trouble. This Drayton woman, maybe she did conspire to kill her husband. But not with that poor little mail carrier."

I looked at Nate. He wore an expression that told me he was processing things. I turned back to Blake. "Is this a slow day for you? Because let me tell you, it isn't for us. We've got work to do. Now do you want some lunch or not?"

"No, I don't want lunch," said Blake. "Is there something I can do to help?"

"I think we've got it," said Nate. "We typically leave all our theories on the board until we can eliminate them. Liz was just saying, right when you came in, that just because we haven't been able to exclude one of them doesn't make it likely. These are just all the possibilities we know of."

"I'm just sayin'," said Blake. "Everything up there related to Poppy Oliver is not possible. Have you met her?"

I threw him a look filled with as much exasperation as I could muster. "We are on her side. She's our *client*, okay?" Technically, she wasn't.

Blake squinted at the board. "Who is Emma Williams? Ryan Sutton? You need me to look into some of these people?"

I stood up, walked towards my brother. "Listen to me. Everything on that board is attorney work product. You don't need to be looking at it, and thank you, but no, we don't need you to look into anyone. We've got this. Now, I'm really sorry, but you cannot be here. You are the Chief of Police for a town in Charleston

County. Good grief—you could compromise the confidentiality of our work."

Anger, confusion, and frustration waged war on Blake's face. "Just make sure you get this right." He stormed out the door.

"What in this world?" I stared after him.

"Poppy makes everyone who meets her want to protect her," said Nate. "There's just something about her. You felt it yourself, you said, the first time you saw her."

"You're right." I moved back to the couch, picked up my drink. "But good grief. He must be bored today. Where were we?"

"We've established that Anne Frances was abused and in contact with Tess and the others through Jacynthe. She was also having an affair with Ryan Sutton, a man with no visible means of support," said Nate.

"I'd bet good money she was somehow keeping him up," I said. "But I can't prove it from her bank statements. I know I'm starting to sound like Daniel Drayton, but I have a strong suspicion she's involved in her husband's death."

Nate said, "Let's walk through it step by step. Our working narrative is that Tess is our client and made the second call to 911."

"And if she was there," I said, "perhaps Sofia and Jacynthe were as well. Somewhere in the vicinity of the accident, they were trying to help Anne Frances and things went sideways. That doesn't necessarily mean one of them hit Phillip with a car, but they maybe had something to do with the other injuries. If he attacked Anne Frances while she was trying to escape with them. It's possible one of the limos actually hit Phillip. We have only the second caller's word—Tess according to our working narrative—that a white SUV was the vehicle involved. Poppy didn't see it."

"All of those women—Tess, Sofia, and Jacynthe—they have a lot to lose, and no reason to tell us the truth if we confront them. We have no evidence. Zero. Only theories."

I pondered that. "Have you wondered why Fraser didn't want

Poppy to know his firm was involved? Didn't want to talk to her personally?"

"I have indeed," said Nate.

"Sonny's right. Privilege and the work-product doctrine will protect Tess, not Poppy."

"But we were hired to help Poppy," said Nate.

"That's what we were told anyway," I said. "Never forget that Tess is Abigail Bounetheau's sister. This could all be an elaborate scheme to protect Tess, not Poppy." Saying that made a chill run up my spine.

"You make an excellent point," said Nate. "Especially given that we can't just take what we learn and hand it to Sonny, especially if it incriminates Tess in any way."

"I hope we're not being used that way. Fraser is quirky, to be sure. But I've always thought he was an honorable man. He wouldn't be a party to that sort of deceit, and he wouldn't be taken in by it."

We both thought about that for a few minutes, sipped our Cheerwine.

I drew a long breath and blew it out slowly. "Bottom line, our working narrative is that Tess was there. Maybe Sofia and Jacynthe too."

"Right," said Nate. "Who was driving the vehicle that hit Phillip—that could be a whole nother thing or not. Do you think Emma Williams is another one of them? Is she connected to Zelda's Safe House?"

"Not in any way I've been able to suss out. But that doesn't mean she's not."

"Any connection to Drayton?" asked Nate.

"Again, none that I can find. But if she'd hit him in that Honda, you'd be able to tell it for sure. And we haven't been able to tie her to any other vehicle. It's strange, the way she keeps popping up. She could be an unstable soul with a beef with Poppy for some unknown reason—a damaged package. Who knows? But we need to eliminate her as a suspect if we can."

"My money is on Ryan Sutton and his white van for the driver and vehicle," said Nate.

"Mine too." I bit my lip. "That van of his could well be the murder weapon. I wonder what he uses that for anyway? With Phillip out of the way, Ryan has much more control over Anne Frances and all the money she inherited. At least as long as she keeps him around. The question is, was she in on it?"

"Her background gets murkier every time we dive into it," said Nate.

"But Ryan wouldn't've used pepper spray, a Taser, and a tactical pen in the process of running over Phillip." I scrunched up my face. "Which takes us back to Tess and her gang."

"Aside from that, the narrative that Ryan killed Phillip makes the most sense to me," said Nate.

"Me too," I said. "At the end of the day, we have to find that white van or an SUV we can tie him to. I don't think he's connected to anyone else involved in this case other than Anne Frances. If it was him, it was either a crime of opportunity—he was staking out the house—or he conspired with Anne Frances."

"And someone else made the first call to 911. That wasn't Ryan on the phone," said Nate. "Our remaining candidates for driver of the vehicle are Mallory and Daniel," said Nate. "I see them as unlikely at this point."

"Me too. We need to make Tess and her cohorts tell us what they know. One or more of them witnessed what happened. We need a better description of the vehicle we're looking for. Right now we don't have enough to even look for it."

"We're going to need a lot of leverage for that," said Nate.

"I'm thinking we'll find some at The Planter's Club."

# TWENTY-ONE

Aside from a couple of old bridesmaid dresses, I had two floor-length gowns in my closet. I decided the red sequin dress would make me stand out at The Planter's Club and not in a good way. I went with the steel gray chiffon number. It was an A-line with a scoop neck, but the top and three-quarter sleeves were made of illusion with pretty beading. It was demur without being dowdy.

"My, my. Mrs. Andrews, I'm not sure I should take you out in public looking like that."

I turned to see Nate propped casually against the frame of our bedroom door. In a classic black tuxedo, he was devastatingly handsome. His blue eyes had a smoky hue this evening. "The feeling is mutual, Mr. Andrews."

"We'd best go before I change my mind. After you." He stepped back, and I proceeded out of the bedroom and down the stairs.

"I've reserved a room at Charleston Place," he said. "Odds are we'll miss the last ferry back tonight. I figure those limos don't typically pick up at budget hotels. Oh, and I called the number Huger gave you. They'll pick us up at six thirty."

"Perfect." At the front door I waited, smiled up at him.

"Yes, you are."


The limousine pulled under the portico by the fountain at Charleston Place at precisely six thirty. A quick look at the tag told me it was the same one that had picked up the woman by St. Michael's Alley.

The passenger door opened, and the same sturdy gentleman climbed out to open the door. "Good evening," he said. "Mr. and Mrs. Andrews?"

"That's right," said Nate. He helped me inside, then slid in after me.

"I'm Louis. Please let me know if you need anything during our trip." He closed the door.

The glass between the front and the back of the car was raised. There was a bucket of champagne and two glasses in the back. Nate poured us each a glass and we sat back to enjoy the ride.

A little more than thirty minutes later, we turned down the dirt driveway leading to The Planter's Club. The road curved sharply to the left and we passed through a manned security gate. Then we were underneath a canopy of giant oaks dripping with Spanish moss. We rolled down the wide drive for a minute or so, then made a turn to the right.

"Notice the cameras?" asked Nate.

"Every other tree," I said.

"That's not historically accurate."

The house came into view and I gasped softly. It felt as though we'd arrived back in time.

It was brick with a raised first floor, double porches, and a row of large white columns. "I never knew this was back here," I said.

"I wonder how long it *has* been here," said Nate. "Could be a reproduction. Weren't most of the plantation houses along the Ashley River destroyed during the Civil War?"

"Yes, except, in a peculiar bit of congruency, Drayton Hall. We passed that on the way in. James said this home was restored. This is amazing."

We pulled to a stop and Louis opened the door. He handed Nate a card. "Just in case. Text or call if you need anything. When you're ready to leave, give your name to any of the service staff and we'll pick you up right here."

"Thank you," said Nate.

As we approached the double front doors, two gentlemen on either side opened them. "Good evening."

The house smelled like old wood and old money. We stood in a wide entry hallway with gleaming hardwood floors and dark, raised panel walls. A round table under a massive crystal chandelier held a towering floral arrangement. We took a moment to get our bearings.

"Shall we try the parlor on the right?" asked Nate.

I nodded my assent. He escorted me into what looked like a gentlemen's club room. More dark woods, comfortable leather sofas and chairs, and a bar at the far end. Nate escorted me to a club chair with a view of the room. "I'll get us drinks," he said.

He returned shortly with club soda for me and bourbon for him, which he would nurse. We needed to fit in, but not get sloshed. I surveyed the room. There were half a dozen other couples having cocktails, most of them somewhat older than us, with one couple maybe in their seventies. All the ladies wore floor length gowns. In another room, someone played "As Time Goes By" on the piano.

"One of us needs to get a look upstairs," I said. "That's no doubt where Anne Frances and the Paxton woman are staying. I don't want to confront them—just get evidence that they're here."

"And then use it when we confront Tess and the others," said Nate.

"Exactly. If we happen to come across anything else helpful, so much the better."

"I take it you want to go upstairs." He raised an eyebrow at me.

"Naturally."

"I'll wait here," said Nate. "When you get back, let's get a table in the main dining room. We'd be poor detectives if we didn't check out the cuisine."

"James said the food was divine." I stood, set down my glass.

"Be cautious, Slugger."

"Always."

He flashed me a look that said *Give me a break.*

I walked back into the main hall like I knew what I was doing. Two other couples hovered, chatting. I'd need to wait until the hallway was deserted to make my way up the grand staircase at the far end undetected. Regulars would know the upstairs was private.

I wandered into the next room on the right, where the piano music emanated from. Double damn. Mallory Lucas and Daniel Drayton sat near the piano. Thankfully they were engrossed in conversation and didn't notice me. Wait. Neither of them had ever seen me without my brown wig and contacts. I stepped back into the hallway and returned to the front parlor to alert Nate.

"That's interesting," he said. "Though to be honest, at the moment, I'm much more suspicious of the widow and her lover than I am of them."

"Me too," I said. "But how are we going to play this?"

"Aw hell, that's right. They know me as Tommy, but they don't know you at all and think my wife is a brunette named Suzanne. This is inconvenient."

"Both of our voices are familiar, mine to Daniel, and yours to Mallory, from when we're in costume."

Nate said, "If Mallory drinks as much as Daniel, that shouldn't be a problem. My sense from having lunch with her is that she does. Still, this could get really tricky."

"As long as they don't run into you, we're good. They're in the next room with the piano. Maybe move so that your back is to the door. I'm going to try again to get upstairs unseen."

"Roger that."

I made my way back into the main hall. But it was even more crowded now than before. I circulated through the crowd, smiling at everyone who met my gaze. The piano player teased a slow, jazzy "Summertime" from the keyboard.

I returned to Nate, who now sat on a sofa facing the far wall.

"I think my best chance to get upstairs might be later, after the floor show starts," I said. "Everyone who's here will likely be in the main lounge then."

"Shall we get dinner then?"

"Let's." I smiled.

He stood and offered me his arm. We walked down the hall to the second room on the left, where a maître d' escorted us to a table by the window. Nate helped me into the chair on the left, then took the one with his back to the room, which was never his preference, but necessary tonight.

Nate surveyed the wine list while I perused the menu.

"They have a tasting menu as well as standard courses," I said. "What's your preference?"

Nate grinned, shook his head. "My preference is that you have your way this evening. And we both know that you want the tasting menu."

"Well, it does take the stress out of choosing what to order."

"That's never stressful for me."

"But it always is for me."

"I know." He laid down the wine list. When the waiter returned, he said, "We'd like the chef's tasting menu, with the recommended wine pairings."

Moments later, the maître d' escorted Daniel and Mallory to a table across the room. "They're seated," I said. "He's facing the same wall I am—I think we can relax."

For the next two hours, we enjoyed a parade of pretty food that tasted as good as it looked.

"I'm hoping James will invite us back when we're not working and can enjoy more than a taste of each wine," I said.

"I'm betting all you have to do is drop a hint."

At nine thirty, we could hear the music change in the main lounge across the hall.

"Sounds like the show's about to start," said Nate. "Shall we?"

"Yes, let's see if we can find a table near the back. It'll be easier for me to slip in and out."

He escorted me into a room that looked like it might be a club in a movie with Fred Astaire and Ginger Rodgers. There was a stage with curtains and tables clustered several deep all around a dance floor. We made our way to a table near the back.

Just as Nate pulled my chair back, Daniel Drayton entered the room, Mallory on his arm. His first expression read like he thought he'd been caught. He looked at Mallory, then back at Nate. Then at me. He looked confused. "Tommy."

"Well, hello. Nice to see you." Nate smiled a thin smile. "This is Liz."

"Hello." Daniel nodded in my direction. "I'm Daniel Drayton. This is...Mallory Lucas." He seemed to feel better once he'd gotten that out. He gave Nate a look that asked for an explanation.

Like any man caught out with a woman who was not his wife, Nate offered him none. He also declined to invite them to join us. After an awkward moment, they moved to a table across the room.

"That could've gone worse," said Nate.

"I'm just glad it's over with," I said. "Maybe they'll keep to themselves now."

We watched the first show number, which might've been a part of a Broadway musical. The singers and dancers were first rate. As the performers transitioned to the next number, I excused myself.

The hall was empty now, thankfully. I hustled towards the staircase.

I noticed movement on my left. Someone had come from one

of the other rooms and was also headed towards the stairs. I pivoted my head and smiled.

It was Ryan Sutton.

How had he gotten in? Why was he here?

He was dressed in a tuxedo, like every other man there. He looked like he belonged.

He returned my smile. From a room behind the staircase, a large man emerged, dressed in a suit like the doormen and the burly guy who'd come with the driver to pick us up. I veered right, in the direction of the ladies' room. I wondered if they had a camera trained on the hallway approaching the staircase. I paused just out of their line of sight, in the shadows.

Ryan kept moving towards the steps.

"Excuse me sir," said the man who worked there. "What can I help you find?"

"I believe my girlfriend is upstairs," said Ryan. "I need to check on her. She's not feeling well." He kept walking.

The burly guy placed himself between Ryan and the stairs. "I'm afraid you must be mistaken, sir. The second floor isn't open to guests."

"That may be so, but my girl is up there, and I'm going to get her."

"I'm afraid not, sir." He touched his ear, said something. He was wearing an earpiece. Of course. Someone would be coming to help him dispense with Ryan.

"Who's going to stop me?" Ryan stepped around the man and put his foot on the first step.

Another employee appeared. How many of them were in the room where they watched the cameras?

The two men each took ahold of one of Ryan's arms.

"Get your hands off me," he said.

"Could you step outside, please, sir?" The employee kept his voice low and calm.

They walked towards the door, dragging Ryan between them.

He struggled and cursed all the way to the door. When they were outside, I looked all around and ran up the staircase.

From the top of the stairs, a wide hallway ran left and right, but also partway back around towards the front of the house, forming a U shape. All of the doors I could see were closed. I needed to get out of sight. Anyone entering the hall downstairs could see me on the landing. I darted down the hall to the right.

French doors opened into a sitting room where two women watched television. On closer inspection, they were watching a feed of the floorshow downstairs. I could only see the backs of their heads, but one was blonde and one was brunette. I opened the door on the right and walked in. Anne Frances and the Paxton woman looked up at me. Neither seemed alarmed.

"Excuse me." Before I got to explaining myself, I casually raised my right arm and rubbed a spot just below my heavy tennis bracelet. It looked expensive, and it was, but not because it was made of diamonds. The cubic zirconia stones were good enough to pass for diamonds if one didn't have a jeweler's loupe handy. What made the bracelet expensive was the camera hidden in the center stone. I pressed a button to snap several photos.

The women still looked at me. Should I warn Anne Frances about Ryan? Clearly, he had some sort of tracker in her purse or her overnight bag. That's the only way he could've found her, wasn't it? Where was our hostess? She was surely smart enough to figure out how Ryan had gotten here. But I didn't know everything there was to know about these people and their situation.

Colleen said another life was in danger. Was that one of these women?

"Y'all don't know me," I said, "and I don't have time to explain myself. But I believe someone looking for one of you placed some sort of tracking device in your purse or your luggage—maybe your clothing or a piece of jewelry. They just hauled a man out downstairs. He was trying to get up here. Said he was looking for his girlfriend. I thought someone should know."

Both women looked stricken.

I turned around and made my way back downstairs.

One of the burly men watched me coming down. "Excuse me, sir," I said, "could you direct me to the ladies' room? I seem to have lost my way."

"Certainly, ma'am. It's right this way." He escorted me to the ladies' room and watched me go inside. Perhaps since he saw me coming down the steps, he figured I was truly lost.

When I came out of the ladies' room, he stood at the bottom of the stairs. With posture that would've made Mamma proud, I glided right by him and returned to our table in the main lounge. Currently performing were scantily clad women doing a Rockette-style kick line.

I glanced from the stage to the table. Daniel and Mallory had joined Nate. Daniel was in his face. For his part, Nate wore a bored expression.

"I thought better of you," said Daniel.

Nate remained silent.

"How could you cheat on a sweet girl like Suzy? The week you bury an old friend—my brother. How could you do that?" Clearly, Daniel had been over-served bourbon.

Nate saw me approaching the table and stood.

Daniel and Mallory looked my way. Daniel scowled. "D'you know he's married?"

I covered my face with my hands and ran out in fake tears.

Behind me, I heard Nate say, "Thanks a lot, pal."

He followed me out. Thankfully, Daniel and Mallory did not.

Nate alerted one of the doormen that we were ready to leave. We waited on the porch. There was no sign of Ryan Sutton.

"You find what you were looking for?" Nate asked.

"That and more."

# TWENTY-TWO

The next morning, I woke up to Nate gently stroking my forearm. "Slugger?"

"What time is it?" Disoriented, I struggled to sit up and prop against the pillows. The Belmond. That's right.

"Seven-thirty. Here." He handed me a cup, wrapped my hands around it. "I brought emergency coffee."

I moaned with gratitude. "Thank you."

"Least I could do." He grinned lasciviously. "I'm the one who kept you up so late."

A slow smile slid up my face. "I don't recall objecting."

"I have breakfast too." He pulled an almond croissant from a familiar bag.

"Christophe's?" I might have squealed a little.

"That's your favorite isn't it?"

"Thank you, Sweetheart." What had I ever done to deserve this man?

"Eat now," he said. "I've got news."

I bit into the croissant.

"I put a tracker on Sutton's Fusion. It's parked at his condo. I can't be sure he's there, unfortunately. Wherever he parks the van, it isn't anywhere within a mile of his building. I did a grid search."

"What time did you get up this morning? The beds here must be made of down from angel wings or something. I declare I didn't stir until you woke me."

"My internal alarm went off at five o'clock. I didn't want to disturb you. Thought I might as well get something accomplished."

"I can't figure these two out," I said. "Sutton and Anne Frances. Clearly, they're having an affair. She snuck off to Kiawah to meet him the day after she buried her husband. But, she was not one teeny bit happy he turned up at The Planter's Club."

"Well, we know where she is. I figure after we get what we need from Tess, Jacynthe, and Sofia, we talk to her next."

"Makes sense," I said. "We know the right questions to ask now, anyway."

"My thoughts exactly," said Nate. "But it's Sunday morning. Tess is headed to church, as is Jacynthe. Sofia had a late night."

"I have photos of Anne Frances and the Paxton woman at Sofia's, in the private part of the club. But I think we may need more to convince Tess and the others to tell us everything. Today isn't the best day to confront the three of them together."

"Agreed. We need to plan that carefully." I chewed thoughtfully. "Would you hand me my iPad?"

"Sure." Nate crossed the room, pulled it from my tote, and handed it to me.

"Why don't we see if we can figure out what role Emma Williams plays in this drama, if any? We may be able to cross her off our case board." I opened the Facebook app.

"What do you have in mind?"

"Give me a second."

While she hadn't updated her page in months, many of the people who tagged Emma with posts offering thoughts and prayers for her husband were from her church, Bethel United Methodist.

I said, "Let's see if she and her family are headed out to church as well."

Nate thought for a moment. "You finish eating and get dressed. It's early-ish yet, not far from here to Wagener Terrace. I'll slip over there and see if I can get a tracker on the Honda."

It was always good to know when folks were heading home if

you were searching their house. "Sounds like a plan."

While church bells all over the Holy City called the faithful to worship, Nate and I watched the Williams's modest white bungalow on the corner of Darlington and Maple. We'd parked on the street along Maple, where we could see the front yard, the side of the house, and the small backyard. Nate had successfully hidden a GPS tracker under the front wheel well of the Honda.

I laid my iPad on my lap. "I've searched every way I know to search. That rickety old Honda is the only car this family has owned in the last three years. They did have a 2012 BMW X3, but they sold it a few months after they bought it."

"What color?" asked Nate.

"Blue, but what difference does that make? They sold it three years ago."

Nate shrugged. "Who'd they sell it to? They'd maybe be upside down in a new car they only had a few months. Maybe they sold it to family."

"Nah—they sold it back to the dealership."

"When did they buy this house?" asked Nate.

"Two thousand ten," I said. "They paid two seventy-nine for it. In this neighborhood, that's a fixer-upper. There's a mortgage for two twenty-three."

"From the outside," said Nate, "doesn't look like they've done much in the way of renovations yet. When the husband got sick I guess a lot of things changed."

The backdoor opened and two pale-haired children stepped out onto the small covered porch. The little girl looked about four, the boy five or six. They were both dressed for church, her in a red flowered dress with matching Mary Janes and lacey white socks, him in a checkered shirt and shorts with a belt.

"What cute kids," I said.

They both looked up as if someone had called from inside. They scampered back into the house. A few moments later, they emerged from the front, followed by Emma, who helped her frail-looking husband down the steps. His suit hung on him, like maybe it was three sizes too big.

"Something is bad wrong with Robert Williams," I said. "I've got a really bad feeling about this."

"Yeah, me too," said Nate.

The family rounded the front of the house toward where the car was parked along the far side.

A heaviness settled in my chest. The children. "We are going to hell for this," I said. "Those poor people."

"We're only looking for the truth," said Nate. "I get that these are sympathetic looking folks, but—"

"I know. Phillip Drayton had his life interrupted. Poppy is innocent. It's just—"

"Maybe there's proof inside that Emma was in Switzerland the night Phillip Drayton died."

"Maybe so."

The Honda backed out of the driveway. I pulled up the tracking app on the iPad as they headed down Darlington. "We're clear."

Nate and I were dressed for church. People didn't generally break and enter in church clothes, which was why it was a good cover. If caught, we were simply friends who had planned to go to church with the Williamses but must've missed them. We slipped on clear latex gloves and got out of the car.

We walked up the sidewalk, climbed the front steps, and made a show of knocking on the screened porch door. After a moment, we opened it and approached the inside door. I had my lock set ready, and as soon as the screened door closed behind us, I handed Nate the iPad and got to work. It wasn't a great lock. It took mere seconds to pick. We were in.

We did a quick tour of the three-bedroom home. I pegged it at around fifteen hundred square feet. The floor plan was simple—the front door opened into a living room. To the left was a dining room, and straight ahead, a hall. The dining room passed through to the kitchen, which also circled back to the hall that led to three bedrooms and a single bath.

"I'll start with the kitchen," I said. "Are you monitoring the car?"

"They're almost there. As soon as they park at the church, I'll set an alarm for when the car moves again. I'll get the master bedroom."

I stepped into the kitchen and started with the small built-in desk. Two framed photos sat near the right corner, one of the family soon after the little girl was born. The new parents beamed with joy while the little boy touched his sister's arm, seemed to inspect her. It was a cute picture, taken before the effects of whatever was wrong with Robert Williams had ravaged his body. They'd been a happy family.

The other photo was in a painted wooden frame with the word "Friends" engraved across the bottom. Emma and three other women of roughly the same age huddled together around a bar-top table with a brick wall in the background. I picked up the photo and examined it closer. It had been taken at the Blind Tiger, in the middle courtyard, next to the outside bar.

I used my iPhone to capture images of both framed photos, then opened the top center drawer. Piles of paperwork were stuffed inside. Much of it was medical bills, explanation of benefits forms, and doctor's instructions for Robert Williams on letterhead from the Hollings Cancer Center.

Then there were the other bills, late notices, and collection letters. This family had all kinds of trouble. I took a deep breath and moved on to the top of a stack of three drawers down the right side of the desk.

Unlike the middle drawer, the top-right drawer was well organized. It held nothing but office supplies. I moved on to the next drawer. Here was a mountain of receipts waiting for someone to have time to organize them. It looked as if they'd just been opening the drawer and tossing things in. They'd be hard pressed to notice if this drawer had been disturbed.

For the next hour, I dug through the pile, looking for anything with the date of August 13, the night Phillip Drayton was killed. Someone must've been looking for something else because the slips were all out of order. I'd almost given the project up for a fool's errand when I found it.

A receipt for $10.82 for one glass of wine from The Blind Tiger on August 13.

The sales receipt was time stamped at 9:15:34 p.m.

The name in the credit purchase section was Williams/Emma.

I laid it on the desk and snapped a picture.

One glass of wine didn't typically make me tipsy, but on an empty stomach, maybe. Had Emma been impaired?

I put the receipt back in the drawer, stirred the contents a bit, and closed the drawer. Then I searched the cabinets. Was Emma a drinker? She'd had no record of DUIs, but maybe recent events had turned her to the bottle. There was a single, half empty bottle of Pinot Grigio in the refrigerator.

Nate came into the kitchen. "Nothing of any relevance in the bedroom. Lots of evidence someone very sick lives here." He stopped, looked at me. "What's wrong?"

I showed him the photo of the receipt from The Blind Tiger.

"That can't be a coincidence." He drew a long breath. His face wore a resigned expression. "You ready to get out of here?"

"Almost." I turned to the refrigerator. Its white surface was covered with kid art attached with colorful magnets. The lower section had a set of ABC magnets for the kids to play with. In the center was a family calendar covered with doctor's appointments and play dates.

The block for August 13 had "Karen's Birthday" written in blue Sharpie.

I took a photo of the calendar.

Silently, we did a walk-through to make sure we'd left no trace, then we made our way out.

Nate started the car. "We still haven't proven anything. But the receipt along with Emma suddenly stalking Poppy, a stranger, certainly moves her up the suspect list."

"It could still be Sutton," I said. "But it surely could be Emma. I hope like hell it's not. But I cannot come up with another explanation that accounts for her behavior and that receipt. The SUV could be registered to the business—maybe she gets a corporate car."

With the iPad, I searched our subscription database for Ridgetech, the company Emma worked for.

"There are no cars registered to the company at all," I said.

"If it's Emma," said Nate, "either someone she knows owns a white SUV, or she rented one. Could've had car trouble, an older car like hers."

"That makes sense."

We did a grid search of the surrounding blocks but came up empty.

I pulled up the Bethel United Methodist Church website to see where they recommended visitors park. We checked behind the church, the two College of Charleston lots off Pitt Street across from the church, and J. Henry Stuhr's lot, which was also open for church parking on Sunday morning.

We found no white SUVs with bush bars.

"It's possible someone took that bar off," said Nate.

"But the only reason they'd do that is if Emma told them what happened." I shook my head. "If it was her—and I still think Ryan Sutton is an excellent candidate as well—she didn't tell a soul. She has too much at stake. If she did this, we're going to have to pry it out of her."

# TWENTY-THREE

At 9:30 Monday morning, Nate and I parked outside the bookshop.

"You really think they'll show?" Nate gave me a skeptical look.

"The last time there was drama and one of them—Sofia—wanted to talk, she left a bookmark, and Jacynthe met her at the graveyard because Tess was tied up at the store. Saturday night, Ryan Sutton showed up at The Planter's Club, plus you know at least one of those ladies mentioned my visit to the second floor. The combination of those two things will make Sofia very nervous."

"What if they got together yesterday after all?" asked Nate. "The bookstore was open all afternoon."

"The bookshop didn't open until 11:00 a.m. yesterday. Tess and Jacynthe were at church in the morning. I'm betting they didn't."

"Do they go to that much trouble every single time they want to talk?"

"If we sit here, we'll find out," I said.

"Well, well." Nate nodded towards the bookstore. "Maybe we'll catch a break."

Sofia Sanchez's Carrera pulled to the curb across the street. She hopped out, looked both ways, jogged across the street and went inside the bookshop. Less than five minutes later she came out with a bag.

"I wonder what they do with all those books," said Nate.

"They don't buy one every time," I said. "They just have to leave a bookmark and then someone has to come by to see where it is. Jacynthe goes in a few times a week to guide a tour. But I guess they do accumulate them. Probably give them as gifts."

After Sofia had gone, I went inside to check the middle book on the display.

"Well?" asked Nate when I climbed back in the Explorer.

"Page eighty. The Lady in White. We're going back to the Unitarian Graveyard."

"Should we wait for someone to come pick up the message?"

"If you want to, we can, but the last time they had a meeting, it was right around eleven o'clock. I'm still not sure about this." I gave him a worried look. "I say we confront them, tell them who we are and what we know and go from there."

"We've been through this. We have to talk to whoever made that second 911 call—most likely Tess. She will not be inclined to be forthcoming. These women have way too much to lose. The photos you took of Anne Frances and the other woman, they might do the trick by themselves—get Tess, Sofia, and Jacynthe to talk. But once we tell them who we are, we won't ever have this opportunity again. We lose our chance to get real leverage. We can only play this card once."

"All right then. Let's go park, get ourselves in place. Be there before them."

"That works." Nate started the car.


We found the Whitridge family plot and picked a spot not too far away, so they could hear us and we could hear them. But we picked it strategically so that it wasn't along one of the main pathways in. We didn't want any one of them to see us before the other one or two of them arrived. Then, we crouched behind a cluster of bushes. Between the tree limbs draped with Spanish moss, the gravestones, and all the vines, it was a perfect place to eavesdrop.

"I've never seen a graveyard like this," said Nate.

"I've never seen another like it."

We heard footsteps, looked at each other, drew a long breath and let it out slowly. I smiled as I watched him doing the exact same thing I did.

After a moment, a woman said, "Sofia? Honey, what's wrong?" Jacynthe.

Sofia let loose a long, animated string of Spanish.

"English." Jacynthe's voice was gentle, but urgent. "Please."

"I'm sorry," said Sofia. "I'm too tired to speak English. I didn't sleep at all the past two nights. I'll tell you all about it when Tess gets here. I don't want to have to tell it twice."

"You're pacing," said Jacynthe. "This must be baaaad."

"Here's Tess," said Sofia.

"Good morning ladies," said Tess.

I nodded at Nate. He closed his eyes, steeled himself. What he was about to do went against every fiber of his being.

We stood but were still screened from the women by moss-draped trees and tall bushes.

Nate raised his voice. "Suzanne, I told you what would happen if you left the house without permission again, didn't I?"

"But Tommy, I—"

"Shut up. Shut up, do you hear me? Get your ass to the car right now. I will deal with you at home."

"No, please, Tommy—"

"You're just making it worse."

"No, I'm not going anywhere with you." I stepped away.

He grabbed my arm, twisted it behind my back. "You wanna bet?"

*"Ow, Tommy, you're hurting me."*

"Release her immediately." Tess stepped in front of Nate.

"Mind your own business, old lady. Walk, Suzanne. *Now.*"

There was yelling in Spanish. Sofia. Where was she?

Nate jerked, let go of me, and fell.

I spun around.

Sofia had tased him.

"*You*," she said. "What were you doing upstairs at my house Saturday night?"

Nate lay on the ground, jerking.

"Oh my Lord." I knelt beside him, sent up fervent prayers.

Sofia talked faster, her accent thicker. "This woman snuck upstairs while security was distracted. She may have been working with another man who they hauled out. It was on the security footage."

Jacynthe stood over Nate with a can of pepper spray.

"*No*," I said. "Leave him alone. Give me that." I stood, snatched the pepper spray from Jacynthe's hands.

Jacynthe looked at me. "Honey, are you sure? That Taser's gonna wear off in a minute. You need a good head start."

"We'll take you someplace safe, if you like." Tess held a puncture pen like a killer in a horror film holds a butcher knife.

I knelt back down, rubbed Nate's arm. "*No one* do anything else to him. I am very serious."

He groaned.

"I knew this was a bad idea," I said.

"Honey, now, I know this is hard for you," said Jacynthe. "But that man is just going to keep on hurting you if you let him."

"The thing is," I said. "As soon as he recovers, we really need to go somewhere and talk privately."

"I'm afraid I don't understand you," said Tess.

I looked at Sofia. "You just tased my partner."

"He was hurting you," she said. "We saved you from him, sneaky ungrateful woman."

I turned to Jacynthe. "You had the pepper spray."

"And you," I looked over my shoulder to Tess, "have a tactical pen. Those are the exact weapons used on Phillip Drayton just before he was hit by a car. We need to know exactly what happened to him. We're your investigative team, Mrs. Hathaway."

She looked at me for a long moment, then at Nate. "Well, you're apparently very dedicated to your work."

# TWENTY-FOUR

"Are you sure you're quite all right?" asked Tess. We were seated in her living room, Nate and me on the sofa, Sofia and Jacynthe in club chairs to our left, and Tess in a wing-back to our right. By Tess's chair, Zelda the suspected Goldendoodle lolled on a green velvet cushion with her name embroidered on it and watched us all. Out the front window we could see White Point Garden. A young woman had brought in iced tea, a tray of assorted sandwiches, and pastries.

All of us had fussed over Nate for the past twenty minutes. I sat with my hand on his leg.

"Yes ma'am," said Nate. "I'm fine."

"I really am sorry." Sofia winced, bit her lip.

"No, please don't be," I said. "We're sorry we had to trick you. But to be honest, we didn't have a choice. The only way we can help Poppy Oliver, which is what we were hired to do, is to find the vehicle that hit Phillip Drayton and the person who was driving it. Anything short of that and I'm afraid the police are going to figure Poppy must've done it. There's a dent in her car, you see."

Tess sighed, looked out the window for a moment. "Yes, I know. This is all my fault. I had hoped to protect Zelda's Safe House, you see. We do a tremendous amount of good. And my friends, of course."

She seemed sincere. I prayed that she was, that she was nothing at all like her sister and protecting Poppy had been at the top of her agenda all along.

"We understand that, truly," I said. "And Mrs. Hathaway, we work for you. You hired us through your attorney. We're here to help. Please let us."

"Well, then," said Tess. "Perhaps we should each tell our part of the story. Jacynthe, would you start?"

Jacynthe nodded, moistened her lips. "Anne Frances Drayton started coming into the emergency room in December of 2010. Every few months. She had injuries consistent with abuse and told stories consistent with wives covering it up. I tried to get her to talk to a social worker, but she wouldn't do it. I did the only thing I could. I told her if she decided she wanted help, she should leave a message at the bookstore. I told her how."

Sofia said, "On the day it happened, she left a bookmark on page forty-five. *The Gentleman Ghost*. That address is 20 South Battery. That's two houses down from here."

"How did you know she left the bookmark?" I asked. "After years of trying to help her?"

"I watched her do it," said Jacynthe. "I was in the store for a tour."

"Do they know what you're doing?" asked Nate. "The folks who own the bookshop, the people who work there?"

"Absolutely not," said Tess. "Polly is my dear friend. I'm in and out of the store several times a week to talk to her about one thing or another. We go to lunch regularly. Between my visits, which don't raise eyebrows, and Jacynthe's, who is a tour guide, and Sofia occasionally picking up a book for a friend, well, we stay under their radar, as it were."

"Okay," I said, "Anne Frances Drayton was supposed to be at 20 South Battery at 2:00 p.m.?"

"That's right," said Tess. "All our pickups are at 2:00 p.m., and if the three of us meet, it's always 11:00 a.m., and it's always the Unitarian Graveyard. It keeps things simple."

"Did someone pick her up?" I asked.

"No," said Sofia. "I came to get her, but she didn't show up. Naturally, we were worried."

"Usually that means the husband caught his wife leaving." Jacynthe looked at her lap. "That's ended real bad twice. We couldn't take that chance."

"What did you do?" asked Nate.

"We met here as soon as we could all come," said Tess. "Jacynthe had to stay late—there were several accidents due to the weather. It was around nine o'clock. We went to check on Anne Frances."

"We could not just ring the doorbell and ask the man if he'd killed his wife," said Sofia.

"We umm, well, I—I did it." Jacynthe looked up like she was talking to The Lord. "I didn't mean any harm. I was trying to protect Mrs. Drayton—all these women. Us too. Our work can get dangerous."

"What did you do?" I asked gently.

"I ordered us protection," said Jacynthe. "The Tasers, the tactical pens, the pepper spray. But the online store also had listening devices. I ordered us these ink pens. You can hear what people are saying. You put the little thingamajig in your ear?"

Hell's bells. "We know what you mean. What did you do with the pen?"

"I slid it in the mail slot," said Jacynthe. "And then I stood on the porch and listened. Sofia and Tess went around back. I had the Taser that night."

"We walked around to the doors that open to the pool deck," said Sofia.

Jacynthe continued. "Anne Frances was there—thank the Good Lord she wasn't dead. But he was yelling at her, just awful. She was crying. It was an awful ruckus. I couldn't make out exactly what they were saying. I should get my money back on those pens. The sound is horrible. Anyway, like I told you, we've had this go real bad a couple times. I tried the front door. It was unlocked. I went in, snuck up behind him. When he grabbed her by the arm I tased him."

"Did Mrs. Drayton see you sneaking up behind him?" I asked.

"No," said Jacynthe. "She was sitting on the sofa, crying. She had her head in her hands. He was standing over her. Then he just reached down and grabbed her."

"Then what happened?" I asked.

"Well, he was on the floor," said Jacynthe. "She was in shock, which was to be expected. She hollered at me, 'What did you do to him?'"

"I told her he'd be fine in a minute and let Sofia and Tess in the back door."

"When we came in, Anne Frances was kneeling by her husband," said Tess. "She must have moved while Jacynthe had her back turned, when she opened the door. Anne Frances was distraught."

Jacynthe said, "I didn't tase him good enough, I guess. It was my first time. He started to come around. I grabbed Anne Frances and pulled her away—"

"You tackled her," said Sofia.

"Well, okay then," said Jacynthe. "Maybe I did tackle her. But it was for her own protection."

"Sofia hit him with the pepper spray," said Tess. "He reached out—he was flailing, grabbing at us. I defended myself with that tactical pen. I stabbed him in the arm. It was barely more than a scratch."

"Finally, I tased him good," said Jacynthe. "He quieted right down."

"What was Mrs. Drayton doing all this time?" I asked.

"She was screaming at us to leave him alone," said Sofia. "Like the way you were in the graveyard this afternoon."

"Well, like I said, the poor thing was in shock at first," said

Jacynthe.

Tess said, "When we told her to come with us, we'd keep her safe, she just started shaking her head, said she couldn't leave him. She wanted Jacynthe to make sure he was okay. She seemed very disoriented, which was not all that surprising given the circumstances."

Sofia said, "We wanted to make sure she had extra time to leave if she needed it, so we started to tie him up before we left."

"And I guess he must've been faking how out of it he was," said Jacynthe, "because all of a sudden, he jumped up, pulled the ropes off, and ran out of the house. We didn't know what he was going to do."

"I followed him," said Sofia.

Jacynthe said, "Tess and I started cleaning up. We grabbed a trash bag and threw everything in it. Even the towels we mopped up the floor with. Anne Frances jumped right in and helped."

"Right," said Sofia. "I followed Mr. Drayton. He went out the back door, through the gate to the driveway. I had one hand on the gate when he ran right out into the street. I don't know if he couldn't see good because of the pepper spray or if he was just running away and didn't look. Somebody turned the corner off of Murray. It was raining so hard, there was no way they could've stopped. It was an accident. They ran right into him. This poor woman got out of the car. She was crying and screaming. I don't know if she didn't have a phone or what, but she searched his pants and found his. She called for help. And then got back into her SUV and left. Drove around Mr. Drayton. I knew help was on the way, but I thought maybe Jacynthe could help in the meantime. So I ran straight back inside."

"And I immediately called 911, to be certain help was on the way," said Tess. "Then I told Jacynthe and Sofia we needed to leave. Jacynthe wanted to help Mr. Drayton. But I knew her family would suffer if she were found at the scene. It was my decision. We all left out the side door. And then we saw poor Poppy turn the corner onto Lenwood."

"The only one of you who saw the SUV hit Phillip was Sofia?" asked Nate.

"That's right," said Sofia. "But the thing of it is, it was an accident. No question about it."

"Then why would she leave the scene?" I said.

"I don't know," said Sofia, "Maybe panic? She seemed concerned. She called for help."

"Close your eyes, concentrate," said Nate. "Tell us about the SUV."

"It was white, and big," said Sofia. "Boxy. Not like a...a...crossover or anything like that. Not long like a Suburban."

"Could it have been a van?" I asked. Maybe Ryan had another female accomplice.

Sofia's forehead winkled. "No. It definitely wasn't a van."

"If you looked at some photos, do you think you'd recognize it?" I asked.

Sofia shook her head. "No, I've tried. It was just raining so hard."

"Anything else you can think of?" Nate asked.

Sofia's eyes popped open. "It had those bars on the front."

"Like bush bars?" I asked.

"Like you see on cars that go on safari," said Sofia.

"What about the back of it," asked Nate. "When it was driving away? Anything?"

She shook her head slowly.

"What can you tell us about the woman?" I asked.

"Not much," said Sofia. "She had on a rain coat with a hood—tan. But the hood came down. She had really long, straight blonde hair."

I pulled out my phone and navigated to Emma's photo. "Is this her?"

Sofia scrutinized the photo. "It could be. The hair is right. But I can't say for sure. I didn't see her well enough. I'm sorry."

Nate and I exchanged a look.

"Who is it?" asked Tess.

"Back to Mrs. Drayton," I said. "Did she ever specifically tell you that her husband abused her?"

It was the ladies turn to exchange a look.

"No," said Jacynthe.

"Why did she tell you she wanted to be picked up on Thursday?" I asked.

"She said an old boyfriend was bothering her," said Sofia. "Turned up after her husband died. She was afraid of him, waiting for him to leave town."

I said, "You obviously spoke with her Saturday evening. I'm guessing your security staff told you about her old boyfriend showing up after they carted him out. But you also knew I'd been there—knew to pull up the security video. Anne Frances had to have told you that. Did she mention how he found her at your house?"

Sofia said, "One of our security guards searched her purse. There was a tracking device disguised as a USB drive."

"Had he ever been there before? With her?" I asked.

"No," said Sofia.

"How did he get inside?" Nate asked. "Your security is top notch. And did she have any idea how he knew how to dress, what kind of place it was?"

Sofia muttered something in Spanish that might've been curse words. "The Draytons are members. Somehow the ex-boyfriend got the phone number and access code. He called for a pickup as a guest of Phillip Drayton. Our system didn't have him marked as deceased. I was upstairs with our guests for most of the evening." She gave me an accusatory look. "He looked like he fit in. Until he tried to get upstairs, anyway."

"Did you ask Anne Frances how he knew enough to pull that off?" I asked.

"She said he must've gone through her husband's desk," said Sofia. "She was afraid the ex-boyfriend might break in—that was one of the reasons she came to us. He could've found Phillip's membership credentials. We do have a brochure with amenities. It includes the dress code."

"Is she still at your place?" I asked.

"Yes, but we've briefed security. The ex-boyfriend won't get back on the property."

Tess said, "We are all extremely aware that our actions, however well-intended, contributed to Phillip Drayton's death. I won't have you think we take that lightly."

"Then why didn't you just come forward—go to the police and tell them what happened?" I asked. "Or stay at the scene to begin with?"

Tess drew her shoulders back. "Our actions were in defense of a poor woman who had been repeatedly beaten by that man. A woman who asked for our help. I'm not suggesting he deserved the death penalty, nor that his punishment was ours to decide at all. We are not some wild gang bent on vigilante justice. We help women in desperate situations every day. But we don't go around killing people. That said, if Phillip Drayton hadn't repeatedly sent his wife to the emergency room, none of this would've happened, would it? Our going to jail won't bring Phillip back. What it will do, however, is destroy a network that helps countless other women and children who are in harm's way, some of whom, without our help, would likewise end up dead. It's a matter of weighing the possible outcomes, both good and bad. Think what you will."

Tears streamed down Jacynthe's face. "I have peace with whatever happens."

For her part, Sofia kept quiet.

"We'll need to give Fraser a full report," I said. As much as I would've liked to, I could not call Sonny and give him what we'd found. I had no idea what sort of deal Fraser might be able to make on their behalf, but at least he would be able to let Sonny know there were witnesses and that Poppy was innocent. How much had Tess told him to begin with?

"Yes, dear," said Tess. "Do that straightaway. He'll know what to do for our Poppy."

"But you could have told him virtually everything we know yourself to begin with." I might have sounded just the tiniest bit cranky.

"That word," said Tess. "Virtually. That word covers a great deal, doesn't it, my dear? I imagine you have much more to tell Fraser than just our part in this."

She was right. We knew who'd very likely been driving the SUV. We knew who'd searched his pockets, found his phone, and made the near-hysterical 911 call. We knew who had hit then run.

"If you'll indulge me," said Nate, "I am curious. How did you ladies meet—come to be working together?"

"Jacynthe and Sofia give generously of their time to the charity I founded, Zelda's Safe House." The regal tone was back in Tess's voice.

"It's a noble charity," said Nate. "But there are many worthy causes. How did you choose this one to devote your life's work to?"

Tess straightened her spine a little further, which I would've thought impossible.

Sofia said, "My sister was killed by her husband. He beat her for twelve years before he put her in the ground. He escaped prosecution. I have no idea where he is, or I would kill him myself. I channel that passion into helping others."

"And your husband, Hugh?" I asked.

Sofia looked outraged. "Hugh is in Honduras. What? You think he beat me and I killed him? Let me tell you this much. If he ever laid a hand on me, I would. He knew better. Hugh and I have a business arrangement that is none of *your* business. But if you want to talk to him, I will FaceTime him for you right now. I assure you he is fine. Probably drunk, but fine."

"Jacynthe?" I said gently.

"I don't mind telling you I was abused for years. My husband died of a heart attack. It took his death to set me free from a life that I wouldn't wish on anyone. I devote myself to helping others in the same situation."

Nate and I looked at Tess.

"Very well," she said. "Perhaps it should be discussed more openly. Domestic abuse is not the exclusive problem of any demographic. I was a battered wife myself. It's not something I talk about. Perhaps I should reconsider that."

"Well," Nate said, "I'm sure Fraser will be in touch soon to let you know what happens next.

They all got real quiet, no doubt considering the possibilities.

I got all their cell phone numbers before we left, just in case.

We dropped in on Fraser, something he was unaccustomed to. Nevertheless, Mercedes showed us right in.

"Miz Talbot, Mr. Andrews. Have a seat. What do you have for me?"

We slid into our customary chairs.

I said, "I'll get you a written report, but we wanted you to know immediately that there were witnesses to the accident. Poppy was not the driver of the vehicle that hit Phillip Drayton."

We took turns talking, told him everything we knew.

"Let me make sure I understand you correctly," said Fraser. "Are you telling me that Tess Hathaway is the woman who made that second 911 call?" His face was contorted. "That *she* stabbed Phillip Drayton in the hand with some pen?"

"Yes," said Nate.

Fraser squinted, sat back in his chair, and looked up at the ceiling.

"I will speak to Detective Ravenel immediately," he said. "I remind you both that you are not free to do so."

"We're aware," I said. "But we need your assurance that Poppy Oliver has nothing else to worry about."

"You have my word," he said. "Now. Finish the job. Find me that white SUV with a bush bar and tie it to the woman who was driving it."

I was afraid he was going to say that. He'd need to hold all the cards he could get his hands on for the game he was about to play.

# TWENTY-FIVE

We needed to be in Charleston first thing the next morning, so we stayed the night. With no business need to be at the Belmond, we checked in to the Hampton Inn on Meeting Street. Except for a few bites at Tess's house, neither of us had eaten since breakfast. We grabbed an early dinner at Closed for Business, then settled into the hotel room to plan the next day.

"Rental cars leave paperwork," I said. "I didn't come across any of that in the desk at the Williams house. She most likely borrowed a car from someone she knows."

"That makes sense," said Nate. "We should do another pass through the neighborhood. Timing is everything."

I did a quick search of Emma Williams's few Facebook friends. All of the women in the photo were there. One of them was Karen Rigsby, whose birthday had fallen on August 13. Everyone except Emma had posted photos from the party at The Blind Tiger, which had started before she arrived and lasted well after she left. None of them owned a white SUV, nor did any of Emma's other Facebook friends.

"We're going to have to do it the hard way," I said.

Tuesday morning we drove the streets of Wagener Terrace again. If a white SUV with a bush bar was there, it was parked in a garage. We pulled to the curb on Darlington near the Williams' home at 7:15. We'd barely been there ten minutes before Emma walked the children to a house diagonally across the street. A grandmotherly looking woman held the door for the kids. Emma kissed them goodbye, helped them inside, spoke to the woman briefly, then waved and dashed back to the house.

Moments later she came back out with her husband, standing by as he navigated the steps. She hovered while he climbed into the passenger side of the Honda, then hurried around to the driver's side and got in.

We followed her over to the Hollings Cancer Center at MUSC, where she pulled into an indented section of the curb on Johnathan Lucas Street under an overhang that seemed to be there for patient drop off. She climbed out, ran around the car, and helped her husband out and inside the building. We circled the block twice, then fell in behind her as she pulled away.

"She probably dropped him off and now she's going to park," said Nate.

But she circled the block, made a left on Calhoun, and followed it back up to Meeting.

"She's going to work," I said. "She dropped him off for an appointment, or treatment, or something, and she can't stay with him because she has to go to work or they don't have insurance." I swallowed hard, took a long, deep breath.

The Ridgetech offices were in the Bank of America building on the corner of Meeting Street and Hayne. The parking garage was immediately behind it, with the entrance on Hayne. We followed her into the garage and drove on past her as she parked, continuing up the ramp. I simultaneously hoped to find a white SUV with a bush bar and hoped not to find a white SUV with a bush bar.

And then we rounded a curve and a white Range Rover was right in front of us.

"I'll look." I climbed out of the car and walked around to the front of the Range Rover. Damnation. It had a bush bar. I took photos of it from every side, then climbed back into the Explorer.

Nate pulled into a parking place and I ran the tag.

"It belongs to Samuel Ridgeway," I said. "Damn, damn, double damn."

"I'm guessing it's his company," said Nate.

I navigated to the corporate website. "It is." I stared at Samuel Ridgeway's smiling face on the About page.

"That poor woman borrowed this car that night and then had the bad luck to hit a man who ran right out in front of her," I said. "She already had more on her shoulders than—I don't know how she walks upright."

"It won't be hard to prove," said Nate. "If Sonny mentions to Samuel Ridgeway that he thinks his Range Rover was involved in an accident that resulted in a death, the first thing he's going to do is tell him Emma was driving it that night," said Nate.

"Her going to jail and leaving her sick husband with no insurance and those kids with only him to take care of them—if he can even do such a thing—is not going to bring Phillip Drayton back." Tears rolled down my cheeks. "And what happens to them if he dies? I haven't seen family swarming around them, helping. Do they even have living grandparents? Aunts? Uncles? I didn't look for any of that."

Nate reached out, brushed my hair back from my face. "We were hired to do a job. This one sucks on all sides."

"She has to be the sole support of that family," I said. "That has to be why she drove away. She couldn't risk being charged."

Colleen appeared in a burst of white light. She sat in the backseat, poked her head between the seats, and touched my arm. "Be strong."

"Why did you get us involved in this?" I asked. "There's no justice to be had here. A man is dead—he was an abusive husband, but he didn't deserve to die. Three women, who do nothing but good, are in big trouble. And then there's Emma, who—Colleen, this hurts my heart."

"It hurts mine too," she said. "But remember, I can see alternate scenarios. Better for people who are responsible in some way to pay for Phillip Drayton's death than someone as innocent as Poppy. So much is going on that we can't know. Too many intersecting stories are unfolding simultaneously for mere mortals—or mere guardian spirits—to comprehend the greater good. We have to have faith in grace."

"And we need to talk to Fraser again," said Nate.

Hope rose in my chest. "He's a good attorney."

"The best," said Nate.

"Faith and the best attorney." I nodded.

"There's my girl," said Nate.

"Sorry, but I have to go." Colleen faded out.

"I'm thinking Tess Hathaway ought to step up for Emma Williams," I said.

Nate shrugged. "Can't hurt to ask."

I dialed Tess. "We've found the blonde driver and the SUV." I explained Emma's situation. "I was hoping—"

"Say no more, my dear," said Tess. "That poor girl. Her bad luck was initiated by ours. This just keeps getting worse, doesn't it?"

"Yes ma'am," I said. "It does indeed."

"There are a great many problems in this life that money cannot solve. And then there are those that it can mitigate. Offer her my assistance, won't you? And Fraser's as well."

"I will," I said.

I called Fraser to let him know we'd found the car and communicate my conversation with Tess.

"I have a three o'clock open," he said. "Tell Mrs. Williams to be here then. Please also advise her to be here in the morning at eleven o'clock. Mrs. Hathaway and her cohorts will be here as well. After we discuss more pressing matters, I am told that these ladies have elaborate plans to assist the Williams family in their time of need."

\*   \*   \*

Ridgetech's offices were on the second floor of the Bank of America building. Nate waited in the parking garage and I went inside and loitered in the lobby until Emma came out at a few minutes past twelve carrying an insulated lunch bag. I followed her downstairs and out the front door and onto the Meeting Street sidewalk.

"Looks like she's having her lunch outside." I wore an earwig, with a thin transmitter coil under my shirt which allowed me to communicate with Nate without holding my phone to my ear, and also allowed him to record any conversation I might have. Though it wouldn't be admissible in court, it might serve another purpose. And there was no way Emma would consent for me to record the conversation I planned to have with her, thereby making it admissible.

She went left on Meeting Street, then made another left onto North Market. I followed her on foot to Concord Street where she turned right. For a moment I wondered if she were headed to Buxton Books. But she walked past it, continuing on to the fountain at the north entrance of Waterfront Park. She smiled at the children frolicking under the streams of water as she climbed the steps.

She crossed the slate walkway and headed out onto the pier. Here, three shelters shaded tables and porch swings from the midday August sun. She walked all the way to the end and settled onto the front swing, facing out across the Cooper River. Here she pulled out a bottle of water and a sandwich.

There would never be a good time for what I had to do. I approached the swing. "Mind if I join you?"

She looked startled, glanced around, probably asking herself if there weren't an empty swing somewhere. Finally, she said, "Sure," and slid over.

"My name is Liz Talbot."

"Emma Williams."

"I know who you are," I said.

The bottle of water stopped partway to her mouth.

"I know what happened to Phillip Drayton."

She hopped up, ready to dart back down the pier.

"Please," I said. "If there's any way I can help you, anyway at all, I will. Please trust that. But I can't let an innocent woman go to jail." Poppy was off the hook, but Emma didn't know that. I needed her to tell me everything.

She stopped, looked at me, eyes large. "The mail carrier?" It came out as a wail. Then she realized she'd spoken, drew back her head, as if trying to suck the words back in.

"Yes," I said. "Her name is Poppy Oliver. I know you've been watching her. Please sit down."

"I have to go back to work. I think you have me confused with someone else. I don't know anyone by that name."

"Please sit down and talk to me," I said.

She took three long strides back down the pier.

"There was a witness who can identify you," I called.

She froze in mid-stride, turned slowly.

"What do you have to do with this?" Her voice trembled.

"I'm a private investigator."

Perhaps somewhat relieved that I couldn't arrest her on the spot, she walked back over, sat back down on the swing. "What do you want?"

"What I want is for none of this to have happened. I'm betting we share that wish. What I *need* is to give my client a complete and accurate report as to exactly what did happen. He is an attorney. A very, very good one."

"I can't afford any kind of attorney." She stared at the boards on the pier. "Much less a good one."

"I know, but there are some extenuating circumstances to this situation. If you will tell your story, an attorney will be provided for you. Very likely other help as well."

She stared at me. "What circumstances?"

"You first," I said. "Start with why you were driving Samuel Ridgeway's Range Rover."

She wrapped her arms tightly around her mid-section, rocked back and forth.

"You cannot let Poppy Oliver go to jail," I said. "You don't strike me as the kind of person who could live with that."

She shook her head. Tears rolled down her face. "I would never have let that happen."

"Talk to me. Tell me about the Range Rover."

"My car wouldn't start," she said. "After work that Thursday. Sam lives a few blocks away. He knows...he knows my situation. The weather was so bad. I needed to pick up the kids. He insisted I take his car. He called someone to come get mine and fix it."

"So you went home," I said.

"Yes. I picked up the kids, made dinner, got them to bed. But, it was my best friend Karen's birthday. I haven't been out with my friends in years. And I wouldn't have gone that night. But I missed her last two birthdays. We always celebrate at The Blind Tiger. Robert wanted me to go—I could tell it was important to him. He wanted me to do something fun. So, I went. Just for one drink."

"And you left a little after nine."

"Yes. I couldn't find a parking space when I got there. A friend of mine has a business across Broad, with a small lot in back. Off Elliott Street. I parked there. But when I came out, the Church Street end of Elliott was blocked. There was a disabled vehicle. Its flashers were on. I had to go the wrong way just as far as Bedons Alley. When I got to Tradd Street, I had to go left, and then I was back to East Bay."

I waited for her to continue.

"It was a crazy night—so much water in the streets. Accidents. I shouldn't have gone out. I should never, ever, ever have taken that risk." She rocked back and forth.

I waited.

Finally, she made a little hitching sound, then continued. "There was a police car. It had someone stopped on East Bay, a little ways up towards Broad. I'd only had one glass of wine. I wasn't even a little bit tipsy. But I was paranoid. I turned right and followed East Bay. I was going to just go around the peninsula, follow Murray, make my way to Lockwood, then get on the Crosstown and head home.

"On Murray, just before Lenwood, I saw blue lights in my rearview."

"You were pulled over?" I scrunched up my face.

"No," she said. "I thought I was being pulled over. I turned onto Lenwood. I thought it would be better to stop there. Murray is busier, and there was so much water. But then the spots at the curb on Lenwood were all taken. I sped up. I was looking for a place to park. I couldn't believe it when the police car accelerated behind me, went on past me down Murray. And then, Mr. Drayton ran out into the street right in front of me so fast—there was no time to stop." She dissolved into tears, keening, rocking back and forth.

I gave her a minute. "What happened next?"

"I got out of the car. I tried to help him. He was unconscious—maybe he was already dead. You have to understand. My husband has Non-Hodgkin's Lymphoma. We have two children. Without my paycheck, my insurance, my family would be on the streets. Literally."

"I understand." What would I have done in her place? If Nate were sick, and those two children in my dream were real?

"I couldn't call with my phone. It was an *accident*. But I'd had one glass of wine. One. Glass. But I couldn't run the risk of my blood alcohol testing above the limit. I was driving my boss's car. I found Mr. Drayton's phone in his pocket. I called for help. And then I left."

"What did you do with his phone?"

"I turned it off right after I called. Later, I pounded it to smithereens with a hammer and put it in the trash." She looked up at me. "You don't know what you'll do to protect your family. Nobody knows. Until they have to make that decision. Until it's their family or someone else's."

I knew she was right.

She shook her head rapidly. "I had no way to know someone else would pull up behind me, get caught up in this. I never would've let an innocent party go to jail. When I heard the letter carrier was at the scene, I figured they'd know she was a witness, not the person who'd hit him. I wanted to make sure she wasn't in trouble, but I couldn't just call her up. So I checked on her a few times, to make sure she was still on her route."

"Did you know Phillip Drayton? His wife?"

She shook her head. "No. I've never met either of them."

"Then why would you risk going to the funeral?" I asked.

Her eyes grew and she raised her hands to the sides of her face, as if she were gripping something inches from her head. In a loud whisper she said, "Because I killed that man. He's dead because of me."

She bent over double, wracked with sobs.

I put my arms around her, comforted her as best I could.

After a few moments, through a swollen throat, she said, "You know I could go to jail for twenty-five years? I looked it up. My husband will be dead and my children grown when I get out."

"Listen, that is the absolute worst-case scenario if you are charged with leaving the scene of an accident involving a death," I said. "Let's take this one step at a time, not get too far down the road worrying about things that might never happen. I'm not an attorney. But given that there are witnesses to the fact that it was an unavoidable accident, I seriously doubt you're looking at a worst-case scenario. Also, you called for help. I would imagine that will factor in your favor. There are many factors that will be considered.

Honestly, I think the outlook may be much brighter than you think." I prayed hard that was the case. Surely this woman would not be held more responsible than the ones who'd sent Phillip Drayton running blindly into the street. Emma's fate would be tied to theirs no doubt. Tess had money and a damn good lawyer. I had to believe Fraser could keep them all out of jail. They might be doing community service for a great many years. But these women had hearts for community service anyway.

She said, "What happens now? I am begging you for mercy. Not for me—for my family. Please."

"As someone often in need of grace, I tend to offer it when I can with both hands. But in this instance, grace is not mine to give. As far as the justice system is concerned, the best I can offer is this." I pulled out Fraser's card. "This is your attorney. His office is on Broad Street. He's the best. You have an appointment with him at three today. Can you make that?"

She nodded.

"Good. You need to tell him exactly what you told me. Then tomorrow morning, there's another meeting at eleven in his office. You'll meet a few more ladies who can maybe help you with some practical matters. I may be wrong, but I would bet the worst of this is behind you. At least you don't have to lie awake at night and wonder when this is all coming down around you."

# TWENTY-SIX

After dinner that evening, we took our wine onto the deck and watched and listened to the surf from the Adirondack chairs. This case had taken a lot out of me. I needed for the bad guy to pay. This case had too many grey areas to suit me.

"You okay, slugger?"

"I will be," I said.

My phone rang. Sofia.

"What now?" I sighed and answered the phone.

Sofia said, "When you asked me if Anne Frances was still at my house yesterday, she was. I thought you might want to know. A little while ago she asked one of the drivers to take her back to Cumberland garage to pick up her car. I guess her ex left town."

"Thanks for letting us know." I hung up and told Nate.

"We know Mrs. Drayton and her playmate didn't kill Phillip. I'm not sure this is our concern any longer."

"I'd really like to know what was going on with those two. We never did interview the widow. I think I'm ready now. How about you?"

He was quiet for a few minutes, then said, "Best to be thorough. We shouldn't close this case until we talk to her. She can corroborate what Tess and the others told us at least. Grab a jacket."

I looked at him, raised an eyebrow.

He nodded. "Best to be safe too."

We went inside and hustled upstairs where we both slid into

holsters for our weapons and topped them with blazers.

We pulled into Anne Frances Drayton's driveway right beside an alarm company truck.

"Hmm," I said. "*Maybe* she decided to up her security since she knows Ryan must've broken in to get ahold of what he needed to get himself inside The Planter's Club."

Nate winced. "It's after nine p.m. *Maybe* she paid them extra to stay late and finish. If they started an install this afternoon."

"Or maybe that's Ryan's missing white van with a magnetic sign on the side."

"That's by far the most likely scenario," said Nate. "We should record audio and video. Just in case."

I switched on my earwig. Nate set up the base unit between the seats. We both flipped on body cameras pinned to the lapels of our blazers.

We climbed out of the car and walked around to the front door.

A loud crash came from inside.

Nate and I exchanged a glance.

Another crash. A man bellowed with anger.

Nate pulled out his phone and called Sonny. "Get over to the Drayton house, now."

He ended the call. "He's on his way back from the detention center. Might be a few."

Something glass broke.

"You *bitch*." Ryan? Maybe.

Another loud crash.

"It sounds like they're throwing chairs at each other," I whispered.

"We need to go in," said Nate. "One of them could kill the other before Sonny gets here."

"I'll go around the side," I said.

"Be cautious."

"You too."

We both pulled our weapons out of our jacket holsters.

Nate eased open the front door.

I darted down the steps, around the side of the house, and in through the pool gate. I crouched low and approached the French doors, which stood ajar. Anne Frances and Ryan were in the large family room just inside. It looked like they'd broken all the furniture they could lift.

She held a gun on him. "Why couldn't you just leave me alone?"

"You kiddin' me? You owe me, bitch."

"For what? Why on earth would I owe you anything?"

"Because I let you live." He snarled the words.

"Hold up there," Nate said in my ear.

"Roger that," I said softly.

"You are a leech," said Anne Frances. "A despicable leech. I've kept you up for the last five years. Bought you a freakin' condo. And all I have to show for it is a stack of hospital bills. I am all done with that. You have hit me and you have violated me for the last time. Do you hear me, you bastard?"

He laughed.

"You should never have come here," said Anne Frances. "You should've stayed in California."

"You should be grateful to me. At any time, *any* time, I could've picked up the phone and called Lucious Carter and told him exactly where to find the girlfriend he's been pining after all these years."

"If Lucious is still alive, he's most likely rotting in jail," said Anne Frances.

"If you believed that," said Ryan, "you'd have sent me packing years ago. Enjoyed your new life with your perfect husband.

Lucious has moved up in the world, I hear."

"Phillip is dead because of you." She screamed the words, closed in on Ryan.

He held up his hands. "Hey, I didn't kill the man."

"You threatened to often enough," said Anne Frances. "And the only reason he ran out into that street—the only reason he's dead—is because you made those women think he was beating me."

*This* was the bad man who needed to rot to jail. He'd set the whole thing in motion. I edged closer to the door.

Nate must've sensed my urges. "Stay put."

"How am I responsible for what those women thought?" asked Ryan.

"What was it you said?" Anne Frances tilted her head. "If I told anyone you blackmailed me into meeting you once a week, where your idea of playtime was roughing me up while you drank the champagne I paid for, in a room I paid for, you'd kill Phillip and incriminate me. You'd already incriminated me if anything happened to him—the people at the hospital thought Phillip abused me. Hell, anyone I came in contact with thought that, which was why I was a prisoner in my own house. And Phillip...my poor husband thought I was in love with another man."

The pain in her voice hit me in the gut.

Ryan shrugged. "Seems more than fair. I let him live and you stay free."

"Free? I haven't been free since you showed up. I couldn't go to the police—after you told them who I was, well, they wouldn't be likely to believe anything else I said, would they?"

He snickered. "You don't make a very credible witness, Nikita."

Holy shit. Nikita? This was Nikki Parks?

"I wish you'd just killed me when you first showed up in Charleston."

"Now where would the fun be in that?" There was a taunt in

Ryan's voice. "It was so much more fun to play with you. And now, we can play all the time. We don't have to hide to do it. Hell, we can buy us a house on the beach."

"There is no we," Anne Frances spat. "There is no us. The only person I cared about in this world is dead and you no longer have anything to hold over me."

Ryan's face shifted, like maybe he realized he'd miscalculated something.

"Phillip was a good man," said Anne Frances. "God knows he was better than I deserved. And I wish I had never met him just because I'm the one that brought you into his life."

"See, Nikki?" said Ryan. "It really is all your fault."

"Bastard," she hissed.

"I am, now that you mention it. But at least I didn't steal a name off my dead best friend."

"I would have done anything to save Annie. But she was dead, and there was nothing I could do about it. I saved myself. Lucious wasn't looking for Annie. He killed her."

"He killed her because she wouldn't tell him where you were," said Ryan.

"Don't you think I know that?" She looked at him with loathing. "We were hours from being free, her, Sasha, and me. Free from the drugs. Free from Lucious. Free from that life. Who told him we were leaving, you slug?"

Ryan grinned an evil grin but kept quiet.

"That's what I thought," she said. "Now, what I want to know, and what you're going to tell me unless you want to die very slowly and very painfully, is who else knows I'm alive?"

"What's it worth to you?"

She laughed, with no mirth whatsoever. "That's not how this is going to go. I'm never giving you another dime. You have cost me more than you can possibly imagine. Slugs like you don't know anything about love. But what you don't get is that I have nothing left to lose that I care anything about. Sasha was the only person who knew who I was. I haven't seen or heard from her since I left Naples. A friend said she went to California. Where is she now?"

A sly grin slid up his face. "Now, see, there's something else you have to thank me for."

Nikki squinted at him. "What did you do to her?"

"I can't be held responsible for what junkies do." He raised his palms "Sasha died of an overdose before I left California."

"If you didn't kill her, you gave her the drugs."

He shrugged. "Either way, she's not going to be telling anyone that Nikita Parks from Chicago is alive and well in South Carolina, living under a fancified version of her dead friend's name."

"Then all I need to think about is how I'm going to kill you—how long I can enjoy that."

"We need to go in now," I murmured to Nate.

"Let me get in position," he said.

"So, what, you just gonna shoot me?" asked Ryan. "You don't have the nerve."

"Wanna bet? See this smile on my face? I'm savoring it. I'm going to leave you to rot in that van of yours somewhere near a swamp. And no one will miss you. Do you know how I know that?"

He just stared at her.

"I know that because you're invisible, just like me. People like you and me, not a soul cares about us. You killed the only three people who ever cared about me—first Annie, when you ratted us out to Lucious, then Sasha, then Phillip. No one has ever cared about you, and no one ever will."

"Put the gun down, Mrs. Drayton." Sonny stepped into my field of vision.

She looked at him, stunned.

Ryan took the opportunity to grab a gun from the floor in front of him and bolted from the room.

Sonny went after Ryan.

I went in through the French doors.

Nikki sank onto the sofa, laid the gun on the floor beside the destroyed coffee table.

I picked up her gun. "Let's get you outside."

Before we could move, Ryan backed into the room, both hands on the gun at his side. Nate walked in front of him, arms straight out, ready to fire. There were only a few feet between them.

"Put down the weapon," said Nate. "Now."

"I don't think I will." He raised the gun, pointed it at Nate's chest.

My ears buzzed. I couldn't breathe. I raised my weapon.

"Sutton, you have three guns on you," said Sonny.

Where was he?

He'd circled back through the dining room. "There is no way out of this except to put down your weapon."

"You're wrong about that." Ryan looked down his barrel at Nate.

I slowed my breathing, ready to fire.

A shot rang out.

Ryan crumpled to the floor.

Nate kicked his gun away from him.

"Are you all right?" I hollered.

"Fine," said Nate.

"Sonny?" I said.

"I shot him," Sonny said to me. Then he spoke into his phone, called for an ambulance and a crime scene unit. He hung up, looked at me, then Nate. "Everyone else all right?"

We all answered yes.

Sonny moved to Ryan, knelt down and took his pulse. He looked up at Nate, shook his head. "He's gone."

I sat down beside Nikki, pulled out one of Fraser's cards. "I don't know if you have a good attorney," I said. "But if not, I recommend you call this one before you answer any questions."

"Thank you," she said. "That's twice you've done me a good turn. How much did you overhear?"

"Enough," I said. "But there's something I don't understand."

"What's that?"

"The night of the accident, why didn't you tell the police the truth? At least about why Phillip ran into the street? All this time I thought he abused you, but he didn't. These women came into your home and attacked him. I know they were trying to help you, but..."

"I did want to protect them if I could. They didn't know what they were doing. They thought they were saving me. More than that, though, I knew if I started telling the truth, I would trip up and tell too much. It was all wrapped up together with Ryan. Everything was all mixed up together. You don't know what kind of people these are. Ryan...Lucious Carter. I've been hiding so long."

"That must've been hard for you. Knowing Phillip was outside in the street..." This part I couldn't wrap my head around. How and why had she come to the door and pretended she'd been asleep?

"I had no idea he was dead," she said. "Sofia said he was injured. I still thought then that I needed to protect him from Ryan. And that meant keeping everything a secret. All I ever tried to do, since Ryan Sutton arrived in Charleston, was protect Phillip from my past—a past he knew nothing about."

"The day of the accident...what was your plan? You signaled Tess and the others to pick you up. What were you going to do? Why didn't you show up at 20 South Battery?"

She drew a ragged breath. "I had to do something. I was losing Phillip. I couldn't tell him what was happening. He would've confronted Ryan. Phillip is unaccustomed to dealing with men like Ryan. Ryan would've killed him.

"Phillip was supposed to go to the Southhampton house for two weeks. He'd had it planned for months—tried to talk me into going with him. Some friends of ours were having a big party. I thought he'd be safe from Ryan for two weeks and I could make a move. Phillip was scheduled to fly out that afternoon. He kept saying it was just rain. They could fly in the rain. I left a message in the bookstore. But then the pilot called and told Phillip there was weather all up the coast and they couldn't fly."

"If he'd gone and Sofia had picked you up, then what?" I asked.

"Tess knows everyone here," said Anne Frances. "Once Phillip and I were both out of Ryan's reach, I was going to ask her to introduce me to her attorney, get his or her advice, and figure out a way to get Ryan out of our lives without destroying everything."

"Couldn't you just have made an appointment and gone to see the attorney?" I asked.

"Ryan watched me," she said. "It was a game for him. Sometimes he'd park across the street and watch the house. Saturday wasn't the first time he used a tracking device to find me. I was trapped. I needed a safe place to stay while I worked all this out."

"The card I gave you...Fraser Rutledge is Tess's attorney."

"I'll call him right now. Thank you again for your kindness."

"You're not invisible," I said. "You said your husband was a good man."

She nodded, crying. "He really was."

"He must've loved you very much," I said. "Hold onto that."

# TWENTY-SEVEN

It's amazing what my Daddy can pull off when he's motivated. He unveiled the family pool on Sunday afternoon. Instead of family dinner, we had more of a pool party. Mamma outdid herself with the spread of food in the screen porch. She was so relaxed that she just put all the food out and let everyone eat when they wanted.

She'd been twice more to the spa in Charleston while Daddy, Ray, Ponder, and the crew Daddy hired finished the yard. And it really did look fabulous. The pool had an abstract shape, more like a lagoon. A waterfall spilled into it from a pile of rocks. Beside the waterfall was a hot tub.

Mamma was in her new swimsuit, in a teak lounge chair with a striped cushion under a trellis. I was right beside her, Merry was on the other side of me. We all had drinks with little umbrellas in them.

"This is amazing," I said. "I may be over here every day to swim."

"You'll have to wear a suit." Mamma gave me the side-eye.

"Where's Blake?" I asked.

"He came by earlier," said Mamma. "He said he was going to pick up a friend, but he'd be back later."

"April, Calista, or Heather?" I asked.

"I'd bet on April." Mamma sighed. "That might be awkward with Tammy Sue here, but what am I to do?"

"I think it'll be Heather," said Daddy. "Pretty girl, umm umm."

Mamma rolled her eyes at him. "With one exception, you have

always enjoyed women a little on the trashy side."

"Mamma," I said. "Heather is not trashy. You have got to get over the fact that she had a previous relationship."

"With a much older man who stashed her in a bawdy house? Sadly, your brother seems to have inherited your father's taste in women."

"Present company excluded," said Merry.

"Well, naturally," said Mamma. "Doesn't Moon Unit have a cute swimsuit?"

"She does. She looks happy, too. I like her and Sonny together. I hope that works out."

Nate and Joe walked out through the screened porch.

"Carolyn," said Nate, "we put the grilled chicken and sausage on the table with the rest of the food."

"I declare," said Mamma. "It's so lovely having a man around who can grill." She eyed Daddy.

The screen door opened again and Blake walked out, followed by Poppy.

We all stared at him slack-jawed.

"Hey everybody," called Poppy.

Colleen popped in and bray-snorted exuberantly. When she stopped laughing, she said, "Do you remember the very first time you brought Nate home for dinner?"

*We were partners, not even dating, but yeah.*

"What else happened that night?" asked Colleen.

I searched my memory. *Chumley. Daddy brought Chumley home.*

"And when Merry first brought Joe home?" asked Colleen.

*Oh, my stars—the rat drama.*

"Yep," said Colleen. "And there were goats for Poppy."

I could not stop smiling.

Susan M. Boyer

Susan M. Boyer is the author of the *USA Today* bestselling Liz Talbot mystery series. Her debut novel, *Lowcountry Boil*, won the Agatha Award for Best First Novel, the Daphne du Maurier Award for Excellence in Mystery/Suspense, and garnered several other award nominations, including the Macavity. The third in the series, *Lowcountry Boneyard*, was a Southern Independent Booksellers Alliance (SIBA) Okra Pick, a Daphne du Maurier Award finalist, and short-listed for the Pat Conroy Beach Music Mystery Prize. Susan loves beaches, Southern food, and small towns where everyone knows everyone, and everyone has crazy relatives. You'll find all of the above in her novels. She lives in Greenville, SC, with her husband and an inordinate number of houseplants.

**The Liz Talbot Mystery Series**
**by Susan M. Boyer**

# BONES TO PICK

Linda Lovely

## A Brie Hooker Mystery (#1)

Living on a farm with four hundred goats and a cantankerous carnivore isn't among vegan chef Brie Hooker's list of lifetime ambitions. But she can't walk away from her Aunt Eva, who needs help operating her dairy.

Once she calls her aunt's goat farm home, grisly discoveries offer ample inducements for Brie to employ her entire vocabulary of cheese-and-meat curses. The troubles begin when the farm's pot-bellied pig unearths the skull of Eva's missing husband. The sheriff, kin to the deceased, sets out to pin the murder on Eva. He doesn't reckon on Brie's resolve to prove her aunt's innocence. Death threats, ruinous pedicures, psychic shenanigans, and biker bar fisticuffs won't stop Brie from unmasking the killer, even when romantic befuddlement throws her a curve.

Available at booksellers nationwide and online

Visit www.henerypress.com for details

# BOARD STIFF

Kendel Lynn

## An Elliott Lisbon Mystery (#1)

As director of the Ballantyne Foundation on Sea Pine Island, SC, Elliott Lisbon scratches her detective itch by performing discreet inquiries for Foundation donors. Usually nothing more serious than retrieving a pilfered Pomeranian. Until Jane Hatting, Ballantyne board chair, is accused of murder. The Ballantyne's reputation tanks, Jane's headed to a jail cell, and Elliott's sexy ex is the new lieutenant in town.

Armed with moxie and her Mini Coop, Elliott uncovers a trail of blackmail schemes, gambling debts, illicit affairs, and investment scams. But the deeper she digs to clear Jane's name, the guiltier Jane looks. The closer she gets to the truth, the more treacherous her investigation becomes. With victims piling up faster than shells at a clambake, Elliott realizes she's next on the killer's list.

Available at booksellers nationwide and online

Visit www.henerypress.com for details

# FIXIN' TO DIE

Tonya Kappes

## A Kenni Lowry Mystery (#1)

Kenni Lowry likes to think the zero crime rate in Cottonwood, Kentucky is due to her being sheriff, but she quickly discovers the ghost of her grandfather, the town's previous sheriff, has been scaring off any would-be criminals since she was elected. When the town's most beloved doctor is found murdered on the very same day as a jewelry store robbery, and a mysterious symbol ties the crime scenes together, Kenni must satisfy her hankerin' for justice by nabbing the culprits.

With the help of her Poppa, a lone deputy, and an annoyingly cute, too-big-for-his-britches State Reserve officer, Kenni must solve both cases and prove to the whole town, and herself, that she's worth her salt before time runs out.

Available at booksellers nationwide and online

Visit www.henerypress.com for details

# SECRETS, LIES, & CRAWFISH PIES

Abby L. Vandiver

## A Romaine Wilder Mystery (#1)

Romaine Wilder, big-city medical examiner with a small-town past, has been downsized and evicted. She's forced to return to her hometown of Robel in East Texas, leaving behind the man she's dating and the life she's worked hard to build.

Suzanne Babet Derbinay, Romaine's Auntie Zanne and proprietor of the Ball Funeral Home, has long since traded her French Creole upbringing for Big Texas attitude. Hanging on to the magic of her Louisiana roots, she's cooked up a love potion—if she could only get Romaine to drink it. But when the Ball Funeral Home, bursting at the seams with dead bodies, has a squatter stiff, Romaine and Auntie Zanne set off to find out who is responsible for the murder.

Available at booksellers nationwide and online

Visit www.henerypress.com for details

Made in the USA
Columbia, SC
30 June 2020